Gather the Bones

Andrea Kresge

THREE MOONS PRESS
Paranormal · Sci-Fi · Fantasy · YA · Fiction · Poetry

GATHER THE BONES

ISBN-13:978-0-9990095-1-2

Published by Three Moons Press.

Cover design by Victor Phillips

This book is dedicated with love to Amy Dubroff Anders, 1974-2017, and to all of my friends with whom I shared the tumultuous years of adolescence.

Part One

1

New Jersey, Spring 1992

"There's a fight outside! Max Munroe just punched out Dan Mullen. His nose is bleeding." My sister Olivia flopped down in the chair next to me, out of breath with pink cheeks. Her strawberry blonde curls flowed around her face like sunlight through red maples in October.

Suddenly, in a rush of skirts and hair, the girls at the table next to us got up and hurried to the Common Area. I had been sitting alone with my notebooks spread out in front of me like surrogate friends while the Nina-Alicias gossiped. I called them that because they were like one being, devoid of individual personalities. They were the meanest girls in school and only seemed to part when they were forced to, when they scattered for Spanish or French, for gym class, for pre-calc. They separated and then came together again, planets orbiting in concentric circles, the convergence of which was their dining room table by the windows. This was where they returned to re-charge each other with the electricity of self-affirming gossip.

"Are you serious? Is Mrs. Gagliardi out there?"

"No, she's in a conference. I think they're still going at it." Olivia paused, looked over her shoulder and then said, "But, get this, Natalie. The fight is over *you*."

My body tensed and my heart began to beat faster. Max was in a fight? Over me? Max was different. He walked through the halls with confidence and an attitude that simultaneously attracted and scared me. What did he think about, long for, believe in? He would slip into the dining room quietly, but his presence had a punch that practically hit me in the center of my forehead. I watched him every day from my table in the corner. I had the perfect view: the windows to the outside, the Nina-Alicia table, and the dining room doors. I saw him come and go, talking occasionally to the girls, never to the boys. I thought maybe he was too good for them, or else he was shy. Maybe it was because he didn't play sports. I pulled myself out of my thoughts and replied to Olivia.

"Quit it, Liv. That's not even funny."

"No, I'm serious. Dan said something about you being a nerdy book worm, and Max punched him."

"Punched him?"

"I guess Dan was saying something gross about wanting to loosen you up. I don't know! Guys are stupid. The point is, Max overheard them and told Dan to fuck off and mind his own business because you were the hottest girl in school, and Dan was just too much of a moron to see it. And then he punched him!"

"No way."

"Yes. But you know he's a dog," she said under her breath.

My mind was racing. When Max first came to Matterson, I wasn't sure about him, but as the days had moved on and I'd watched the way his body moved underneath his cotton shirts and khakis, I started to want to know what it would feel like to reach underneath that cotton, glide my hand along his animal arms, his skin, which looked to me like it must feel like a smooth canvas. His hair was brown and fine, and hung irresponsibly in his eyes. He never brushed it away, just stared through it. My mother said it was a sign of dishonesty. She didn't like a boy who couldn't look her in the eye. To me he was perfect: his body was like the trunk of a tree, his arms were branches, his legs were roots. I wanted to climb him, etch my initials into his skin.

There were places where I'd imagined walking with him, in the woods behind my house, on the large campus, places where we would we would kiss, and declare our eternal love for each other. Maybe we would make love in the leaves, and if my parents were in the house making dinner or reading the paper, or if the Headmaster was lurking around the corner, better yet. I wanted to be as reckless as possible. I needed something to shake up my life, to take control for myself. I knew I was very naive, and still a virgin at seventeen (which was rare at my school). I'd only heard about sex from the voices in the hallway, and from the looks on the faces of the Nina-Alicias.

"Come on!" urged Olivia. She pulled on my arm. I shoved my notebooks into my bag.

We rushed through the dining room doors to see a crowd gathered at the other end of the Common Area. I could see the flurry of Max's fringed, sheepskin coat and his dark head of hair rising and disappearing behind the crowd of prep school teenagers starved for some public school action. I caught a glimpse of Max's face and there was blood running from his nose.

"We have to stop them!"

"Don't, Natalie. Stay here," warned Olivia. She grabbed at my dress as I dashed away, trying to keep me from getting into the fray, but I was too strong for her and I pushed through the crowd.

"Max!" I shouted. The Nina-Alicia's turned and looked at me with disbelief. I rarely spoke up in school. I wasn't in student government, I never sang in the school musical. I was the girl who sat in the corner reading. At the sound of his name Max froze mid-punch and stared at me. Dan leaned against the wall wiping blood from his cracked and bleeding lip. Before I could get to Max, Mrs. Gagliardi burst from her office like a frantic water buffalo. She was calling for back-up while her wide hips moved as quickly as they could toward the crowd. I could hear the sound of her stockings rubbing together.

I stared at the spectacle in amazement. Maybe I had missed the signs. I should have known. Max had started talking to me in the hall. We'd both joined the poetry club. He told me he read TS Eliot and Ferlinghetti. He would brush up against me when we were at our lockers and it would electrify me for the rest of the day. When he talked to me I felt like I had been verified. *Yes, Natalie is a living, breathing, teenage specimen. She lives! She breathes!*

He'd punched my shoulder before he walked away. *See you in History, Catgirl.* I'd smiled a smile that felt like it was going to crack my face in half. I stayed up late at night writing in my journal or listening to my radio through my pillow. It was lights out at 9:30, and no music either, so I took my small radio that ran on batteries and put it under my pillow with the speaker directly under my ear.

When I heard parental feet pattering across the floor, I'd reach under my pillow and turn the volume down. I got very good at this, my hand darting like a gecko on a brick wall. Every time I did it, my heart rate sped up a little. It wasn't until Princeton University's last radio show ended after midnight that I'd turn it off and relax, drifting into what was usually fitful sleep.

I'd never cared much about clothes, but as I spent more time around Max, my clothes took on new meaning. I wore what I thought he'd like. I had a bra that made my boobs look bigger. I wore it a lot. I found go-go boots at the Better Threads thrift store for five dollars. My knees peeked out of them revealing a daring amount of skin, sometimes some thigh. He told me he liked the hideous plaid shirt I wore with my jade Buddha necklace. I wore it once a week, on the days when we had chorus together.

My mother berated my fashion sense. *You look like an orphan in that thing. At least iron it. You're wearing tweed with that?* I wore it anyway. My dad told me the Buddha was inappropriate. *You should go to Church this Sunday,* he would say. *It'll be good for you.* Good for me like a multi-vitamin was good for me? Like cabbage was good for me? I skipped Church and slept in, sleeping most deeply between 6 and 10 am. The house was quiet then.

Mrs. Gagliardi was yelling. "Mr. Braithwaite, a fight! A fight!" Her voice cracked with surprise at the behavior of at least one of Matterson's best students. Mr. Braithwaite's footsteps pounded down the shiny, institutional green hallway. Soon they were both upon the crowd, parting the sea of hormonal arms and legs to get at the perpetrators, Maxwell Munroe and Dan Mullen, trust fund baby of Silas Mullen, the owner of Old Mill Valley's only winery. Mr. Braithwaite grabbed Max by the back of his leather coat and yanked him away from Dan, through the crowd to the Headmaster's office. Mrs. Gagliardi helped Dan, the obvious loser, stumble to the nurse's office.

The crowd turned to watch the fighters leave the room, staring in dumbfounded appreciation for the show. These things did not happen at Matterson. Olivia and I had become two of the many loitering onlookers, and I felt rather ashamed of our fascination. I was trembling with excitement and disbelief. The Nina-Alicias saw the whole thing. They were vibrating with agitation, peering at me out the corners of their eyes, whispering with their hands covering their mouths.

Nina, in particular, was glaring at me from the corner of the room by the sofas. She had her fists clenched. The Nina-Alicias were all the same. Their fathers were all lawyers, doctors, and realtors. They lived near the country club in large houses made of creek stones. The all got cars for their sixteenth birthdays with vanity plates that say dbl trbl and 2cute.

Max's wasn't like them, and maybe that was why I liked him so much. He had a strange mother who hovered like a lion in the parking lot after school. He was either her cub or her prey, I wasn't sure which. She clawed into him with the strange ferocity only a mother can have. Like a mother cat biting down on her kitten's neck, she'd open the car door for him and suck him in. He'd disappear into the upholstery. I knew she was a nurse, and that she was strict. I watched them, even in the morning sometimes, if I was lucky enough to get to school early. I watched him kiss her goodbye through the open window of the car.

The crowd dispersed and classes resumed, but Max was suspended from school. I wanted to talk to him, to ask if the fight was really about me, but I didn't have to. It spread through Matterson faster than an outbreak of mono or strep throat. It was no longer a mystery why the Nina-Alicias grew quiet when I walked into the dining room. It was whispered about on the school bus, in corners of hallways, by the lockers, in secluded corners of the 70-acre campus. "Did you hear what Max did? Max likes Natalie

Watson. Can you believe it?" The words echoed through the corridors of the school.

I'd known Max for four months to be exact, though I couldn't really say I *knew* him. Not the way I'd like to. He transferred to Matterson in the middle of our junior year. Everyone wondered why. I figured it had something to do with Public-School-Colleen. She stopped dropping by Matterson once Max's mother began giving him rides to school.

Max would sit alone at lunch like me, studying his food and his notebook with delicate, intense concentration. His long eyelashes almost crisscrossed in front of his brown eyes. He often wrote straight through lunch period. I think the only reason the Nina-Alicias didn't shun him was because of the way he moved. He'd cock his head to the side as if to say that he was more of a man than any of the other boys at school. No one knew if this was true. Maybe Public-School-Colleen did, but I was certainly not going to ask her.

He swaggered when he walked. It was subtle, kind of a lope, like the stride of a lone wolf you might see on a nature program. Max had wild eyes, too. In his eyes I saw the sort of kindness that can melt you into a pile of mushy knock-knees and the uncontrolled wildness of an animal that's never been socialized to live with humans. The combination scared me a little, but I liked it.

2

Serena had a sleepover party at her house the weekend after the fight. She was pretty much my only friend. She would get high in-between classes in the bushes behind the school buildings and talked a lot about a guy named Ed, a band called Ministry, and Zipperhead, a store in the trendy little town of New Hope. Ed was a "couch surfer." I wasn't exactly sure what that meant, so I pictured him standing on a couch in Hawaiian shorts, feet dug into soft cushions, arms stretched straight out, and bracing for a wave.

I studied Serena, taking mental notes on how to be cool like her. While the Nina-Alicias were admired by most of the school, I admired Serena's rebellion. I was never quite as daring as her, but she seemed to understand, or at least respect my need to sit alone at lunch, to read Hesse's *Demian* and Rilke's *Letters to a Young Poet* rather than discuss Mindy's new Lexus or Nina's near overdose on coke. Our friendship was founded on our desire to be different, and we spent time together whenever we could.

A girl from Matterson named Jayne was also invited to the sleepover. My parents thought it was good for me to make friends and they approved of Serena. I guess it was because her parents were prominent members of the community. Her dad was a writer for Newsweek and her mother a classical piano teacher. What my parents failed to realize was that Serena and I wanted to be nothing like our parents.

We gathered at Serena's house at seven o'clock on Friday night, watched TV with our feet squeaking on the glass coffee table, and helped Serena bleach her chin length hair, whispering in the bathroom until her parents fell asleep. It took hours, but by 11 her father's snores rattled the modern house and the bathroom reeked of chemicals. The moon hung framed in the windows of her living room, a thin sliver, like a fingernail clipping. Jayne and I resembled each other in jeans, flannel shirts, and boots. Serena had slipped into fish net tights with holes in them, cut off shorts, combat boots and an army jacket. We both admired her silently, feeling conspicuously normal next to her and her hair, which glowed as white as the moon.

Serena had arranged for us to meet three boys someplace down the road. They went to public school and were in a band, which exempted them from the evaluations we normally put boys through: they were automatically cool. We slipped out the front door, skirted through yards and driveways, over a fence, and hurried down a dirt road that lead to the bridge. The night was dark and cold with only that thin moon, so we were practically invisible. I shivered as the dampness cut through to my skin. We reached one of those old colonial bridges that had been blocked off because it was unsafe to drive over. It was down the creek from an old mill, which was one of the many relics that were Old Mill's namesakes. The bridge stretched over the water like a black creature in the night. I could smell the damp earthiness of the muddy creek and the faint hint of musty wood from the bridge. At that point, the creek was a weak version of its larger self, waiting for the spring rains to swell it up the banks. The rains were late that year and everything was stretching and gasping for sunlight and water. It was a place my parents would never go, and that made it all the more intriguing.

We walked toward the bridge. Skunk cabbages had emerged late that year and the mud that was usually an April phenomenon was still sticking to our feet in May. Our feet made obscene sucking and slurping noises as we stepped slowly through the mud and we laughed, immediately hushing ourselves for fear of a lone adult who might just be passing by. Truthfully, it was no place any average adult would choose on a Friday night just shy of midnight. It was only teenagers and weirdos who needed to gather under damp bridges on cold nights: most adults had bars and living rooms where drinking and smoking were allowed, and making out was normal. People probably drove to the bridge during the autumn to take in the colors, or to fish when the water was high, but that night we found it to be deserted, exactly what we wanted.

"Here," said Serena, "give me a light." She held a lighter out to me and put a cigarette in her mouth. I held my hand up to the flame to protect it from any wind that might pick up, but the night was still. She inhaled and the end crackled to life, the small red embers the only light in the woods. She exhaled a puff of smoke. "You want one?" she asked.

"Yes," I replied. Jayne declined. It wasn't my first time smoking. That first time was also on a dirt road, but it was with my friend Cassandra from Old Mill. Cassandra was the reason my parents sent me, and consequently my sister, to Matterson. Cassandra was a "bad influence."

I chuckled to myself as I thought about how naive my parents were.

"What?" asked Serena.

"Nothing."

"What are you laughing at?"

"I was just thinking about the first time I smoked."

"How old were you?" asked Jayne, a faceless voice in the darkness.

"Fourteen. Cassandra Reynolds and I were sitting on the hood of her car back Birchwoods Road."

"That dirt road behind Kramers?"

"Yeah," I said as I exhaled a mouthful of smoke.

"That's where Mark and Dean Whitmore used to take me to smoke," replied Serena.

"Yeah, it's totally safe. Nobody ever goes there," I replied.

"I think it's creepy," added Jayne. "There's that old paper factory."

"You would think that!" laughed Serena. "Here, just smoke one, Jayne. You have to."

"Fine," she said with slight annoyance, though she laughed just a little too. Serena could be bold and pushy, but we liked that about her.

Once Jayne's cigarette was lit and she had recovered from coughing, we started walking again. As we neared the bridge, we heard voices.

"They're already here," whispered Serena. "Now remember, don't mention Ed, ok? I think I might hook up with Carl. And I have beers in my backpack, but don't say anything. I want to see if they held up their end of the bargain."

"What's the bargain?" asked Jayne.

"They're supposed to bring the weed," Serena explained. I knew no more than Jayne, but I acted like I did and nodded my head in agreement. I knew "weed" meant marijuana, but that was as far as my experience went.

We followed their voices and found them sitting under the bridge on the concrete foundation, black, inky shapes just inches away from the shallow trickle of the creek. We waded through a cluster of mayapples, rustling their leaves, alerting the boys to our presence. It smelled of stagnant water. I couldn't really get a good look at them, but they *were* boys and they'd followed through with their end of Serena's bargain, so the introductions were made and the beers handed out.

I'd had beer once before with Cassandra at an Old Mill party. My parents found out about the alcohol and grounded me. I couldn't be friends with Cassandra anymore. That was the beginning of the end of my time at Old Mill High, the public school. I kept my head down and stayed out of trouble until Serena entered my life this year. Once we became friends, my life picked up its pace. Matterson could be such a stifling place compared to Old Mill. I was intellectually stimulated, of course, but the other kids were predictable and nothing exciting ever happened.

We gathered, some of us sitting cross-legged, some squatting like Neanderthals around a fresh kill. The sound of crisp, cold cans of beer being opening disturbed the night's syrupy quiet. It was a sound that reminded me of summer and I anticipated the thirst-quenching beverage. Instead, the beer tasted like bitter, metallic tap water. Serena said it was Coors, which meant it came from the Rocky Mountains and that made it good, but I was not convinced. Phil, boy number three, pulled out a small ceramic pipe, pressed something into it, and lit it up. The pipe was passed around, and when it came to me, I mimicked them, pretending I knew what I was doing. Noticing my inexperience, Serena told me to hold it in my lungs for a while. I inhaled deeply and it burned. I sat there with my cheeks puffed out and my eyes bulging like a sad clown. I finally let it out after an excruciating and self-conscious eternity with a long exhalation. I coughed and coughed, thinking I would never be able to stop. The smoke smelled like rotten skunk cabbage.

I felt justified in my rebellion. My parents believed that they were the world's best authority on all things academic and religious. They were educated, but not in anything that I found interesting. They taught math and political science at the community college. I was failing Algebra II and I had a C in Biology, and I hated politics. My parents rode me incessantly in the evening, nagging me to do my homework, picking on the state of my room, the clothes on the floor, the posters, and the junk.

My sister Olivia was good at math. The irony was that my mother taught math, but she wouldn't help me. If Olivia could do it without her help so could I, she said. So, my little sister tutored me in math. I think my parents tried their best not to show favoritism, but they failed miserably. I was the difficult child. "Natalie, why can't you just go along with the program? Natalie, your sister isn't complaining. Why don't you take a little lesson from her?" Their fuddy-duddy church friends would come over for dinner and I would hear them downstairs, their voices echoing through the dry wooden house, "That Natalie. She's such a wild thing. A tomboy— nothing like her sister."

Olivia and I got along as well as two sisters close in age could. I liked her, despite the whole goody-goody thing she got into. We bickered and argued, but with an unspoken understanding that we really did appreciate each other. Olivia just always did everything right. It was no effort for her. She always agreed with our parents, and was *actually* attracted to the "good boys." She volunteered for good causes, her activity being candy striping at the Hospital that summer. I rolled my eyes at this. I thought about getting a job at the record store in Old Mill, but I didn't. I preferred to flop around the house, lazy and uncooperative.

My parents made us go to church every Sunday. Old Mill Community Church was the bane of my existence. Olivia at 14 was an acolyte wearing her little white robe, grinning and lighting the candles in her strawberry blonde curls. I'll never forget her cherubic face. I had to do it too, actually, but I didn't enjoy it like she seemed to. They "strongly encouraged" us go to Sunday school, but it was really not an option. I sat through it sullen and pouting. The Pastor told us that anyone daring to fornicate would undoubtedly face judgment. We all shrank in fear. On the bright side, each one of us could repent and seek forgiveness from Jesus Christ. At least it was a relationship between me and God, rather than me and a Priest. Serena had to go talk to a dark screen in a little box when she felt guilty. I never really repented, though. I'd never fornicated either.

The conversation bounced around from one uninspired topic to another. The boys called their band Oedipus Sex, which seemed cool at the time.

"Is that supposed to be a reference to the Oedipus complex?" I asked.

"Well, yeah," replied Carl, who was growing his hair long. It was still too short to put behind his ears, and it hung in his eyes. He was constantly brushing it out of the way. It reminded me of Max.

"So what does it mean?" asked Jayne.

"It's just cool," answered Ron.

"Isn't Oedipus the one who does it with his mom?" asked Serena.

"He married his mother and killed his father," I added.

"So, then Oedipus Sex has to refer to Oedipus doing it with his mother," said Jayne. "That's gross."

"Dude, think about it. It's kind of weirdly cool," said Ron through snorts of laughter.

"It just sounds good," offered Phil, who hadn't said a word until then. "Plus, the story of Oedipus marrying his mother is from the Greek story *Oedipus Rex* by Sophocles. The other ideas come from Freud."

We were all silent. Ron made a few snorts and sputters, and erupted into laughter. We all followed.

The conversation moved to parties at Old Mill and when Oedipus Sex was playing next. They were currently doing a tour of living rooms and garages. Phil leaned over to me and whispered in my ear.

"Do you wanna take a walk?" he asked, breathing into my hair, tickling my ear. My mother's breath did that when she whispered to me in church. I always pulled away. With Phil, I didn't flinch, but allowed him to finish his request.

"Yeah, sure," I replied. I took the last gulp of my beer and grabbed another cigarette from Serena's box of Camels. My fingers and toes were tingling and my head felt like it was five feet above my body. Right between my eyebrows on my forehead I felt like there was a third eye opening, like all my awareness had collected right there in that spot. My vision was a little blurred, but I felt good, not so cold anymore, and sort of numb. I stumbled up the bank behind Phil.

He skipped ahead and spun around quickly. He reached inside his jacket and pulled out a small bottle.

"Here, try it," he said as he walked backward. I could see his face faintly in the moonlight. He was smiling. His hair was also semi-long, and he tossed it out of his eyes with a quick movement of his head. I guessed from the length of their hair that all three boys had started growing their hair at the same time, maybe six months ago.

"What is it?"

"Blackberry brandy. It's sweet. Much better than beer. Try it." I took a sip. It warmed my entire throat. I could even feel the burn of alcohol in my stomach. "Have some more," he said. "Let's walk over to the mill. It's abandoned, you know. We thought about playing here, but we need a power outlet. There's rats and stuff inside."

"Yuck." I took another sip of brandy.

"Hey, I've got some more pot. Wanna smoke with me?"

"I guess, but not too much. I can't feel my eyelids."

"You're just buzzing. It opens all your chakras."

Chakras? He pulled what looked like a cigarette out of a plastic bag and lit it. He took a long puff and then passed it to me. I did the same. I felt the earth spinning very fast underneath my feet. The night was as black as the sticky tar that bubbled on my road in the summer and the air seemed almost as thick. It was like the clouds had descended upon the earth. What was that expression? You could cut the fog with a knife. I pictured myself with one of those large cleavers I've seen the chefs use at a Hibachi grill my parents took us to. I imagined swinging it at the air, chopping it up into chunks. The air fell to the ground like pieces of coal. I swayed back and forth a little, feeling almost like the air was holding me up.

I thought maybe that was what it felt like to get close to God. I'd thought I felt the presence of Christ once. I was thinking about him for some reason during a performance in my high school auditorium, which doubled as a chapel. It was like His spirit came down and filled me. My hands got hot and my arms wanted to rise up out of the constricting seats like white, feathered wings.

Mostly, though, it was more earthly things that I felt, that gave me the compulsion to fall down on the ground and roll in it, breathe in moss, and dry leaves, dip my head in creek water, poke mayfly and dragonfly nymphs with a stick and roll down hills.

My parents worried for my soul. They didn't understand anything about my impulses. All things holy in their lives were of the mind. Their god was transcendent. Mine was everywhere. They were happy in fancy clothes, bowed before the white altar. I preferred dancing in the damp garden. They kept the Lord's Prayer in pastel needlepoint framed on the wall. They thought the fear of God would do Olivia and me some good. I *did* want them to approve of me. I wanted them to think I was good, but in a way it was futile. I would never live up to Olivia. I had a wild streak, the part of me that couldn't be controlled, and that's what made me.

"You don't party much, do you?" Phil asked.

"Oh, I party. Why?" I asked, slurring my words.

"You're just wasted off a beer and some pot, that's all."

"I had that brandy, too."

"Yeah, and that. Come here," he said, and pulled me to him. He started kissing me. I was so surprised that I kissed him back even though I didn't even know if I wanted to. I didn't even really know what he looked like.

I'd only kissed one other boy, John. His family lived closest to my house on Lomink Road. He had braces then and I had a retainer and it was repulsively sloppy. At the time I'd had visions of our teeth getting stuck together like kissers in hundreds of rumors that circulate through any school. Serena had heard that two kids from Frenchtown got their braces stuck together and were rushed to the ER lip locked. The Frenchtown Frenchers, we called them. No one knew if it was true or not, but it was fair warning for anyone daring to kiss with metal on their teeth.

Phil moved his arms around my waist and I let my hands hang away from our bodies, not sure I wanted to touch him. He started walking slowly forward, guiding me backward. I put one foot carefully behind the other. Soon I felt the wood of the old mill against my back. I was suddenly hit with the absurdity of the moment as a vision of Max entered my mind again and I started to wish I was kissing him instead.

"Let's go back and see what they're talking about," I suggested.

"Why? They're just high and stupid. Isn't this why you're here?" he asked, and kissed me again.

"I just wanted to take a walk. Let's go back."

"Well, I didn't bring this pot for nothing!" he said loudly.

"I'm sorry. I just want to go back," I said, stumbling over my words.

I ducked under his arm and started running back toward the bridge. I could barely control my movements. My head was a water balloon and my legs were rubber bands. I tripped over a root that was sticking out of the ground and landed on my knees and hands, tearing a hole in my pants. I still had the brandy bottle. I picked myself up and kept running.

They were all still under the bridge. I scrambled down the bank, and sat down next to Jayne, breathing heavy.

"Damn, what happened?" she asked.

"Nothing."

"Looks like a lot of nothing!" said Ron sarcastically. "Looks like you've been doing something! Woo hoo!" he shouted. *Idiot*, I thought to myself.

I pulled my knees up to my chest and hugged them to me. I thought about Max again, this time with even more conviction. I *had* to talk to him. The thought of kissing Phil suddenly made me sick. I took another sip of brandy.

"So Natalie, we all want to know what you think of mysterious Max punching out Dan," said Jayne with sarcasm.

"I don't really think anything."

"I heard he's pretty screwed up," Jayne added.

"Who'd you hear that from?"

"From Allyson Fitzsimons. She said his parents are freaks."

"Whose aren't?" asked Serena.

"How would she know?" I asked.

"She just knows," answered Jayne. "She says they're abusive."

"That can't be true. Parents don't really do that anymore, do they? Not to kids our age," added Serena, who was sucking on a cigarette. "He's too big to beat up. Too old."

"Well, Allyson said that his parents hit him and they made him transfer to Matterson because he got caught with some girl. And they're really religious."

"You're kidding," I said quietly, taking a gulp of brandy. "I don't believe it. It has to be some weird story that Allyson made up."

"No, I'm serious. Allyson told me all this. It has something to with that blonde girl who used to come by school to meet him," insisted Jayne.

The sound of Phil's feet trampling the mayapples disturbed our conversation.

"Dude, where were you?" asked Ron.

"Just having a smoke by the mill," he replied, glancing in my direction.

"I just can't believe all that is true," I mumbled, drinking more brandy. A slight breeze was rustling the tender spring leaves. The heavy fog was moving out and tattered clouds were visible around the moon, which hovered like a white sickle blade above us. I stared out at the water knowing on some level that there was probably some truth to what Jayne said, but I also knew that Max hadn't been at Matterson long enough for anyone to know him. And truth be told, I felt like I knew him better than anyone else. I felt like I had dibs on his secrets. The voices of the others faded into the background as I sipped Phil's brandy and stared.

I woke up slowly, like crawling through thin tendrils of bubblegum being peeled off a sidewalk. It felt like a jackhammer was pulverizing my skull. I stretched and rolled onto my side and felt cold, dusty concrete underneath me. As I became more awake, I smelled mildew. I looked around and saw a surreal gray, dusty room with a boiler and a sump pump. A basement. I was laying on a dirty piece of tan carpet with a pastel crocheted blanket draped over me. I crawled upstairs.

Over breakfast Serena and Jayne told me that I unfortunately kissed Phil goodbye, gave him my phone number, and then stumbled back to Serena's house, only to throw up on the front lawn and then insist on sleeping in the basement because it was too hot in the house. I didn't remember. They teased me and gave me winks as if I've scored big-time, but I was completely freaked out as I sat nauseated over my bowl of frosted flakes. Apparently, mysterious impulses were lurking just underneath my conscious mind.

3

Max was suspended for four days. I kept thinking about that night under the bridge with the boys. The feelings of danger and excitement had ignited something in me. I bought a box of clove cigarettes at the Tobacco Barn in Old Mill and started smoking them out my bedroom window.

I was lucky that my bedroom was in the loft. I guess it was the privilege that came with being born first: Olivia's room was on the second floor, closer to watchful parental eyes. The house was a regular farmhouse with the exception of a triangular embellishment in the attic area — my room. From the outside it resembled a steeple and from the inside it was a curved bay window. The best part about my room was that I could crawl out the side window, drop down onto the roof below and shimmy down an old oak tree to the ground. I snuck out successfully for the first time the night before Halloween when my cousin Leanne and I met for Mischief Night. We'd toilet-papered our neighbors' houses and rubbed soap on the windows of the neighbor's car because he supposedly bit the heads off of pigeons, though we'd never seen him do it.

I wanted to sneak out again. My parents were in typical form, picking on me like carrion birds on a carcass and ruining my appetite at the dinner table. I hated them when they were like that. I pictured them both with sharp little beaks and drab feathers, hopping around on an empty road, their heads bobbing like chickens pecking the ground. Peck, they were relentless.

Before dishing out the food, my mother always said grace.

"Dear Lord, we thank you for this food, and for providing us with everything we need, including your forgiveness. We look to you for guidance. Please bless these girls as they prepare for school tomorrow, and keep them out of trouble. Amen."

"Amen," we all echoed.

I sat at the table thinking about the word "Amen," saying it over and over in my head as the early summer sun sent long shadows across the front yard. Have you ever noticed that the more you say a word the less sense it makes? Eventually it becomes utterly absurd. What the hell does Amen mean?

"Why do we say Amen?" I asked, daring them to answer.

"Because, it's just what we say, hon," answered my mom.

"But what does it mean?" I asked again.

"It means thank you," said Olivia. She started running her fingers through her hair, and examining the ends.

"Olivia, don't do that at the table," said my mother, who was scooping a heaping spoonful of vegetables out of a white porcelain bowl. She slid them onto my plate.

"It doesn't mean thank you, Livvy, it means something else, 'let it be so,'" said my dad. "It's Hebrew."

"Have some of the roast, Natalie," my mom said.

"I will. But why do we say it? It's not even an English word."

"Why don't you just eat your mother's cooking?" complained my father, avoiding the question. "It's not attractive for a girl to pick at her food like a bird."

"I eat fine, Dad."

"Do you eat like that at Matterson? I hope you get our money's worth from that dining room. You know you're lucky to be able to sit in such a lovely place and eat food like that," said my mother.

"Food like what?"

"At Matterson."

"Their food sucks, Mom," offered Olivia.

"Well, it may not be my cooking, but I'm sure it's good," my mother replied.

My father stabbed the grayish roast with a fork and sliced off another piece. The china plate it was perched on moved back and forth on the tablecloth as he sawed.

"Keep that plate still, Jerry! You'll spill grease on the table," snapped my mother.

"Natalie, I hope you'll be a little more focused next year," my dad said sternly, ignoring my mother.

"This year was fine," I muttered to the vegetable mush on my plate.

"Well, we don't want to see math grades like this year's. I'll be interested to see what you get on the final. And Biology, too. You really need to work on your sciences. Would you want to get a tutor? Maybe you should make an appointment with Ms. Gagliardi. You're facing college applications, you know," said my mother.

"Ms. Gag!" said Olivia, pretending she was choking. "You have to see Ms. Gaaaaag!"

"Shush, Olivia," hissed my mom. "I'm serious, Natalie. Maybe it would be a good idea. You're going into trigonometry."

I shrugged, pushing my food around on my plate.

"Trig can be challenging for students with a low aptitude for math. I know you did okay in geometry, but trig is a different story. It's more like algebra, and you know how that's been going."

"I know, Mom."

"Why don't *you* just help her, Mom?" asked Olivia.

"I'm busy, too, Olivia. A tutor can be very good. I thought maybe we could get by without one, but now I think it's necessary, don't you Natalie?"

"Let's wait and see how it goes, ok?" I said quietly.

"Also, Pastor Steuben is starting a new group at Church. It's for teens to talk about the issues and pressures you face. I think it would be good for you to go, Natalie. We don't want a repeat of this year," said my mom.

"Why do you keep talking about this year? This year was fine," I said.

"Well, your attitude needs a little work," said my father.

"Why don't you guys ever pick on Olivia?"

My father was mute. My mother fumbled for words. "She's… She just hasn't really…She just never… She's just not like you."

I fumed with rage as I ate the last of my mushy vegetables. I asked to be excused and left the table, pounding up the stairs. I locked the door behind me and made sure I had my house key tucked securely in my pocket so I could get back in if my parents went to sleep. I put on a tape by The Smashing Pumpkins to create the illusion that I was in my room studying for finals, reading *All Quiet on the Western Front* or *Richard the Third* and slipped out the window. Of course, I could just walk out the front door, but there was some power in pulling the screen out of the window, and sliding down the tree, knowing that my parents thought I was safe in my room.

I took my cloves with me. The woods hadn't yet expanded into their summer fullness and the night was quiet without the strange chorusing of insects. There were two weeks left of school. I walked the familiar path to my rock, hidden among the birches and beeches. I leaned against the beech tree that I liked to climb during thunderstorms and lit my cigarette.

I felt guilty every time I smoked, but I did it anyway. I was proving some kind of point to myself, I guess. I inhaled and closed my eyes, tasting the sweet brown paper. When I opened my eyes, I saw, for a split second, a human figure move in the pines. I shuddered with fear and my nervousness tripled. "It's nothing," I said to myself. I took another puff and my head began to swim. I sat down on my rock, spacing out, staring into green nothingness. A breeze licked the paintbrush boughs of the white pines and in that slight hissing of green needles I heard something call my name. It wasn't a human voice, but a whisper, almost identical to the voice of the breeze. Right after I heard it I decided it was nothing more than the wind, but I couldn't quite convince myself.

I sat up straight and looked for my cat, Ladybug. She had disappeared into the underbrush and the sun was low enough now that I was being bathed in the gray-blue ink of dusk, and the shapes of the foliage around me were beginning to look like creatures moving toward me, stalking. It had to be my imagination, but my heart raced anyway. As I moved to get up, I heard my name again. I turned and raced back to the house, faster and faster, sure that something was following me.

∞

"Natalie, get down here and eat your breakfast!" bellowed my mother up two flights of stairs. I had to be at school by 7:45 and my stomach lurched. I grabbed my notebooks and hugged them to my chest as I turned off my stereo and trampled downstairs. Olivia sneered at me as I walked into the kitchen, which was white and blue, and lots of gingham with embroidered and quilted curtains, place mats and rugs.

"Nice dress!" announced Olivia.

"Shut up, nerd," I snapped.

"Yes, honestly, Natalie. Do you think that's appropriate? At least iron that dress. I don't want you going to school like that."

"I don't care, I think this dress is cool."

"But do you have to wear those old boots?"

"Yes!" I said loudly, as I stormed out the door with my car keys and a piece of buttered toast in my hand. My boots were black with a three-inch brown wooden heel and zipped up to my knees. They smelled like mildew and someone else's feet, but I didn't care, because they were so deliciously, hideously cool. The dress was a purple, cap sleeve A-line with red buttons, and it brushed against my legs luxuriously. It was bare leg weather finally, and I was excited for Max to see me in the dress. Matterson had a dress code: no denim, no jeans, no untucked shirts, no T-shirts, no sneakers, and the boys had to wear ties. There was, however, no rule about good taste or thrift store bargains.

∞

In the lunch line, meatloaf and mashed potatoes were slathered onto my plate. I picked out the red Jell-O for dessert and mixed hot chocolate with coffee. I settled down at my regular table with a bird's eye view of the dining room doors, the Nina-Alicias, and the windows to the outside. I'd seen Max already that day, but we had only checked each other out with cautious interest. I knew that lunch was when we would talk. I ate some of the meatloaf, pulling it apart and spreading it around my plate with my fork. The Jell-O was the best part of the meal, so I pushed my plate aside and ate dessert. I saw Max slink into the dining room. He stood by the doors briefly, examining the room. Ignoring the Nina-Alicias who began to twitter like cats watching birds, he walked right over to me.

My heart began to race. My hands started to sweat so much that my pen slipped between my fingers. He was wearing a butterfly collar shirt and an olive tie. In fact, his entire outfit looked like it was from the Salvation Army. I stared with appreciation. His hair hung just slightly in his eyes, and he slouched a little too, as if he wasn't sure he was allowed to stretch into his 6 foot tall frame. He stood across the table from me.

"Hi," he said.

"Hi."

"So, I wanted to talk to you."

"Yeah."

"About the other day, this is kinda weird, I guess. I just get mad sometimes. Dan's a moron."

"What did he say that made you mad?" I asked.

"He was saying stuff about you. I think he likes you actually, but he's too dumb to understand the fact that you like to read a lot is a *good* thing."

"It is?"

"Well, yeah. I mean, you're interesting. You're not like the other girls over there, bubbly and annoying and shallow." He glanced toward the table where Nina, Dina, Alicia and Mindy lean in toward one another whispering in their secret language of judgments and conclusions.

I devoured him with my eyes. I consumed his profile as he looked their way, I drank his lips as he talked, recording their movement, digesting his eyelashes, thick and dark, his crooked smile and the dimples on his cheeks. His nose wasn't small, but had an attractive square shape at the end. His eyes were hazel green, and his lips were full with chiseled definition in that little part that connects the top lip to the nose. His ears stuck out just a little. I could smell him — some kind of cologne and laundry detergent. I could barely breathe. There was an awkward but charged silence.

"Can I sit down?"

"Yeah, just let me move this." I pushed my tray out of the way, putting a crumpled napkin over the mutilated meatloaf.

"It's true, you know. What I said to Dan. You are the coolest girl in school."

I laughed. "Ok, if you say so. Thanks for sticking up for me."

"I wanted you to know. I was really mad at Dan, but I was hoping you'd find out why I punched him."

"Well, I did. Everybody did."

"Yeah, and now everybody knows I think you're hot." I laughed again. Max was grinning at me mischievously. "You wanna take a walk?" he asked. We still had 45 minutes left of lunch period. It seemed like taking walks was all boys ever wanted to do with me, lately.

I got up, dumped my tray and threw my books into my backpack. We stashed our bags in our lockers and slipped out the front doors of Willard Hall. Matterson sat on a large campus in the middle of the small town of Matterson, New Jersey. It was a boarding school as well as a day school, so it was populated by kids from as far away as Pennsylvania, Delaware, Maryland and New York. The entrance to the campus was embellished by two large pillars bearing Latin phrases about knowledge and morals that I could never remember, and beyond the pillars was the town.

At the other end of campus were the soccer fields, the woods and then the cornfields. Matterson wasn't like some high schools where you were pretty much marooned inside all day except for gym class. If you didn't have class at Matterson, you were free to wander the rolling arboretum, or even leave campus to get lunch someplace in town as long as you showed up for class on time. It was like being in college. Almost.

I was sure the Nina-Alicias and maybe Dan Mullen were watching us leave Willard Hall. The day was warm and the trees on campus were in various stages of flowering. As we walked down the sidewalk we passed Allyson Fitzsimons who scowled at us, leaving me feeling rather unsettled. But as Max pulled me around Sadie Hall, and into a small cluster of dogwoods, I forgot about her. He sat down in the grass under a tree, and picked up a white petal, playing with it in between his fingers. I sat down too, crossing my legs, trying to keep my dress from revealing too much leg. I don't know why I did that: wore a dress that was too short and then spent the day feeling conscious as the white of my thighs was revealed when I sat, or when the wind blew. Half of me wanted Max to notice and half was obsessively pulling my dress down.

"So, do you like it here?" I asked.

"Yeah, I like it. I dig the prep school thing. My old school's not great. There are a lot of shallow assholes."

"Yeah, well this place has them too, trust me," I said rolling my eyes. "Where did you go before?"

"Warren."

"Oh. That's kind of a long drive, isn't it?"

"Yeah, but it's not too bad. Most days my mom drives me and picks me up. It just means I have to get here really early and leave right when school ends. But they have a Jeep they let me drive and I can use it this summer. If I don't screw up before then."

"Why would you screw up?"

"Oh, I won't. I'm just saying…"

"So, how come you transferred here?"

"It was a deal I made with my parents. They said this one girl I was dating was a bad influence." My stomach did flip-flops. Maybe it *was* like Jayne said.

"My parents did the same thing to me!" I said, feeling like we were suddenly bonding.

"Yeah? Not quite the same, I bet."

"Well, yeah, I don't know all the details."

"I was dating this girl from Old Mill, Colleen Fenstermaker. And they caught us."

"Caught you?" I knew what he's going to say.

"Yeah, you know, *doing it*," he said with slight pridefulness.

"Oh." Goosebumps invaded my skin, and I shivered. "That's different than my story. I got caught drinking with my old friend Cassandra. She's kind of a party animal."

Party animal was an understatement. Cassandra was one of those girls who innocently or otherwise had acquired the reputation of being promiscuous. Kids called her Loose Legs, Slut Butt and a number of other awful nicknames. Most of my ex-school mates perpetuated the rumor that Cassandra "slept around" and even had an abortion once. It was all muttered in clandestine voices over beefaroni and milk cartons, or in small groups at the mall when she strutted by in her stretch pants and baggy sweaters. I always tried to be open about people and I liked her. She was always laughing, always cheerful, and I respected her despite her supposed extracurricular activities.

"Cassandra? From Old Mill?" He asked excitedly.

"Yeah."

"Cassie Reynolds?"

"Yeah. You know her?"

"Know her?" He laughed. "Um, yeah, like, I only partied with her every weekend last semester. Me, Jeremy Miller and Colleen and Bonnie Fenstermaker."

Apparently I'd missed quite a bit of partying since I started going to Matterson. "Wow. I can't believe that. I can't believe we never met before," I said, trying to comprehend what this connection meant. We both got quiet and I began picking at the grass, pulling clumps of it out of the soil.

"Seems like it's meant to be, doesn't it?" said Max. "Hey, so you like TS Eliot?" he asked, changing the subject.

"Yes! My favorite is *The Love Song of J. Alfred Prufrock*. 'Let us go then you and I when the evening is laid out against the sky…'" I said in a dramatic voice, gesturing with my hand.

"Right on. I like that one too. I like this other one, what is it? Oh, 'This is the way the world ends, not with a bang, but a whimper.'"

"*The Hollow Men*. I love that one. My parents have an anthology that I read sometimes. My favorite in there is Robert Frost, but there's this cool book by Ginsberg and another by Ferlinghetti that I like a lot."

"Awesome. Can I read a poem of yours sometime?"

"Yeah, I'll look for one that's good. I only just started writing, though. It might be corny."

"I bet it's not. I won't mind anyway. It's a good way to get to know each other better, don't you think? To share poetry? I've never known a girl who liked poetry before."

"I'll find one for you to read. Maybe we can take another walk and share poems before school is over."

We sat there examining each other like two creatures just discovering that there was another being like us in the universe, the common threads of our lives slowly intertwining. It was exciting except for the little nagging voice in the back of my head. It was mostly Jayne's voice saying he was screwed up, but also something else, more elusive. What she had said wasn't false. He *had* been caught with Colleen. And he partied with "Cassie." I knew the kinds of guys she partied with. I stared at the trees around us and at his wide 1970's tie, trying to sort out the implications of all this.

"You're like a cat, you know that? Like a mink," he said with the confidence of a man, breaking the silence. I snapped out of my thoughts and I felt my cheeks flush.

"Wow, thanks."

"Seriously. I can't believe you don't have a boyfriend." He scooted across the grass to sit right in front of me. "Unbelievable." He grabbed my hands, which I'm sure were sweaty, and looked me right in the eyes. "Natalie Watson, will you go out with me?"

"Yes," I squawked, though my mind was racing with thoughts I couldn't even give voice to yet.

"Cool, Catgirl, See you in History," he whispered. "I'll call you tonight," he said, leaning in close before he got up and walked back to school, leaving me sitting there in the dogwoods in my purple dress and go-go boots.

4

It progressed like any normal teenage romance—quickly and intensely. We made plans to go out the following weekend and he stopped by my house in his parents' Jeep to pick me up. He walked up the path hanging his head low. His feet were clumsy and he inadvertently stepped on two of my mother's pansies. I saw her cringe and bite her tongue. We all watched him walk up the path. "Make sure you invite him in!" shouted my mom from the kitchen. "So you can scrutinize him," I whispered under my breath, but I did what she asked. He was taller than all of us. He sat at the kitchen table like a specimen ready to be dissected.

"So, how are you liking Matterson?" asked my dad in his puffed up King-of-the-House voice.

"I like it. The teachers are really nice, and the students are cool," Max said through a false and toothy grin.

"Do you have a favorite subject?"

"I guess Bio and English are my favorites. I really like science, and I'm also into literature. Well, and then there's music. I like to play the guitar and sing."

"A well rounded lad!" announced my dad.

He loved to talk in that regal tone of voice. I guess it was the professor in him or something. We were all trying to make light of the situation in our own way, because everyone knew this was my first real boyfriend. That in itself charged the atmosphere with a feeling loaded with assumptions and fears on my parents' part. I paced around the room as they made small talk. I looked at my watch, fussed with my hair, picked at my fingernails. I gave Max the "let's bolt" look and he stood up, his chair scraping across the floor. The sun was resting on my mother's African violets and blue glass bottles on the windowsill. Ladybug watched tentatively from the stairs, not wanting to come down with a stranger in the house.

"Well, have a nice afternoon," said my mom with a listless, "I can't stop you even though I want to" kind of voice.

"We will!" I grabbed my bag and slipped it over my shoulders. My mom stared at the red Jeep with apprehension.

As we bounced along the gravel driveway leaving the confines of my family, he popped a tape in the deck and stretched his free arm across the chasm between our seats. He was only touching my headrest, but the back of my neck tingled with the thought of his hand brushing my hair or resting on my shoulders. The tape deck was playing *Orange Crush* by REM.

We drove south along the Delaware River. I'd decided that I want to experiment with black and white photography, so we stopped now and then when I saw something I wanted to photograph.

"Let's drive back Birchwoods Road," I said.

"Where the old paper mill is?"

"Yeah, I've always wanted to take pictures of it."

Like Stuteskill Bridge, Birchwoods Road lived a double life. It was the dirt road of choice when people wanted to do anything illicit or illegal, but that was usually at night. During the day it was simply a scenic drive with maples and oaks leaning in from all sides. We pulled up to the gate that led to the old paper mill. There was a chain across it with a sign that said, "Condemned, State of New Jersey."

"Condemned, wow. I didn't realize it was condemned, I just thought it was abandoned."

"Same thing," Max replied. "It just means it's not safe to enter, I think. Any old mill that's not in use anymore is probably unsafe. Let's go check it out!" He jumped out of the Jeep, his keys jingling in his pocket. I put my camera around my neck and ducked under the gate. The small factory was a cluster of dirty and crumbling red brick buildings with smoke stacks and strange cooling mechanisms across the slanted roofs. A creek gurgled behind it and I saw an old water wheel, unmoving in the slow, dark water at the back of one of the buildings.

It was a gray but luminous day, perfect for black and white. I took a few pictures, and while I was standing still Max walked up behind me and put his chin on top of my head. He was exactly a head taller than me. We were at that point in a relationship where we weren't comfortable touching, though we were both motivated by an electric urge to devour one another. I could feel us both trembling just from a light touch.

We walked around for a while taking pictures. I paused by one of the buildings.

"Hold on a second," I muttered as I rummaged through my Guatemalan cloth bag. I pulled out my tin of cigarettes and popped one between my lips. I held it there and deftly lit it with a green lighter.

"You smoke?" he asked, raising his eyebrows.

"Yeah, sometimes. Serena got me into it. Is that ok?"

"Yeah, it's great! I love cloves. I thought you might be more of a good girl than that."

"Oh, I don't know if I'm a prude or not," I said, grinning. In retrospect, I probably should have been a little offended by that comment, but instead I felt enigmatic, powerful. We stood in a haze of smoke.

"Can I have a puff?" he asked.

"Sure." I inhaled one more time and handed him the cigarette. I felt dizzy. "This place is weird, isn't it? I swear it feels like there are ghosts here." The cigarette crackled as he inhaled. "Oh, stay in that position! Let me take a picture of you!" I said, suddenly. He posed, head lowered out of the wind, pointer finger and thumb pinching the cigarette. "You remind me of Jack Kerouac!"

"Oh yeah? Well, you remind me of a sex goddess." He moved close and hugged me, lifting me off the ground and spinning me around. I buried my face in his neck. He put me down and held the cigarette up to my mouth so I could take a puff. I inhaled and before I know it his lips were on mine. He circled me like the smoke, a tall tree extending branches around me. His fingers were all over my back, in my hair moving from the base of my neck up along my scalp. I put my arms inside his coat where it was warm. We were like twin bolts of lightning, harbingers of an ensuing thunderstorm.

He pulled away. "You are amazing, Natalie. Thank God you exist." He pulled me to him in a tight hug. I was on my tiptoes, my neck straining to rest my chin on his shoulder. I looked up, and to our mutual shock, I let out an involuntary shriek.

A man's face was looking down at us from an upstairs window in the building behind Max. The man's eyes were wide with urgency. Max let me go and I stumbled backward.

"What is it?"

"There's someone up there watching us!" I pointed to the window and he turned around to look up.

"I don't see anyone."

"Well, I swear I saw it. It looked like an Indian man." My heart was pounding. I was afraid it was a watchman, a murderer, or even worse, a ghost. "Come on, let's go."

"Awe, I was just getting warmed up!"

"Let's warm up somewhere else. Come on." I ran back to the Jeep. He followed and we got in, panting. As I looked back, I saw a human shape dart between the buildings. Dust flew as Max tore back onto the road heading toward the river.

We drove in silence for a few minutes and then he turned on the radio again.

"So, you really saw something?" he asked.

"Yes! It was so creepy. I felt creepy the moment I walked in there."

"You believe in ghosts?"

"Yeah, I guess so. I mean, I think I just saw one." I laughed nervously.

A frown crept over Max's face. It made me uncomfortable, so I shifted my gaze. I looked at his hands on the wheel. He had very long thin fingers and large knuckles. The skin was smooth and his fingertips were blunt on the end, not pointed like mine. I liked his hands.

"I believe in ghosts," he said quietly. "Sometimes I think I feel my grandfather around me. He died two years ago."

"Oh, I'm sorry."

"It's ok. I think he comes by to protect me."

"That's cool. What does he protect you from?"

"My parents mostly. They can be really strict and mean sometimes. I mean, I love them, they're good to me, but I feel him come around when my mom gets into one of her moods."

The more I got to know him, the more I learned that what Jayne said under the bridge was most likely true. I envied Allyson for knowing him better than I did and was jealous that Jayne heard it first. I also noticed something new about Max: an underlying sadness that was subtle, but very much there. I hadn't noticed it before, but now that I was becoming familiar with him, I saw that he seemed to be in a quiet pain. It showed in his eyes. I found it intensely attractive for some reason. I think maybe I thought I could help heal him or fix him. I know now that you can't ever fix a person.

We drove through Upper Black Eddy and on into Frenchtown. I loved that part of New Jersey. The small, down home and gritty towns along the Delaware oozed personality and subtle intrigue from the drab olive houses and dirty streets. He parked the Jeep along the street in Frenchtown and we hopped out, ready for lunch. We found a place called Marcie's near the canal where we could watch people walking by. It was small and a little steamy inside from the kitchen. I ordered a turkey club sandwich with lemonade and he got a meatball sub and coke. A waitress named Genevieve smiled at us with a mouth of missing teeth.

I had a boyfriend. I sat across from him and said this to myself in my mind. It was hard to explain the combination of elation and fear that I felt. The feelings mingled with each other so that I couldn't tell if I was electrified from fear or excitement. What I did know was that I could see the rest of my time at Matterson improving considerably. I'd have a date to my senior prom, someone to sit with at lunch, to walk with on warm days, to go to lacrosse games with. I wouldn't be weird, bookish Natalie who'd never had a boyfriend. I'd entered the members-only status of the experienced. All I had to do was wait for the right person to come along. I didn't have to try desperately to fit in like so many kids at school. Just being myself had worked out after all.

"So, Max, I wanted to ask you something." I said with hesitation.

"Shoot." He took a big bite of his sandwich and chewed, his right cheek bulging out with a mouthful of meatballs and bread.

"Do you get along ok with your parents? I mean, do you fight a lot?"

"We get along, mostly. They've always had interesting ways of disciplining, but otherwise we get along great. My mom and I are really close, and my dad and I have stuff in common."

"What do you mean by interesting ways of discipline?"

"My mom at least, sort of believes in corporal punishment."

"What's that?" I sipped my lemonade.

"That's when you discipline by hitting."

"You mean your parents hit you?"

"My mom mostly. Though, now that I'm taller than she is, it's changed a bit."

"Your dad doesn't?"

"Nah, my mom rules the family."

"It sounds like abuse to me," I suggested boldly, thinking of Jayne.

"Don't call it that. I'm weird enough as it is. I don't need people thinking I'm abused."

"But it sounds like you are. And you're not weird. Don't say that."

"Now that I'm bigger it's fine. It's different now. I love my mom."

"It just seems freaky to me. I don't want you to get hurt."

"I'm already hurt enough. There isn't anything I haven't seen, Natalie, but I don't really want to get into this now. Let's just have a nice day, ok?"

His hands were trembling a little as he talked. He made eye contact and then glanced away as if holding my gaze for too long freaked him out. I knew I could win a staring contest with him. How could anyone hurt this beautiful person? I couldn't imagine it. My stomach churned and I couldn't finish my sandwich.

We spent the rest of the afternoon talking about poetry, and kissing in dark corners, behind trees and buildings, as if we were sneaking around, still on campus. I was becoming addicted to his lips, breath, tongue, eyes and hands. His mouth tasted a little bit like chocolate, because he'd been eating a Three Musketeers bar. We nosed through a used bookstore, pointing out poetry books that we thought looked interesting. It was one of those times when every other phrase out of our mouths was "Me too! Me too!" We felt like soul mates. Maybe we were. There's no rule that soul mate relationships have to be easy, or healthy, right?

It was after dark when he dropped me off at my house. We kissed in the front seat of the Jeep and I could see shapes moving around in the kitchen. It was probably Olivia spying on us, or one of my parents trying to catch a glimpse of something they could scold me for, but the lights were off in the Jeep. They couldn't see in. We were beginning to understand each other and the way our mouths moved and fit together.

"I think I'm falling in love with you," he whispered when he pulled away to take a breath.

"Me, too."

"I'll call you tomorrow."

I opened the door and jumped to the gravel driveway. "Bye" I said wistfully, closing the door gently and walking backward up to my house, waving as he pulled away.

∞

Over the next two weeks, we became inseparable. A level of trust started to grow between us that he didn't seem to have with anyone else. It was exactly what I wanted. It felt like it was just how it needed to be, and he rapidly became my best friend. It seemed kind of fast, but our feelings were strong and real.

My mother, on the other hand, said he smelled like trouble, and that he seemed like he had "problems." She was right, but he didn't seem more troubled than any other kids to me. And anyway, I felt troubled myself. I felt like we were puzzle pieces that fit together.

5

During our last week of school, Max constantly asked me to take walks. I didn't say no. Why would I? I was getting to know the locker room and the dark room of the photography classroom very well. He was skilled at finding secret hiding places. I should have been studying intensely, preparing for my exams, but instead, I was gazing out the windows at leaves curling their small pea pod heads out of the tips of twisted branches. I stared eyes glazed over, not focusing on anything but the cathedral of color, and the emotions that were moving through me like a river about to flood its banks. When I tried to concentrate on biology or algebra, my brain sputtered and popped like an engine ready to die. I was a lost cause. I kissed getting A's goodbye. And I didn't care.

I think people are most exciting while they are an unknown entity. In that unknowing, they contain unlimited possibilities. Max was still unfamiliar enough to me that he embodied all my fantasies. He was anything I wanted him to be. My heart frequently felt like it was ready to split open, it was so full of what I thought was love. I needed to release my feelings, so I poured them onto paper. I wrote him poems late at night while my house expanded and contracted with the faint shiftings and sputterings of my sleeping family and slipped them in his locker in the morning. I wrote him notes during my classes and slipped them in his pockets and his backpack. Our lockers became the busiest post office in the county.

Many of the poems I wrote were too syrupy to be worthy of reiteration. But, I had a fantasy. It thrilled me and terrified me. I loved this strange juxtaposition of feelings. I didn't necessarily want it to come true. In fact, I really didn't want it to, but putting it on paper felt good. My pen flew across my notebook with a fervor.

> When no one is looking,
> when we are alone,
> nothing to stop us,
> you push me up against the lockers,
> we intertwine like vines,
> behind the coke machine,
> the lockers shake,
> your hands in my hair, holding me there,
> we are one being
> against the lockers
> mint green metal doors
> clanking as we move together.

It's not that I liked the idea of being forced to do something. I just like the idea of him being strong, of him finding me and saying, "I want you and must have you now, even though we're at school and the headmaster could walk in at any moment." The fantasy never really got very far. I never imagined us ecstatic in the throes of sexual intercourse. It was just the thrill of doing something with the risk of getting caught. I slipped it into his locker the next day, feeling nervous and excited by my daring.

It was the very last day of school and Max insisted that we take a walk. We rushed out the glass doors of Willard Hall, down through the dogwoods and across the soccer field to the pond where goose droppings peppered the ground. He was upset, almost frantic. We stopped by a dead tree that stretched half way across the pond. I thought about walking out on it. Would it sink?

Max wasn't touching me. Something was wrong. "We're in trouble. I mean, I'm in trouble," he said.

"Why?"

"You know that poem you wrote me? The locker room one?"

"Yeah?"

"Well, my mom found it."

"She did? Is that bad? Where did you leave it?"

"She searched my room, I guess. I had it in my desk drawer. Yeah, it's bad. I mean, I promised I wouldn't date any girls for a while, until after I get into college, pretty much. It's what they made me promise when they sent me here. And now she found this. She thinks we're doing it. I spent the last night locked in my room. No food, no water."

"What? Why?"

"For punishment."

As I looked at him more closely I saw the hint of a bruise across his cheekbone. "Your parents did that to you?"

He nodded.

"Can't you just refuse to let them?"

"It's way more complicated than that. It's better to just go along with them sometimes than to be stubborn. It makes things worse in the long run. I learned that a long time ago."

"That is insane. They could probably get arrested for that."

"But they're my parents. I love them."

"I guess, but it's hard for me to see anything loving about *that*."

"I know, it's weird," he mumbled. "So anyway, I'm not allowed to see you anymore."

"But we only just started going out!"

"I know, well my mom thinks we're fucking already. In fact, we might as well start since she already thinks we are."

"That seems like a weird reason to do it."

"Yeah, but what the hell. It can't get more screwed up than it already is, right?" He laughed and stared across the field, biting his lip. Both his fists were clenched tightly at his sides.

"So, what happened with Colleen that freaked your parents out so much?"

"It's my mom, really. She's the one who freaks out. They went away to a Bible conference type thing for parents of teenagers last August. I stayed home and Colleen came over a lot. They came home early and found us right in the middle of… well, you know."

"Oh. Right." I cringed at the thought.

"It's a sin, I guess. A big one. But it's hard, you know? To resist…"

"I don't think it's a sin. I mean, yeah, they say it is at church, but I have my own beliefs."

"You do?"

"Don't you?"

"I guess. I just don't think about it."

"You don't have to let them control you, you know. So what are we going to do?"

"I'll just sneak out a lot this summer."

"Can you do that?"

"Yeah, it's easy. I've been sneaking around all my life."

My mother started to look at me with suspicion. I think she could see that I was in a constant state of arousal. The spring flowers swollen with pollen were drab in comparison to the bright beacon glowing from within me. Around her, under her scornful eye, I felt like a harlot, like some floozy who should be standing on a street corner in the red light district of Old Mill, if there were such a thing. She saw what was looming on the horizon. So, when Nora Munroe called her and explained that she thought it was best that Max and I not see each other over the summer, my mother happily agreed.

I could tell she was upset. Her lips were pursed slightly in the frown of disapproval I'd learned to recognize. She'd been clanking around in the kitchen, banging pots in the cupboards, running the dishwasher, mopping the floor. She always cleaned when she was ruminating. It was a Sunday and I knew something was going on. My stomach clenched into knots. Finally she called me downstairs. She was sitting in the living room. Pictures of Olivia and me were perfectly arranged on the mantle. I stared at a picture of myself with my hair in a feathered 1980's coiffure. Ugh. There was another one of the two of us in matching red, gingham dresses, posing in front of a fake farm scene.

"Max's mother called this morning. We agreed that it's best if you two don't see each other this summer. Nora told me a little about Max's activities last summer and I think you should really try and focus on some other friends." She said it all in one breath. She was acting calm, but I knew she was seething underneath. How should I respond?

"You know Mom, she's kind of nuts. You should hear the stuff he tells me about her. You can't believe that what she tells you is true."

"Well, she wants him to be able to focus on some work he's doing at the College this summer: a science project of some kind. She thinks you're a distraction for him."

"Yeah, so?"

"Well, I think it might be good for you to spend the summer with other friends and do some reflecting. I don't like the sound of some of the stuff he was up to last summer. And that poem you wrote, *honestly* Natalie."

"That poem doesn't mean anything. Anyway, it was private."

"I don't want you focusing on thoughts like that. I think you need to spend some time reflecting on how you feel about relationships and spirituality."

"What's that supposed to mean?"

"I think you're too obsessed with him, Natalie. There are better things to put your energy into."

"I am not obsessed with him. He's my first boyfriend."

"You know, we've never really talked about this, but I want to stress how important it is that you save yourself for your future husband. There's no need to rush into sex. I was a virgin when I married your dad, and I think it was best that way. Plus, your husband will be able to tell if you're not."

"Was Dad a virgin when he met you?"

"Well, no, he's a man." I sat there momentarily mute. What? "So, from now on, you are not to see Max anymore. There are plenty of nice boys out there who you can spend time with. Like Evan Falcone at Church. He's such a nice young man," she said it wistfully, staring off into the space behind me. That was the last straw.

"Evan Falcone is so *boring*! I can't believe you would do this to me!" I stormed out of the room and pounded my feet as hard as I could up the stairs, each step an exclamation of my displeasure, intended to tear at her heart. Each step sent little bursts of adrenaline through my body. My heart was pounding and my hands were cold. My body didn't know how to react. Cry? Punch my pillows and mattress? Throw things? Write about it? I dialed Max's number. His mother answered, sounding winded and distressed. "No, he's not home. Don't call again." I felt desolate and desperate. I lit a cigarette and smoked it out the window.

I called Serena and told her what happened. She stopped by around 4:00 to pick me up. Serena's car was dirty and full of candy bar wrappers and mixed tapes. A Suicidal Tendencies tape kicked around at my feet.

Her parents weren't home. She got out her bowl, some stale pot, and put *Dark Side of the Moon* on her stereo. I loved the crackle of burning leaves — any kind, and this time I wasn't nervous. I was angry and I wanted to escape. I wanted to hurt myself. Maybe that would be a good way to get back at my mother for siding with a psycho like Nora Munroe. We laughed for hours. We looked through the JC Penney catalog drawing mustaches on the women modeling bras. We also ate two frozen pizzas and a tube of raw cookie dough. I felt like Serena and Max were the only people in my life who understood me.

6

In 1992 there was a blossoming alternative music scene in some of the local towns, especially near the University. It was a summer night and my friends and I were packed into a small basement club called Gone with the Wind. Max had snuck a call to me earlier in the week and we'd conspired to meet there under the guise of *other* social engagements. He was there to see a band called *Thumbnail*, because his friend Jeremy Miller's older brother was the keyboardist. I was there to hang out with Serena. We'd developed a secret phone call. He would call, let it ring twice, hang up and then call again. If I heard it, I knew it was him and I could race to the phone. It worked well in theory, though twice my Dad had picked up and heard nothing but a click on the other end. It seemed very logical to us, and before the days of cell phones and e-mail, it was one of the only ways to communicate secretly. It hadn't occurred to either one of us that all that sneaking around might have been a sign that it was either not meant to be, or that our parents had any kind of a clue about what was good for us.

Gone with the Wind was hot and stifling inside, but we all endured it for the sake of making the scene. Jayne was standing in the corner with Serena, always in her paint-splattered jeans, old T-shirt and long hair. Max was all over me, his large hands on my shoulders, my waist, laughing a loud breathy laugh. The set was ending and he pulled me up the stairs to the street. Outside the club, kids were smoking and mingling in combat boots and clouds of combusted tobacco. I rested against the brick wall of the building and he leaned in on one hand next to me. I pulled out my cigarettes and lit one seductively. I wasn't really addicted; I knew better than to get addicted. It just made me feel powerful. I know that might seem weird, but it was something about being able to say, "I choose this. Even if it might be bad, I have the power to choose it."

Max leaned in close. "So, Catgirl, I want to see you a lot this summer."

"Yeah, me too."

He started playing with my hair, tucking it behind my ear with his finger. "I can use my Jeep and you have your Jetta, so we can both drive places if we need to."

"Yeah, I think so. It makes me kind of nervous, but I can probably pull it off, especially if Olivia will keep secrets for me, instead of gossiping like she usually does."

"Well, we need to have a plan. Like, are you really ok with sneaking out? We can go someplace for a while in the car. We could probably go to Jeremy's house too. We're gonna have to lie a little bit. Can you lie to your parents?"

"Yeah, I can." I felt guilty, but I buried it. I was embarking on an adventure. I was breathing into myself, stretching into my skin, and testing how far I could push. I knew more about myself than my mother did, anyway. Locking me up in the house with dreams of wholesome Church boys and saving me for my future husband was not going to work. I made up my mind to never do what she wanted me to do. She was stuck in the 1950's.

"Ok, so tomorrow night let's meet up. I'll tell my mom I'm going out to study at the Community College library and instead I'll pick you up. You tell your parents you're going out with Serena. I won't pull up all the way into your driveway, so you just meet me around the bend and we'll go out someplace. That way we just avoid confrontation."

"What time?"

"7:00, give or take a few minutes."

"Ok. Where will we go?"

"Do you want to meet Jeremy after all my funny stories? His house is cool, really laid back."

"Yeah, ok." He leaned in and gave me a lingering kiss.

"Be ready to have a wild time. Jeremy's pad is *cool*..."

I laughed as he pulled me back down into the basement club.

∞

I was nauseated and nervous the next day, thinking of our clandestine date. I needed to be able to leave with "Serena" without my parents being near the front door to see me walking down the driveway. It would definitely seem strange to them, so I had to be positive they weren't around. It had occurred to me that I could even tell my parents that I was staying over at Serena's and they wouldn't suspect a thing. The thought of spending the night with Max sent ripples of excitement and anxiety through my nervous system. I called Serena to tell her what I was doing in case my parents called her house for some reason.

"You know what's gonna happen if you stay there!" she warned.

"Maybe not!" I insisted. I didn't want to seem easy.

"Natalie, that's not the kind of guy Max is. He's going to put the moves on you, I know it."

"Well, maybe I *will* do it then!"

"You should, girl. You'll never stop once you start!" she teased. She certainly hadn't. She'd called me with quite a few pregnancy scares. I figure she and Ed just weren't responsible. I planned to be very careful. I didn't like the idea, that once I started I wouldn't be able to stop, as if it was a drug. I could always just do it once as an experiment to see if I liked it.

"I have to get ready. So, here's the deal. If my parents call tonight, I'm at your house and I'm in the bathroom or the shower or something. If they say I need to call them back, call me at Jeremy Miller's house. You have the number. I'll call them from there. Oh, and Olivia knows and she's cool." I was afraid I'd let some important detail go.

"I've got it, Natty. It'll be fine. Don't worry so much."

"Ok, I'll call you tomorrow."

It was getting warm outside, but the nights were still cool, so I put on a pair of Levis, a red T-shirt and brought my navy blue hooded sweatshirt. I packed a small bag with clothes to sleep in, some toiletries and my hairbrush and pulled on a pair of brown leather strappy sandals that Olivia called my "Jesus sandals." My hair hung almost to my waist then, with golden blonde streaks. I felt good, like I'd imbibed an elixir for excitement and arousal.

I ate dinner with my parents, and they didn't suspect a thing, even though I could feel every nerve in my body tensing up. Why would they suspect anything? After dinner, they parked themselves in their usual positions in front of the evening news. Olivia and I were hanging out in the kitchen, which had a view of the driveway. Olivia was going to stand guard and try to distract my parents from walking into the foyer or the kitchen while I was walking down the driveway. At seven, I yelled into the living room.

"Bye! I'll see you guys tomorrow!"

"Ok, bye hon. Have fun. See you tomorrow," they both muttered from the sofa and easy chair.

"Have fun in church tomorrow, Liv!" I teased.

"I will. Be careful."

"I'll be fine as long as you don't rat on me."

"I won't. See you tomorrow," she muttered.

"Bye!" I whispered, poised like a sling-shot, ready to run out into the woods.

The early summer evening was blurring into a pink and salmon colored sunset. The air was cooling off and a clear night with the chatter of crickets was not far off. The sky was hazy, and the rolling hills were thick with green leaves. I slipped into the woods and cut through them to the curve in the driveway, weaving through scrubby wild blueberry bushes and sassafras. Max wasn't there yet. The driveway stretched out like a pale, graphite colored snake and I sat down on a rock, nervously looking back toward the house to see if I was within view. I could see Olivia watching like a ferret from the kitchen window. When I heard the roar of his Jeep I started running toward it. He stopped abruptly, dust kicking up from the dirt road, and I hopped in. He did a quick turnaround and we were off.

He breathed a deep sigh of freedom and put his hand on my knee. We were free for a few hours. We could have kept driving forever and I wouldn't have cared.

"Jeremy's parents are sort of hippie, artist, country people. They're much cooler than any parents I know," he said.

"I figured they were. You told me about the farm and the goats and stuff. My family is like that too, sort of. I've spent lots of time at the fair looking at cows."

"Well, his parents are pretty lenient about stuff. They let him drink beer sometimes, smoke weed, and we usually have the rec room to ourselves, plus there's the pasture and the woods."

"How far away is it?"

"It's a long walk from my house, in Warren County." I'd never been to Max's house, which felt strange, but, I understood why. I didn't want to come face to face with Nora, anyway. She seemed to think I was Satan's daughter.

Jeremy's house was a dilapidated green farmhouse set back from a long driveway. The porch was decorated with wind chimes and pots full of geraniums, asters, and variegated coleus plants. A homemade ashtray made of blue glazed clay sat on a white plastic table along with a newspaper that fluttered in the breeze. It smelled like incense, ashes and spice. There was a beaded curtain hanging in the front door that jingled in the breeze so we were circled by the tinkling of wind chimes and beads. Somewhere a horse's lips fluttered and a goat kicks in the mud. The crickets were gearing up and the air felt close and hot with just the slightest chill easing in. We walked through the front door without knocking. Inside, it was eclectic with tapestries on the walls, and bundles of dried chili peppers hanging from various dark corners. In fact, in the living room, there was a string of plastic chili pepper lights strung along the ceiling, illuminating the room with a reddish light. A poster of Billie Holiday smiled at me from the wall.

"Someone here likes peppers," I said quietly, conscious that we'd walked unannounced into someone else's house.

"That's Jeremy's dad, Len. His specialty is enchiladas."

"This place is even cooler than I expected," I whispered.

"Isn't it?" Max seemed pleased with himself. I looked around some more, wishing that my parents were cooler, comparing the house to my own. An entire wall of the living room was filled with old vinyl records accompanied by a stereo system that looked like it could blow the roof off the house. An electric guitar leaned against the wall.

"Who's the musician?" I asked.

"That's Len too. He's in a blues band. Jeremy's mom sings."

"Wow, you didn't tell me that."

We walked through a hallway that stretched from the front door through to the back of the house. At the end was a back door and also stairs that lead down. There were paintings of abstract nudes in the hall, and the wooden floor creaked under our feet. A voice was echoing up from someplace downstairs.

"Yo Munroe! Is that you and the chick?"

"Chick." I wasn't sure if my spine bristled in offense or amusement at the sound of that word.

"Yeah! Watch out, we're coming down!"

I followed Max down a steep staircase into what would be a basement, except it was covered from the floor up to the ceiling with an orange shag carpet. There were vinyl bean-bags on the floor and a blue futon was positioned in front of the television. They even had a pool table and a little area with a sink and a cabinet full of liquor.

Introductions were made. Jeremy had a girl with him named Nadia who went to his high school. She and Jeremy couldn't have been more different. She had a small diamond nose ring, her skin was dark and smooth and her hair was pulled back tightly in a shiny black ponytail. She was petite and was wearing a gauzy turquoise dress with no bra, and I could see her dark nipples through the fabric. It made me feel a little embarrassed, but I pretended not to notice. Jeremy was one of the blondest guys I've ever seen. Even his eyelashes were nearly white, and his eyes were robin egg blue. He was freckled from head to toe, and was wearing round tortoise shell glasses. He was wearing an old, faded T-shirt that said "Turn on, Tune in, Drop out" in psychedelic colors, and a pair of off-white pants made of a thick, natural looking fabric. Nadia was about five feet tall, and Jeremy must have been six foot three.

For some reason all of it made me feel like a prude. Jeremy and Nadia oozed maturity and overindulgence in a variety of things normally off-limits to teenagers. I felt like a tightly wound rubber band. The room smelled subtly of dogs and mildew, but there was incense burning, and I adjusted to the smell. The TV was on, and we did what all people do when there's a TV in the room. We stared and stared through long moments of silence. I decided that Jeremy and Nadia were probably high. Max and I had flopped on the bean bags, and I leaned over to whisper to him after about fifteen minutes had passed.

"I forgot to tell you that I can spend the night."

"You can? Seriously?"

"Yeah, though I guess you can't."

"Well, I probably can if I go back really early, before my parents get up. Or, maybe I could tell them that I'm spending the night at someone else's house, like this professor I'm supposed to be working with at the college. That might work. They like being in denial in some ways."

"Ok, well if you want me to, I can stay."

"Oh, yeah, I want to you to!"

I leaned back on the beanbag and rested my head on my arm, inhaling a big breath full of nag champa incense and basement air, and wondered just what I was getting myself into.

7

The four of us decided to go outside and watch the stars. It was a clear, crisp night and there were rumors of shooting stars. A certain kind of wildness was barking at the back door. None of us could sit still. Jeremy was a gregarious, laughing, poke-you-in-the-sides kind of guy who loved to play host. He grabbed a cooler, some beer, and a sack with various items to smoke and munch on. He also brought a blanket for the grassy field. Behind the farmhouse was a lawn with a clothesline and a small dog house for their border collie, Harley. He jumped and leapt at our faces, pawing and barking for attention. Beyond the lawn stretched a path that led through a thicket of trees, and then opened to the pasture. There were sheds to our right where the goats and pigs slept, and a pen for chickens. I could see their fat bellies illuminated in the field by the waxing moon, horses with their heads down chewing on tough grass and weeds. It smelled of that sweet and slightly sickening odor created by grass, hay and manure. The goats muttered in the dark as we stumbled by.

The pasture sloped up into a dark island of nothingness. Jeremy directed us to walk further ahead to get out of the area where there might be droppings from the animals. We walked through the horses who sputtered and hiccoughed at us. One stomped its foot restlessly. The moon was bright, and lighted our way enough that we could move roughly toward the center of the hillside. The only sounds were the occasional howl of a dog, or a whippoorwill, the rustlings of the animals. The sounds seemed to bounce off invisible walls in the dark. It felt like the universe had edges.

Jeremy opened a blanket with orange and red zigzags on off-white wool and shook it in the air. It opened like a sail and fluttered to the ground in a perfect square. I could smell stale tobacco. He pulled out four tall skinny candles in jars and set them on the corners of the blanket and handed out bottles of beer. We all stretched out on the blanket, beers in hand, and stared up at the sky. It was as if the dome of the universe had opened right above us, spilling out a whitewater river of stars. We could see the Milky Way: a cloudy streak across the ceiling of the universe. We smoked stolen cigarettes while the world spun beneath us.

I couldn't tell if time was passing quickly or slowly. My only barometer was how fast my bladder was filing up from the beer I was drinking. My eyelids were numb and my mouth was dry despite the beer. I really had to pee, so I got up and walked across the pasture to the edge of the woods. As I squatted, butt bare and glowing white to the world, I had the distinct feeling that I was being watched. The trees were fuzzy dark shapes nearby, and my eyesight was poor in the thick tar of the night air. I stared and stared trying to see into the woods. I couldn't pee. I was tense, too conscious of myself, too aware of the silent and stoic trees, and the eyes that I swore were watching. I had to relax and concentrate.

I heard voices echoing from my friends on the blanket and felt like an outsider. They were over there with their unspoken knowledge of something I didn't connect with. Maybe it was the summer carnivals and tractor pulls that I never went to, the backyard barbecues that Colleen attended with Max at her side, or the Old Mill parties that until recently hadn't interested me that much. Whatever it was, I was more at home by myself in the woods on the edge of the pasture, watching from a distance.

The horses were below us and every now and then one sounded off with a snort or a whinny that sounded more like a human laugh than a horse. I pulled up my pants, adjusting the waist of my jeans and walked back to them slowly, trying to focus on them in the dark. They were simply dark shapes lumped together between small flickering lights. Even when I returned it was like slithering back into a black ship in the middle of an invisible sea. I flopped down next to Max and the blanket was spinning. They'd been in the midst of a conversation, and their chatter ebbed and then picked up again as I returned.

"Have you ever heard of dark matter?" asked Jeremy, surprisingly close and clear in the vacuous dark.

"Yeah, I think so. It's something to do with astronomy, right?" answered Max.

"Right, only it's more mysterious than that. Scientists have discovered that there is a substance in space that they know is there but they can't see it. Like, the way we currently perceive things in space doesn't work. It's there, but we can't see it," Jeremy tried to explain.

"Wait, how do they know it's there if they can't see it?" I asked.

"They can detect it because of the way light refracts off of it and the way other objects move around it. So, they know there is a substance there, but they literally can't see it with scientific instruments."

"Maybe it's a black hole," offered Nadia.

"It's not a black hole. It's something else, but there are only theories as to what it is. No one knows. Isn't that weird?" Jeremy was getting excited.

We all stared up at the sky in silence for a while. A shooting star flashed and was gone before I could point it out. I watched for another one, but the sky was still.

"So, what do you guys think it is?" asked Max.

"I think it's God," said Nadia.

"I was gonna say that too," I replied. "But it doesn't quite make sense. The answer to God couldn't be that simple. And anyway, it's weird to think of God being just black lumps of stuff out there in space. I mean, God would be something more spectacular, don't you think?"

"But some people are suggesting that the stuff has consciousness," said Jeremy.

"How do they know that?" I asked.

"Don't know," he replied.

We were silent for a long time. I started to think hard about how there could be something imperceptible to humans, but that existed as fully as anything else around us. How many other things existed, but couldn't be seen? It could be endless. There could be whole invisible universes within our visible one. Suddenly nothing seemed like an impossibility.

"Think about the time before microscopes. No one would have believed then that there was such a thing as microscopic life, or atoms. Maybe there are other universes in the dark matter. Maybe they're like entrances into other worlds," I suggested.

"Could be," said Max.

The other two were suddenly wrapped around each other, oblivious to us. My perception of time was off. It made me anxious. I tried to relax.

"Max, don't you think, if there's stuff like that out there that exists even though we can't see it…" I was talking slowly, trying to work it out in my mind, "that there could be things here on earth that we can't see, but that are real?"

"Yeah, I think so. Why not? You mean like spirits? They say we only use ten percent of our brains."

"Right. So, maybe at some point, with telepathy or something, we will be able to see the dark matter," I said.

"Yeah, but I don't think it's God, do you?" he asked.

"Not really. I think God *is* the universe. I think God is everywhere at once."

"That's so deep."

I started to giggle. It turned into more giggles that fed off one another endlessly. I didn't know why I was laughing. I was nervous and cold, and maybe laughing made me feel better. Jeremy leaned over to us.

"We're gonna go back to the house and make some food. You wanna come, or stay out here?"

"I don't know," I hesitated. I was sorry they were leaving. I felt an uncomfortable combination of fear, curiosity and apprehension.

"Let's stay a little while longer," said Max.

"Ok. We're gonna make fajitas. You can have some when you come in," said Jeremy.

Once they were gone, Max sat up. "Natalie, check it out." He pulled a condom out of his pocket, winking at me.

"Now? Are you sure this is the right time?"

"Yes! I love you, you love me. What are we waiting for?"

"We haven't known each other very long."

"There's nothing to be scared of. You'll love it. I promise."

He kissed me and I began to warm up to the idea a little, but then the night seemed to become more still and I felt like I was being watched again. Maybe it was because of our conversation earlier. Maybe the stars were watching, or people were peering in from parallel universes. A train moaned somewhere in the distance, rolling over the rails, a great single eyeball of light beaming into the night. It was creepy and mournful and I loved it. As his hands wandered over me, my mind wandered. I thought that I was probably a little weird to get turned on by the sound of a train and the chill it sent up my spine, a little weird to think of trees having eyes, of parallel universes. It also scared me that I was excited by the fact that Max might be a little dangerous. I didn't really know why I felt that way. I had no reason to. He was just a young guy with a dysfunctional family. How dangerous could he be? And yet I felt that thrill of vulnerability.

He unbuttoned my jeans and tried to slide them off of me. It's hard to explain. Deep down inside I was really terrified, but I denied my fear. My stomach was rigid, not softening into his closeness, but other parts of me were responding to him. I had a knot in my throat, a chill in my bones. It boiled down to an intellectual decision. My body was giving me contradictory feedback. At least logically, it seemed like the world was telling us to go ahead and get on with it. Serena, Jeremy, Nadia and Max - they all thought it was a great idea. My jeans were off and he had my shirt pulled up over my breasts with my bra undone. I felt like an Easter ham on display at the dinner table. I should have had an apple in my mouth. My skin glowed white with goose pimples. I looked at my watch: 1:00.

"Don't you need to call your parents?" I asked. Max paused. He had his pants down and was sitting back on his haunches.

"No. Not now, anyway."

"You're gonna get in trouble aren't you?" I realized I was trying to scare him into stopping.

"I don't really care right now." The condom crackled like a candy bar wrapper. I had stifle a laugh as the absurdity hits me. He loomed over me, smiling with urgency. We were like two children experimenting with a new toy.

"I'm cold, aren't you?"

"Come on, don't be a tease. This'll warm us up." He rolled on top of me and pressed his weight against me. He didn't wait long. His weight held me down, his force opened me up. It hurt, and I felt like crying, but I was mute.

That was it. I'd been unsealed. Like the stars in the Milky Way rushing out in a torrent of silver, I was open to the wind carrying seeds, open to the night's blackness. But who had opened me? I barely knew him. Suddenly he seemed unfamiliar. I felt like he didn't have the right to do it. The stars had more right than he did, and that was where I first focused my attention. I liked to think that the stars were alive, that they could see me and that they were acknowledging me, their daughter, harpooned like a white whale, blade buried deep in flesh.

I could see the birches on the edge of the woods in my peripheral vision. Almond shaped crinkles of bark stared out, wall-eyed. My mind wandered to the dark matter. What was that stuff, anyway? I faced the sky, staring up at the stars, almost as if I was above my body, floating up there with them. For a few moments I was totally separated from what was happening to me. I glanced over toward the trees again and I saw the figure of a man standing there, half hidden in the shadows of moonlight, but very clearly there. I gasped out loud.

"Oh yeah, baby!" said Max loudly. It might have been sexy, or even funny under different circumstances, but it was neither. The figure by the trees had long dark hair with white feathers hanging from it. I could see his eyes and there was kindness in them, but also intensity. His chest was bare, and he was wearing what seemed to be a buckskin loincloth with more white feathers. He raised a hand as if in greeting and held it like that for a few moments. He knew I could see him! I blinked and he was gone. I couldn't believe it. Was I hallucinating?

My consciousness was coming back to Max on top of me. He was really enjoying himself. I didn't really feel much at all. I wondered if every girl felt like this the first time. Suddenly Max froze for a few seconds, flopped on me and immediately relaxed. He sat back from me and examined my face.

"Don't you feel good, Natalie?"

"I feel ok. It kind of hurt, though."

"Well, it won't always be like that. Next time you'll feel better." He held my face with his hands. He did care about me.

"Max, I saw something weird."

"Yeah? When?"

"Just now, a few minutes ago over by the birches. I saw a man standing there."

"You did? You saw a man when we were kissing at the paper factory, too. Do you hallucinate when you're getting it on or something?"

"No, I don't think so. Maybe it was the beer, or the cigarettes. I don't know."

"Weird. Well, are you ready to go in?" He buried the condom under some loose grass.

"Yeah, let's go." I pull up my pants and helped him fold the blanket and gather the candles, which had burned down low. My inner thighs were sore when I walked. I couldn't quite wrap my mind around what just happened. I expected to feel profoundly changed. Instead, I really didn't feel different at all, except sore inside. I was telling myself "you just lost your virginity," but on every other level, I just couldn't access my feelings. It was like I'd lost part of myself, and I guess I had. That was the only feeling I could really identify. We walked back to the house. Jeremy and Nadia were still awake in the rec room.

"Yo kids! What up! Looks like you guys got busy!"

"Right on, Jerm. You have some food for us? I'm starving," said Max jovially.

I have to admit, I felt a little insignificant at that point. I looked over at Nadia, who was sunken into a bean bag. She just shrugged. I suspected that they had been doing the same thing we just did.

"We can cook up some more fajitas," said Jeremy.

"Where are your parents? Are they here sleeping?" I asked.

"No, they had a gig tonight. They'll be home pretty soon, probably."

"Will they care if we're here?" I asked.

"They won't mind. They like me to have friends over. As long as we're *careful*."

"Right," I said, and headed for the bathroom. I sat down to pee, and it burned like hell. I closed my eyes, and wrinkled my face, as if that might make the pain stop. I could hear the television murmuring in the other room. When I opened my eyes again, I noticed that the small bathroom's walls were decorated with brown and gold wallpaper and the floor had that same orange shag carpet: hideous. It also smelled subtly of urine and dog. I looked down at my underpants as the stinging subsided and they were stained with blood. I finished quickly and went out to whisper to Nadia. She was on one of the beanbag chairs.

"Do you have any pads with you?" I asked cautiously, bending down to her so the boys wouldn't hear me.

"No, why? Did you get your period?"

"Not exactly."

"Are you ok?" She sat up quickly. "Did he hurt you?" She asked urgently, a look of fearful concern creeping across her pretty face. I was surprised by the intensity of her reaction.

"No. Not really. Not on purpose anyway. I just never did it before. You *know…*"

She didn't seem to want to talk to me anymore. Maybe I'd made her uncomfortable. Maybe she was perpetually high. It didn't matter. I actually felt a little violated, but I wasn't sure why. Some days I had so many wild, rushing feelings that it was hard to tell what was really significant.

We ate the fajitas with sour cream and guacamole and eventually went to sleep on the floor on top of sleeping bags, and under piles of blankets. I couldn't sleep. I couldn't stop thinking about the man I saw in the woods, and I was subtly aware of the soreness in my legs. I kept drifting off only to be awakened by the heavy thud of anxiety, my heart racing. Had I felt that same man watching me when I was trying to pee? Why? The rest of night was the same. Max was sound asleep, completely oblivious. I think the loneliest feeling on earth is to be wide-awake in the middle of the night while someone sleeps peacefully next to you. It's nice to believe in the interconnectedness of life when you're awake, but at night, in the dark, quiet hours before dawn, if you're the only one awake, it feels lonelier than actually being by yourself.

The light started to peek through the narrow windows near the basement ceiling somewhere around 5 am. I was already awake listening to the sounds of the house, which were new and strange. I heard Jeremy's parents come in, and go right to bed sometime before dawn. I nudged Max to wake him up, worried that he would get in trouble for staying out all night and that I would get in trouble as a result. We got up quickly and stumbled to his Jeep with sleep still in our eyes. He dropped me off at home after a long goodbye full of kisses and I love yous. You know how if you say it too much, it begins to lose its meaning? That's how it was. But at the same time, I longed to hear it. If he didn't say it, I started to wonder if something was wrong. I crawled up to my room. Everyone was gone for early church, so I had a few hours to myself. I sank into the mattress, luxuriating in the springy softness of my bed, settling into what had happened.

8

The summer was breathing and expanding, a huge sigh of fertility. Max and sex were electrifying, but troubling. Nothing else occupied my mind. I fantasized about misty, humid nights and of being taken ferociously by some mysterious man: someone who was powerful, who could conduct the wind, the clouds and my body like an orchestra. The things I fantasized about were more about mood and setting than actual intercourse. I lay in bed at night thinking a lot about this. I loved the subtle fear that Max inspired in me. I still don't really know why. Maybe it was a sneaky form of self-sabotage. Is that why girls like "bad" boys? Could it be because we don't really like ourselves?

On Monday I had a cramp in my right side. I knew nothing about my body. I worried that maybe something inside me was broken. Maybe I was more fragile than I thought. I snuck into my parents' room and found my mom's copy of *Our Bodies Ourselves,* a classic women's health book first published in 1971. It fell open to a page describing "ectopic pregnancy." I began to panic. I read the whole section and convinced myself it was possible. Max called later with the special two-ring warning to see if he could come over after my parents went to sleep. I didn't tell him about my freak-out and we made plans. My parents had no idea that I was seeing Max and it seemed like it was going to be a typical summer, aside from my new sport of sneaking around. They were gone regularly, teaching summer classes. Olivia and I were talking about volunteering at an organic farm called Silver Lake Farm.

Max drove to my house and parked his Jeep at the end of the driveway. At 11:00 I slid out my window and shimmied down the tree. I was wearing a long Indian print skirt, which turned out to be a bad idea, because the rough oak bark scratched my legs. The moon was full and bright and I felt like a ripe honeydew melon just like the ones that swelled in my mother's garden. I don't know how else to describe the feeling I had. My body felt more alive than usual, my mind was active. It felt mysterious and magical. I was in the mood to talk more about dark matter, god and spirits. I dropped lightly from the tree onto the ground, and started walking through the moonlight toward the driveway where Max was waiting.

He was leaning on the Jeep with the headlights off. The night was quiet and my footsteps broke the silence with the crunch of rubber soles on gravel and leaves. He saw me across the field that stretched between the woods and the front of my house. He walked over to meet me, swept me up with his arms, and spun me around. He always had so much emotion pent up in his tightly wound body that he seemed to shiver when he hugged me. He often had a gaze that seemed to hold much more information than he ever shared. There was a silent pain in his eyes, and also an urgency that I never understood. I mistook it for power, but that's not what it was. It was more like agony, I know now.

We walked through the field toward the woods behind my house. The woods to the North stretched out flat for a distance and then sloped down to Hennessey Creek. The moon was so bright that it was easy to see. It was exciting to meet like this, in the dark velvet of the night when no one knew about it except us. It was an intoxicating feeling, like we were alone in the world and that together we embodied every possibility imaginable. The power of adrenaline, of ecstasy and creation: all these things felt palpable, tangible. I could taste them on the tip of my tongue, smell them in the perfume of the woods. A whippoorwill sounded off in the distance. Years later, I miss that sound.

We penetrated the woods like a herd of cattle in the dry leaves. We trampled toward the stream, nervously aware of the noise we were making. I was afraid my parents would hear it and turn on the outside light on the lookout for a bear. We were surrounded by birches again, which grew closer together than the larger oaks, and pines. Max paused and turned to me in the middle of the birch grove.

"Let's hang out here for a while. It's nice."

"Don't you want to go down by the creek? It's so pretty down there. My cousin used to take me for rides in his Jeep down there. I can show you."

"Off-roading?"

"Yeah, it was fun. That was before he got married."

"Let's just stay here for a while first."

"Ok," I shrugged. He seemed to have an agenda.

He had a light blue acrylic blanket that looked like it came off his bed. He opened it, mimicking Jeremy's motions with the Mexican blanket and it fluttered, settling on the ground. He breathed into my ear. "Let's lie down and look at the stars." I sat down, leaning on one elbow.

I took the opportunity to bring up my thoughts on spirituality. "You know, I've been thinking about the universe a lot lately. And I was reading this book on Buddhism, about desire and non-attachment and it seems like such a great way to try and not be so emotional about everything. It's all so fascinating. There's all this interesting stuff they don't tell us about in school, you know? You should really read some Bu -" His lips were on mine before I could finish the sentence. He was ferocious; his hands in my hair, tongue filling my mouth, rolling on top of me, his weight forcing the breath out of my lungs. I managed to get my mouth away for a moment. "Max, stop. You're acting crazy."

"I was just going nuts today. There's just something about you that drives me crazy. And now tonight in the moonlight… now I know what moonlight is for." Those were some smooth words, but he was starting to pull down my underpants.

"Max, wait."

"I just want to get closer to you."

I sighed. Maybe it was a sigh of surrender, I don't know. I didn't want to risk losing him. Socially, I needed him. He was one of my only friends. I needed the Nina-Alicias to look at me with respect. I needed someone to sit with at lunch. "Max, I want to wait a little while before we do it again. I'm still kind of sore."

He wasn't listening. He grabbed my arms with both hands and pinned them against the ground.

"No, come on. We need this. I need you."

"Let go of my arms."

"Don't you like it like that? Kinda like your locker room poem?" He moved my right wrist into his other hand, so that he was holding both my wrists together. He uses his other hand to spread my legs. I whimpered "wait," but he didn't. I struggled to get away, but he was bigger and heavier and stronger than me.

He started talking again in those funny phrases he liked to use. Even though I didn't want to, my body reacted to his touch. It was the first time I'd ever felt those kinds of feelings: my hips moved unconsciously into a rhythm with his, feeling the intricate mechanics of our motions. But I was also mad as hell. He just *had* to have what he wanted immediately when he wanted it. He was arrogant and selfish.

I stared up at the sky like the first time in the pasture. Have you ever seen those pictures where the photographer is standing underneath tall trees, and they look up and snap the photo like that? It's like the trees lean in toward one another in a circle of intertwined fingers. The moon was practically in the middle of the spinning trees, high in the sky, with a ring around it in blues and greens, the penumbra. I said the word over and over in my head.

Max stopped and kissed me for a long time, which made it seem ok. He rolled over on his back. We're lay there like two dying fish, worn out from flopping too long in shallow water. There was a moment of silence in which the woods seem to pulse like a subtle heartbeat. I took a deep breath, inhaling the peppery leaves, the fresh earth. Clouds are licked the moon, moving swiftly.

"Oops," he said, laughing a little.

"What?"

"We forgot protection."

"What do you mean *we*?"

"I mean, I didn't think of it."

"Well, what were you thinking of?"

"You know, I was just into it. We'll be ok. I mean, just because I didn't wear anything doesn't mean you'll get pregnant. People do it all the time."

"That's true," I tried to agree. "I don't even know if I can."

"Yeah, maybe you can't. That would be good."

It was disgusting, but I was trying to forgive Max even as I yanked up my cotton underpants. In fact, a strange and complicated connection had been forged between us. We didn't discuss it again. Ignore it and it will go away.

∞

I opened my eyes and saw bars surrounding me on all sides. A wooden roof stretched only inches above my head. I was in a cage. My arms and thighs were covered in open wounds. I winced. I was bleeding. Someone was outside the cage, pacing rhythmically, feet in patent leather shoes, tapping on the hardwood floor. As I focused my eyes beyond the bars I saw that the red velvet seats of my high school auditorium were filled with students I recognized. I was on the stage. The person with the tapping feet moved around the cage dragging a whip. He stepped closer and my eyes slowly followed the length of his body up to his face. His cape was black and lined with purple satin, his hair greased back with pomade, his face menacing and purposeful - Max's face. He cracked the whip. I cowered like a wildcat. The crowd jeered. Max unlocked the cage, cracked the whip, and clicked his shoes. "No!" I shouted at the unsympathetic crowd. "NO!"

I didn't get to experience the delicious in-between time that often happens right after waking from a dream. Instead, I felt a sickening heaviness accelerating toward me, faster and faster, my pulse speeding up to the moment when the anxiety hit and I couldn't tolerate lying in bed. I had to get up and move around, to flex my muscles, to distract myself. What did the dream mean? Did it mean anything at all? The questions didn't matter. Whether it meant something or not, it was the kind of dream that washed me with a feeling I couldn't shake. Who was Max? What was I doing?

I didn't eat breakfast. I looked out the window, calculated that it was threatening to rain. I threw on my gray T-shirt, old jeans, and blue rubber boots. Avoiding my sister, whose music escaped through the crack in her door, I slipped out the front door and walked into the woods. My cat Ladybug followed me voicing quiet chirps. "Are you okay?" she seemed to be asking. I scooped her up and we walked back a narrow deer path toward my rock. I avoided the birches.

I looked up at the trees, the bright green, full leaves of summer curling out of the tips of branches, green fronds rising up out of the dry sediment. If only I could've just been one of those trees. If only life were simpler. Ladybug sniffed a log and turned back to look at me, her mouth half open in that funny expression cats get when they smell something particularly putrid and delicious. Something nasty was percolating in the pit of my stomach. It was a slow, brooding kind of despair. I wanted to talk to my mother about what was happening to me, but I couldn't. She would be so disappointed in me. I also couldn't stop seeing Max. I just couldn't. He was my lifeline in school, my ticket to a social life that wasn't agonizing. I knew it was ridiculous for me to give him so much power, but on the other hand I'd never known pain like the pain of feeling outside the social network of high school. I didn't know what Max did during the day, or on nights when we didn't meet. There were a lot of things we didn't talk about.

I stared into the pines, ruminating, thinking myself into a state of near unconsciousness, ungrounded and spaced out. My eyes relaxed and got blurry, my breathing slowed and quieted, and right there in the baby white pines, I saw the man again. He was standing about ten feet from me covered in white feathers. I could see his face: he had brown skin and a gaunt face. I could see the trees right through him. His eyes were deep and dark and his expression was neutral — not friendly, not menacing. Our eyes met. Some kind of energy stretched from his ghostly retina to mine. I was glued to the ground, too freaked out to move. His mouth didn't move, but I started to hear words in my head.

"Listen," I heard first. Then, "Follow me. Your light called to me. Don't be afraid. I can see your light from a distance."

"Who?" I asked. "Who are you?"

"I see you. I am Whitefeather. You have a bright light. I need you to follow me."

"Follow you where?" He didn't answer. I blinked, focusing my eyes and he was gone. Only Ladybug scuffled out of the brush. I sat there stunned. My pulse was racing. I'd really lost it. Was I hallucinating? Who was he? Were those his words, or was it my imagination? Maybe I was going insane.

∞

Over the next week, I started having panic attacks. I would wake up in the middle of the deep, quiet night with fear hitting me like an eighteen-wheeler flattening my Volkswagen. Sometimes I would cry, and sometimes I would hyperventilate. My breath was quick, short, and unsatisfying. Sometimes I would get up and walk around my room, careful not to step on the parts of the floor that creaked. I looked at myself in the mirror and didn't recognize the deep green eyes, the small nose, dimpled chin, golden hair. In the half-light of the early morning, I was a specter, a spook, a freak. I felt like I was only half a person. Somehow my interior landscape had been sucked dry and violated. I tried not to think much about what happened between Max and me on that full moon night in the birches, or Whitefeather's insistent request. It was just something that I wanted to forget. Thinking about it gave it life. And yet I couldn't forget. Instead, it boiled up when I was asleep, waking me in a pool of sweat, with a pounding heart.

I was starting to think there was something wrong with my body. My breasts were sore, even when the soft cotton of my nightgown brushed them, or when I ran down the steps. I kept looking for signs of illness. I figured maybe it was PMS, and hoped it wasn't something worse like gonorrhea or those other weird diseases we learned about in health class. I examined myself with a mirror hunched over the toilet, convinced that anything I saw was a sign of some terrible venereal disease. I had a pamphlet from the school nurse's office that described the various symptoms of each STD. I read it over and over, hoping that with each inspection I'd find something new and enlightening, something that would finally put my mind at ease.

Days and then weeks went by. Max and I snuck out once a week, sometimes twice. I'd become very familiar with the vinyl seats of his parents' Jeep and the way my skin stuck to them. When I peeled away it made a fart sound, but we never laughed. I couldn't be with him in my woods anymore. I was afraid Whitefeather would appear to me again. I'd become a slut like Cassandra, promiscuous like Serena. I felt worn out like an old dishtowel that was washed and rung dry too many times.

Also, I didn't want to admit it, but my period was late. Really late. I had no proof, but I didn't need it. *I knew.*

9

Getting pregnant at seventeen was a strange kind of humiliation that snuck up my spine and swelled in my belly like a sickness I couldn't shake. While being the obvious repercussion of having sex, I felt caught in the middle of a shameful and filthy act. Having sex and not getting pregnant was much more forgivable. The girl who got pregnant was somehow more foolish than the girl who took the same risk and just got lucky.

My own body became my enemy. It attracted trouble and then created more. I felt the moment it happened that full moon night as the birches leaned toward us. The earth swelled around me in subtle puffs of leaf litter. I heard the whippoorwill cry while Max's strong hands held me there. I felt it move into me, and felt that electric transformation. I was paralyzed in a way, though I was conscious, I was caught, a speared fish flapping, opening its mouth for water, finding only dry, harsh air. I spent the beginning of July full of anguish. What had I done?

I needed an outlet for my self-loathing. I bought black lipstick at the costume shop and dressed myself like a gothic freak in mourning. I moved into darker moods, frightened my family, sulked in my room. I wanted to be nothing, fall into a deep, frothing sea of nothingness, disappear into the shadows in corners of rooms, and blend into the scenery like one of those stick insects that freezes on the screen-door in the summertime. I sat on the toilet willing the blood to start flowing, pressed on my belly, thought I could push it out, did jumping jacks, laid in bed praying for cramps. Nothing. I thought maybe if I never said anything, never did anything, it would just go away. I knew that wasn't true, but denial is powerful. Denial is like a sweet and forbidden candy, decadent because you know it's a rare and temporary treat, a quick fix that will leave you hurting.

I started to think about Cassandra. She was just a girl like me with bad luck, who dated assholes. I had the sudden compulsion to call her, to tell her she was really a good girl after all, that it wasn't her fault, that she deserved better. What I really needed was for someone to say that to *me*. I'd started throwing up in the morning. I was still having panic attacks. I'd become a sister to Regan, the possessed girl in The Exorcist by the looks on my parents' faces, though they had no idea why. I was transforming.

I had to tell Max. The nausea and the sickness were too much for me to ignore. I decided to tell him on one of our regular sneak out sessions in late July. We'd pulled the Jeep up into a clearing along Haneyville Road. I'd spritzed myself with a perfume called Poison. As usual, the summer insects were orchestrating their song, and the creek gurgled a few feet from the Jeep as it splashed on slime-encrusted rocks. I was trembling and my hands were clammy. I didn't want to suffer any longer so I just blurted it out before the Jeep's engine even settled itself.

"I'm pregnant."

"What?"

"You heard me."

"No. How? I mean, when? That one night? Shit." He paused, staring out the windshield at the woods and the creek. His hands still gripped the wheel. I could see the blood leaving his knuckles as he squeezed it. His arms began to tremble. "Oh my God. This totally sucks. Are you sure?"

"Yes, I couldn't be any surer."

"How long have you known? I mean, how much, how far?"

"Over a month, but I wasn't sure until I started puking."

"Well, I have some money saved. I can give you some for an abortion." His arms relaxed a little and he let them drop from the wheel to his lap. "That's what we'll do. I mean, girls do that all the time. Did you know Cassandra had one? Why are you looking at me like that? It's easy. They just suck it out."

I'd become suddenly and ferociously protective of this life inside me. I moved my hands to my stomach. "No. I can't. I won't do that."

"What do you mean you *can't*? You can't keep it! How fucked up would that be? Us as parents? Forget it. You have to get rid of it."

"You don't understand. You don't have this thing inside you. It's a baby, Max. I'm going to have a baby. I can't just 'get rid of it.'"

"But girls do it all the time."

"You think it's that easy? I mean, yeah, I thought about it, but now I don't know. I kind of like the idea. Someone for me to love. Someone who is all my own, a part of me. I like that."

"You have me to love. Isn't that enough?"

His words enraged me. "I'm talking about something different, Max."

We sat in silence. Max was drumming his fingers on the steering wheel in an irritating rhythm. I twisted the strap of my purse between my fingers and crossed and uncrossed my legs. He flipped on the radio and then turned it off again.

"This is fucked up," he said, and suddenly got out of the Jeep. "This is so fucking fucked up!" The Jeep shielded me from the full volume of his voice. He began repeatedly punching the trunk of a white pine. His arms moved like they were made of rubber, like an athlete. I tried to focus through the dusty windshield. His figure was blurry and I couldn't make out his expression. I didn't want to, anyway. I was afraid to get out of the Jeep. He'd never hit me, but I had a feeling he was capable of it. I was beginning to discover that when Max got angry, he got violent.

He got back in the Jeep and his hand was bleeding where the bark cut through his skin.

"I'm sorry. I get mad sometimes. I have to let it out. I just can't fucking believe this." As he says the word "fucking" he hits the steering wheel with his bleeding hand, rocking the Jeep and honking the horn by accident. We both jump, startled.

"Max, calm down. It'll be fine. This stuff happens. Lots of kids are just accidents and lots of teenage girls have babies."

"Yeah, but not *me*. This stuff doesn't happen to *me*."

"It didn't happen to *you*, Max, it happened to *me*. I'm the one who has to squeeze a kid out of me!"

"Yeah, but just you wait and see how my parents react to this. Holy fucking Jesus."

"I'm taking you home. I can't get in the mood now."

"Well, neither can I!" I shouted, folding my arms across my chest.

I was watching myself from above. The hardest part was convincing myself that it really was happening. Telling Max helped a little, and my body was constantly reminding me that something miraculous was going on inside it. I never thought of myself as a fertile woman. I was barely a woman at all, but somehow I was incubating a baby. I toyed with the idea of marrying Max and living happily ever after, but I knew that wasn't going to happen. I knew he would never be my husband. I wasn't even sure if he was still my boyfriend.

∞

After I got home I stood in front of the mirror staring into my eyes. I can't remember where I heard it, but someone told me once that it is a great and powerful thing to stare at yourself in the mirror. I mean, really stare, making eye contact with yourself. As you stare, tell yourself "I love you." Say it out loud. I tried it once, and felt embarrassed. It's a scary thing to really stare into your own eyes. Sometimes it's terrifying. I stood and examined myself. It was like someone new and unfamiliar was emerging slowly, along with the umbrella ferns and mushrooms and katydids. The more I stared, the less I recognized myself. I felt different and at that moment I was somewhat at peace. I put my hands on my belly expecting to feel its fullness. Nothing - flat as a pancake.

The next morning, after a night of vivid dreams, I got up as usual, and was greeted with the familiar woozy head and queasiness. I stood for a moment in my mint green summer pajamas spinning between my pastel walls and shelves full of teddy bears before I had to bolt to the toilet and puke. Olivia heard me.

"You OK?" She peered around the corner of the bathroom door. I quickly considered whether or not I wanted to tell her what was happening to me. I had to admit I needed someone to confide in. I could tell Serena and I would eventually, but at the moment I was bursting with the need to talk about it. I stood up and wiped my mouth, flushing the toilet and hoping she didn't see that I had been throwing up.

"No I'm not, Liv." She came in, still in her nightgown, hair in a mess of matted waves, sleep in her eyes. Her nightgown was pink with capped sleeves and cartoon cats. She reached down for my hand.

"Come on, get up and rinse off your face." This was something our mother always did for us when we were sick. She guided me to the sink and turned on the water for me. The cool water on my face felt wonderful. My eyes cleared a little and I swooshed the water around in my mouth, rinsing out the bitter taste that lingered. My throat felt scratchy from dry heaves.

"Is it the flu?"

"I don't know."

"Do you know anyone who has the flu?"

"No."

"Maybe it's morning sickness!" she said heartily and way too loudly.

"Shut up!"

"Whoa." She lowered her voice to a whisper. "You mean it *is*?"

"I think so. But you have to keep your mouth shut. Don't tell them."

"Are you sure? Have you taken a test?"

"No. I guess I should. Want to go with me to the store? I could use some company."

∞

I sat on the toilet holding the little white cylinder underneath me. I felt obscene trying to pee on it. The box came with two tests, so I peed on both. Olivia and I waited tensely for the first one. I prayed for one pink line, which meant negative. Two lines was the other option, which I was dreading. We paced through the house, the hardwood floor creaking under our feet while the tests sat on the sink in the downstairs bathroom. When the time was up I brought them out into the kitchen. We both looked at the same time: two pink lines. Test number two delivered the same result. 100% pregnant.

"Are you gonna keep it?" she asked me with quiet excitement.

"I guess. I mean, I think so. I kind of want to. Should I?"

"I don't know, I mean, what will you do? What will the kids at school think?"

For the first time I thought about going back to school. I might not be able to. In fact, of course I couldn't go back there. Not in my condition, not in the condition I'd be in soon. I imagined walking through the halls with a growing belly. While students talked about lacrosse, tennis, homework, the school musical, I'd be remarking on how the baby was kicking, and how my ankles were swollen. I couldn't face school with a huge stomach, while Max went about his regular flirtations, unaffected and skinny. He might lose interest in me if I got huge.

"Shit, I don't know, Liv. It's just gonna suck no matter what."

"Why did you do it?" She whispered, as if it would soften her question.

"I didn't do it. I mean, it just happened. I can't explain it. It wasn't on purpose."

I couldn't tell her about that night. It was too hard to explain how it happened without feeling like it was somehow my fault. The pregnancy was shameful, but admitting how it happened felt even worse.

She rolled her eyes. "I *knew* you guys were fooling around. It was pretty obvious. I mean, everyone at school could see it."

"Thanks, but I don't need to know that."

"What no one could figure out was why you went out with him, knowing what a dog he is. I told you he was."

"He is not a dog."

"Natalie, face it, he is. Every girl in school has been hit on by Max Munroe. I'm surprised he didn't hit on me! Did you know, the last week of school by the lockers, Max was coming onto Kerri Kowalski and Dan Mullen came up to him, grabbed him by the neck and pushed him up against the lockers saying something like 'If you ever hurt Natalie, I'll kick your ass for real.' Max just hung there frozen."

It was like Olivia had been dying to tell me this, but kept it to herself for months. Now, finally she was telling it, and she was talking fast with her hands, her face animated.

"Kerri Kowalski? She's gross. Are you kidding? Dan did *that*? Why didn't you tell me that before?" I asked, horrified. This added a whole new dimension to things.

"Well, I don't know. You were so crazy about Max. I assumed you'd figure it out."

"I didn't think Dan gave a crap about me."

"Apparently he does. He can be a jerk, but underneath, he's a really nice guy. I bet you there was more to that fight than Max let you know about."

"Maybe." The reality was slowly settling in. Max might have been cheating on me. The whole school knew, and yet no one had the decency to tell me. Not even my sister.

I walked to the front door and looked out, trying to calm down. My mother's apple trees had fruit that year, though they were never very good — always tart and tough. There was a blue bird nest in one of them. Our house was heating up like an oven. I took a deep breath, but it wasn't enough. I walked into the kitchen, opened the refrigerator and stared at it, hoping for an insight. Nothing. I walked to the living room. Pictures from my childhood were gathered on the mantle and I hated them. I hated the outfits my parents dressed me in. Not because they were ugly, but just because I needed to hate something. I opened a window and a slight breeze lifted the curtains. I could hear a wasp buzzing. All these small pieces of life continued on in their tiny worlds while mine slowly crumbled.

It was a hot day, reaching nearly 100 on my dad's outside thermometer. My anger festered and grew as we hung around the house overheated and lethargic. I kept going over it in my head, picturing Max with Kerri, with Colleen, with Allyson, with the multitudes of girls I'd seen him talking to at school. As the heat escalated, my walls began to break down. I couldn't talk without choking. I couldn't talk to Olivia anymore.

I ran up to my room and grabbed the first thing I saw — my alarm clock — and threw it at the wall. It shattered into pieces of white plastic, batteries and colored wires. The plastic still read "Dream Machine" on the floor. I pushed my white dresser, rocking my pink lamp back and forth. It threatened to fall off. At a loss, not wanting to break anything else, I punched at the air as long overdue sobs erupted out of me. I hated crying. I leaned into the dresser with my back against it and slid slowly down to the floor. "What did I do to deserve this?" I yelled at the room.

10

I was growing along with the forest as the veronica protruded in fuzzy wands and purple coneflowers stretched their necks. The nights were hot, sticky and full of insects. There was a new dog someplace over the hills that barked at night. It sounded forlorn. I lay in bed for hours listening to the new sound, the way it echoed through the hills, muffled by full trees and grasses and the distant roar of cars on the far roads. I hadn't forgotten that there was an enormous detail that I needed to share with my parents. I just couldn't bring myself to do it.

The Franklin Street Carnival had arrived in Old Mill. Teenagers flocked to it like ants to a sugary spill on the sidewalk. Serena invited me to go with her, Ed and Jayne on Friday night. I hadn't told Serena about my situation, though I knew I should. Serena might have been able to offer some comfort, but ever since hearing that the entire school seemed to know that Max was a "dog" except me, the thought of telling her had made me feel so ashamed. I agreed to go to the carnival, and decided I would tell her there.

The carnival was held in an open field adjacent to the trailer park, "the other side of the tracks" according to my dad. Olivia was going too, but with her friend Jay and a few other friends. We got ready together, primping in the bathroom, experimenting with hairstyles, discussing which tank tops made our boobs look bigger, and which shorts were the most flattering. For Olivia, these decisions were of utmost importance. I was beyond the days of caring what I looked like. Looking good was the last thing I wanted. Looking good was what got me knocked up. I wore a long black skirt and a black tank top. My look was completed with black nail polish and black lipstick. I didn't need any other color.

The street was lined with cars squeezed together like sardines, some with two wheels up on the curb, others eased partway onto people's private driveways. We parked a few blocks away and walked. The first thing I saw was the Ferris wheel illuminated in the distance. We all stared, transfixed, like pilgrims arriving at our Mecca. The smell of funnel cakes wafted through the air and my stomach growled. The mix of people at these carnivals was always the same. There were men with the classic haircut — long in back, short in front. Their counterparts almost always wore white, fringed boots, and sported the wall of bangs that went out of style in 1989. Juxtaposed against these carnival regulars were the upper middle class doctors, attorneys and local realtors who went there to rub elbows with the hoi poloi. We ignored everyone except the other kids our age. They were all that interested us.

Ed's hair was spiked and he was wearing a shirt that looked like it was made out of Serena's fishnets. Serena had on socks that went up over her knees in black and white stripes. We bought funnel cakes and cotton candy. I was so hungry, I devoured my funnel cake, leaving powdered sugar all over my face and fingers.

"Damn girl! You hungry or something?" asked Serena. "I haven't seen you in so long, it's been like, a month!"

"Yeah, I've been busy."

"Doing what?"

"Nothing, really."

Ed stood defiantly in his ripped shirt. "Let's do something cool. Like, the Salt and Pepper Shakers," he suggested.

"I can't go on those, they make me puke," said Serena.

"I'll go," said Jayne. Serena and I glanced at each other in amazement. Jayne wasn't the type to be so daring.

"That's fine, Natalie and me will walk around and talk. Meet us at the Tilt-a-whirl in like half an hour."

She hooked her arm in mine and pulled me away from them. We walked toward the games where men with old T-shirts yelled at us from behind the counter. "One Dollar! Try your hand at this! Come on ladies, give it a whirl!" and on and on. We stuck our noses in the air.

"So, what have you *really* been doing? I bet you've been getting it on with Max all this time."

"Not exactly. I haven't talked to him for a couple weeks, actually."

"Really? You break up?"

"No, well not officially. I don't know exactly how to say it. I'm…" I pulled her behind a building where people were shooting at pieces of paper with red stars on them. I whispered. "I'm pregnant."

"What?"

"Yes."

"You're kidding, right?"

"No."

"A bunch of times I thought I was, but I wasn't. You really are?"

"Yes. I took two tests."

"What are you gonna do?"

"I'm gonna keep it. Did you know that Max might have been cheating on me?"

"Cheating? Nah, I just figured you guys had an open thing going on. Ed and I are kinda like that."

"No! It was not an open thing at all. Why didn't anyone tell me?"

"Well, you never talk to anybody. No one knew the details. Anyway, you guys hadn't been together that long. It was only like three weeks or something and school was ending. Are you really going to have this baby?"

"He was gonna give me money for an abortion, but I said no. I think he's mad at me now."

"Oh man, Natalie, you should've taken it. Shit. That would have solved everything."

"I just didn't want to. You know how they do it? They suck it out of you."

"Yeah, but imagine *pushing* it out of you later?"

"Whatever. I'm having it. I think it's a girl."

The sound of BBs shredding paper ceased for a moment and at the same time, Serena's eyes widened. She was facing the current of people walking slowly around the carnival. "Natalie, Max is *here.*"

"Shit, I thought he might be. I just knew it somehow. I just *knew* it."

"He's with Allyson."

"Oh god, no way." I turned to look, and there he was, leaning over Allyson, who beamed up at him, olive skin and brown hair pulled tightly into a barrette. "What does he see in her? She just never goes away." My pulse quickened, and my mouth went dry.

"Are you gonna talk to him?"

"I don't know. Should I?"

"Well, yeah! Dude, he's the father of your baby!" She put her hand over her mouth. "Oh my god that is so weird!"

"I hate her. I hate that girl."

Beyond the carnival, the low mountains were thick with leaves. The hills were filled with rhododendron. The crickets were laughing at me. The fat men soliciting could see right through my soul. Allyson was going to take one look at me and know my innermost secrets.

"I can't do it."

"Yes you can!" shouted Serena. She gave me one big push and I emerged from the shadow of the building into the stream of people, dodging them as they moved past me. Serena put her hands on either side of her mouth. "Max!" She yelled above the hum of machinery, people and games. "Yo Maxwell!"

My brain began to feel like it was floating in a bowl of water. When I moved, I could feel waves sloshing in my skull. I started to feel nauseous. I looked around at the people walking past me. It was a sea of faces, and slowly, every face was beginning to resemble the ghostly man.

"Are you ok?" shouted Serena from behind me. I turned around to answer her and saw Whitefeather, as I'd started to call him, standing behind her. He raised a hand in greeting and said something, but I couldn't hear him. He began to dissipate into the air, leaving nothing but the darkness of the canal on the edge of the carnival. "Natalie!" She yelled. Her voice echoed in my ears long after she mouthed the words. I began to lose my balance, I felt like I was going to puke. "I need to sit down." Everything was going black. I blinked my eyes. Nothing.

Max had turned and was looking in our direction. He saw me teeter and fall into the crowd. Some people stepped around me and some stopped momentarily saying, "Is she ok?" and then walked on, leaving the responsibility to someone else. Max and Serena ran to me at once, shielding me from the persistent feet. Max pulled me up off the ground and half-carried me behind the buildings to the water.

"Natalie, what the fuck? What's going on? Are you on something?" Max's voice was pulling me from the deep recesses of my unconsciousness. Like swimming through milky water, I surfaced, opened my eyes and saw the silhouette of his messy hair hanging down around his face. He was holding my head in his hands. Serena was standing behind him.

"Did I faint?" I asked groggily.

"Yeah, dude. You went down," said Serena from the shadows.

"Did you smoke?" asked Max, turning toward Serena, looking for an answer.

"No, man, she's pregnant. She wouldn't do that."

"What happened?" he asked as I lifted myself up on my elbows.

"I just got dizzy. I needed to sit down. I thought I saw the man again."

"It must have something to do with being pregnant. Maybe this happens to pregnant women," he suggested.

"Maybe, but I feel ok." I wasn't dizzy or nauseous anymore. I stretched my legs and Max helped me stand up. "I thought you might be here," I said, peering through the darkness, trying to get a good look at his face. "I didn't think you'd come with *her*, though."

"Allyson? We were just studying Bio at her house and decided to come over here." Max looked around. "Where did she go? She must have left. Shit." He examined the crowd beyond the temporary buildings and turned back to me. "You look so beautiful." He bent down and wrapped his arms around me in a tight hug. "I missed you."

"You did? You haven't called for a while."

"Yeah I did, you just never answered."

"I'm home all the time"

"I've been studying a lot at the college."

"With your imaginary professor?"

"No, with a real one. Allyson is helping me. What's with the third degree?"

"Nothing. I just heard stories from Olivia."

"Your sister makes stuff up. She doesn't like me."

"She said Dan Mullen defended me in the locker room."

"Dan? No way. He's a moron. It's the other way around. He was talking shit to Kerri about you and me."

My mind was spinning. Who was I supposed to believe? I wanted to believe Max, but Olivia wouldn't lie. Would she?

"I need water."

"I'll buy you some lemonade. Come on," he said. Serena followed us through the crowd.

I didn't know if I wanted to laugh or cry. I was losing my mind. I couldn't get it out of my head that Max and I were meant to be together, even though I also couldn't accept him the way he was. It was hard for me to comprehend that I had a long life ahead of me full of other lovers, other friends. We were having a baby together. He would be the dad. I kind of liked that picture, but I didn't know if it was healthy or not. On some level I knew it wasn't, but my impulses won out.

Max bought me a fresh squeezed lemonade. He was taking care of me and I liked the feeling. I relaxed and held his hand. We walked as I sipped my lemonade. Soon we were on the edge of the carnival and the sounds were a little muffled. It felt private.

"I missed you."

"Yeah."

"This is a nice spot." He began kissing me, sending me back to those first few days when everything seemed so magical. Before my life began to fall apart. "Everything's gonna be ok, Natalie."

"It is?"

"Yeah." His hands were inside my clothes. His hands were like fleas getting inside your clothes before you even knew it. Like heat seeking missiles.

"I need you. It's been so long. I'm ready to explode."

"I bet."

"You should move with me to college after we graduate."

"What?"

"Yeah, you and the baby."

"Oh, I bet your parents would love that!"

"We don't have to tell them."

"I don't think so, Max. Not unless you go to school around here. I'll probably stay here with my parents so they can help me. If they don't disown me."

"They won't disown you. They aren't like my parents." He laughed nervously. "Well, I'm applying to Swarthmore, Harvard and Columbia."

"Can you really imagine a baby at any of those places? No, I'm staying here. Maybe you should too."

"I can't *not* go to college!"

"I haven't really thought that far." I'd had enough of his college talk. I needed to feel alive and okay. The bright lights of the carnival offered escape, and some kind of affirmation even though I couldn't articulate it. Serena had disappeared. I felt a pang of guilt. I should've stayed with Serena. Max and I walked around for at least half an hour and finally found her. She was with Jayne and Ed near the Tilt-a-whirl. Serena was distant, Jayne suspicious.

∞

It was a Friday, I'd fainted at the carnival a week ago. I was sitting at the porch table with Olivia when I started to get cramps. Cramps weren't right. I never got cramps. My belly clenched tightly and then eased up a bit. I relaxed. It was probably nothing. I put my book down, dog-eared the page and looked at her.

"What?" she asked.

"I need to tell you something freaky."

"Okay," she said with apprehension.

"I've been seeing things. Not a thing, a man."

She raised her eyebrows at me.

"I mean, I've been seeing a spirit."

"Like a ghost?"

"I'm not kidding."

"Have you told Mom?"

"No way. Are you crazy?"

"She'd take you to Pastor Steuben. Is it scary? I mean, maybe you *should* go to him."

"No, I don't want to talk to him. It's not scary. It's just like this guy appears to me sometimes, and once he talked to me."

"You sure you're not making this up?" She laughed nervously.

"No. Why would I?"

"I don't know, for attention or something."

"I think I get enough of that around here, don't you?"

"I guess. Where did you see him? In the house?"

"No, I saw him when Max and I were on our first date, then again in the pasture at Jeremy's, and then I saw him again in the woods behind our house. Then again at the carnival."

Cramps were starting up again and my stomach seized with pain.

"You don't look so good. You feel ok?" Olivia asked.

"I just have some cramps."

A few minutes of silence went by as we both just stared at the yard, listening to the sounds of summer.

"Have you seen Max lately?"

"I saw him last week at the carnival. That's when I fainted," I said.

"So what's up with you guys?"

"I don't know. He's busy with some research project at the college, and we haven't been seeing each other as much. I think he's mad that I'm keeping the baby. I honestly don't even know if we're still together."

"It kinda makes sense."

"He hasn't told his parents yet. I think he's really afraid of what they'll do."

"Well, he'll have to tell them eventually. So will you."

"I know. The longer we wait the worse it's gonna be."

"Are you still in love with him?"

I had to think about that. "I guess, but I don't know why. It's stupid. Maybe if he goes off to college like he plans to, and meets a new girl, then it'll be easier. Because I'm pretty sure that will happen. He might pretend to be faithful to me, but he won't be."

"Doesn't that hurt your feelings?" Olivia asked cautiously.

"Not anymore." I paused, sensing more cramps. "I'll be right back."

The screen door squeaked as I opened it. My denim shorts were sticking to my sweaty legs. Ladybug scooted through the open door as I walked inside. I went into the bathroom and slowly pulled down my pants praying there wasn't blood. How strange. Three months ago all I wanted was to bleed. Now it was the complete opposite.

There was blood. Not a whole lot, but enough to make me nervous. I knew what it might mean. I wasn't naive anymore. Miscarrying was kind of a good thing, right? But I didn't want it to happen. I wanted this baby, but I was afraid to call anyone or go to the hospital. This wasn't how I want the world to find out. The house was quiet. Both my parents were at the college. I could smell my mom's spices from the herb cabinet in the kitchen. The humidity made everything more pungent.

"Liv, something's wrong," I said when I went back out to the porch. "I'm bleeding a little bit."

"You are? Is that normal?"

"I don't think so. I'm gonna keep an eye on it. I don't feel right."

She smiled at me with pity. I don't think she understood what I was saying. "Let's watch a movie. Want to? I rented *The Doors* yesterday," said Olivia. "Let's make salads and watch it." Olivia had started mothering me, which was a little odd, since she was two years younger. She had that kind of personality — stable and dependable and generally level-headed. She wasn't predisposed to wild moods, or the sullen gloom that I got into.

I needed to take my mind off the thoughts that were tumbling around inside my head. Olivia didn't seem to want to hear my stories about the mysterious man. I think she sensed that I was moving into things that were not only un-Christian, but potentially dangerous. I didn't expect her to understand, but I wanted to tell her anyway. We moved into the kitchen. I pulled out a bag of red leaf lettuce and got out two plates. I piled mine with lettuce, a chopped tomato and some tuna salad. I finished it off with black olives and dressing. Leaving a mess that our mom would have scolded us for, we moved into the living room. It was so humid, our feet stuck to the tiles making sticky, slapping noises as we walked. The movie unfolded with a swooning Val Kilmer as Jim Morrison. I shoveled the salad into my mouth, eating more out of habit than hunger.

I started to get cramps again. It began as a dull ache that I hardly noticed and gradually built up into a painful clenching — a contraction.

"Pause it. I have cramps again." I hurried to the bathroom. I hadn't been taking any painkillers because I was trying to have a natural pregnancy, but I was seriously reconsidering. I sat down on the toilet and the contractions started to get worse. After all this, with no warning, she was leaving me.

"Are you OK?" implored Olivia's voice from the other side of the door.

"No!" My voice was breaking with tears. For the first time in almost three months I felt totally alone. My body was expelling her, my baby girl. At least I thought she was a girl. I'd never know for sure. The tragedy and the irony of it consumed me. I began to sob. After all the worry, the nasty scenes and the conversations, she was leaving me. The pain rolled through me. I turned around to face the toilet and threw up. The room started to spin and then space... blue space and violet swirls of birds, like the view out of the cockpit of a space shuttle as it leaves the atmosphere, washed over my mind. I was floating and spinning. The floor was no longer made of cold wood. It was soft, pillowing clouds. Suddenly Olivia was screaming.

"Natalie! Wake up! Come on, wake up, please!" She was in the bathroom shaking my shoulders. I'd fainted again.

"Shit, just... hold on. I'm calling an ambulance." She was crying. She left the room. *No, don't leave me. I don't want to be alone.*

Her voice echoed through the farmhouse. "Yes, Hunterdon County, we're the second left on Lomink Road, off of Hennessey Creek Road. It's a dirt road. Yes, Jerry Watson. What? My sister. There's blood and she got sick and fainted. I will. Ok, bye."

Her feet pitter-pattered through the kitchen, down the hall and then she squatted in front of me.

"It's gonna be ok. You're gonna be ok. I called an ambulance. They'll be here soon." She sniffled and ran her hand over my hair. She'd seen a lot for her age, I thought to myself. Almost as much as me. "Try to get up. Ok, wait, I'll get you a pad." She rummaged through the cabinet under the sink. "Here, put this on."

I did what she said and pulled up my pants. The blood was relentless. I'd ruined the bath mat. Soon there was a commotion and three people in EMT uniforms were helping me onto a stretcher. They wheeled me into a white van. Olivia rode along.

"I'm ok. I don't need to go to the hospital. I don't want Mom to know." The EMT technician closed the ambulance door.

∞

"She's awake," whispered Olivia.

"Natalie. Welcome back," said my mother. Her lips were pursed making her mouth look like a prune. I knew that face. "You have a lot of explaining to do."

I was still trying to figure out what was going on. My belly felt like it had been walloped by someone's angry fist. My eyelids were heavy as if I'd been drugged. The three of them were sitting in chairs across the room. My dad had a paper cup of coffee, which he was nursing slowly. Olivia looked tired and worried. She was still in her tank top and jean shorts. My mom and dad were both dressed in their office clothes. My dad always wore jeans with a sports jacket. This time it was a dusty red linen jacket. My mom had on a purple jumper and a white blouse. It's interesting what you notice when you're in an altered state. Mostly what I focused on was my mom's necklace. It was a gold heart-shaped locket with pink and green swirls. I was wondering how they got the pink and green colors onto the gold.

"What happened?" I asked. My mom got up and walked over to my bed. She sat down and her weight made the bed bounce just a little.

"Olivia told us everything. You lost a pregnancy. You were hemorrhaging. That's why there was so much blood."

I started to cry and she reached over to pet my head. She was quiet and I could feel her emotions building. She was a stoic person and didn't show her true feelings much. When she did, it scared me a little because it felt so unusual, like she was losing control. There was always a touch of blame in her when she cried and this time was no different. She began to sniffle. "Oh, honey I wish you would have talked to me. I could have helped you." Her voice cracked. I was ready to lean into her, to surrender to my mother's rare compassion, but then she added. "It's for the best, though. Thank God the Lord knew what was best and gave you a blessing. I just can't believe you didn't tell me."

Anger began to rise in me. "How could I tell you? And you think it's for the best?" I pulled away from her. "How can you say that?"

"Well, it is, honey. You know it is. I'm just glad it happened like this, instead of you having to drop out of school. What were you thinking, anyway? That it would just go away? I mean, did you think we wouldn't notice?"

"No, I didn't think that."

"And how did it happen? I mean, who?"

"Max, Mom, who else?"

"But you weren't seeing Max this summer."

"*Right.*"

"Well I see that conversation did a lot of good!"

"Mom, I love him."

"Sometimes love is just a passing mood, Natalie. You don't love him. You don't even know him."

"Well, I'm beginning to."

"I guess you are. At least in one way. You will *not* see him anymore. Your father and I forbid it, and we will put a call in to the headmaster if we have to." She paused for dramatic effect. I had no response. "By the way, I called Max. He knows. He was quite relieved."

"What?" My fuzzy mind was trying to comprehend it all. I sniffled and blew my nose. "Did you talk to Max or his mom?"

"Max. Promise us you won't see him again. God, Natalie, what a mess. All because you just couldn't control yourself."

"Mom! It wasn't like that!"

"You think I couldn't see what was going on with you? I mean, I thought you would respect our wishes and stop seeing Max, but I see now that you don't respect us at all. I think you're going to need some time to reflect on your behavior. At least your little secret problem is solved now. It's time to move on and thank God that you're healthy and that He forgives you for this... this sin you decided to commit, because that's what it is young lady." She sighed with frustration.

Did I sin? All I could figure was that I must have done *something* wrong. Something I couldn't identify. I must have eaten the wrong things, or maybe on some level, I didn't want a baby, so I unconsciously got rid of her? Maybe it was the coffee I'd been drinking? The herb tea? The hiking? What was it? Max had never told his parents. He forced himself on me, got me pregnant, I miscarried and they would never know. I went through agony, day after hot, sticky day that summer, and he was probably fucking Allyson the whole time.

∞

I should've told him off. Instead, I decided to pack.

I was done with New Jersey. I loathed everyone. Max hadn't even called. Of course I was grounded. Grounded for something I didn't even ask for. I didn't ask for any of it. They thought they had it all figured out. *Natalie the harlot. Natalie the whore. She couldn't control herself. She has no respect. What a wild thing. Nothing like her sister.* They didn't know either one of us. I was going to get out of there. Just for a little while. I'd go visit my cousin Karla in California. She'd been living there since college. She was twenty-four. She'd let me stay with her for a little while. It was only August. I'd just drive out there to clear my head. Other kids had done cross-country drives. They raved about it. I wasn't going to tell my parents. I would just leave a note. "I'm visiting Karla in California. I'll be back before too long. I'll come back in time for school. "I'll be right back."

Part Two

11

No one was awake when I snuck out of the house at 4 AM. Only Ladybug saw me leave. It was so quiet, every step seemed to vibrate through the house. I had a duffel bag and a small backpack. My heart pounded with adrenaline, because I only half-way believed that I was really doing it. I just kept going through the motions. I'd gathered snacks, tapes to play, and my journal. I'd saved a little money over the last year, and I tucked it into my wallet. I'd taken my mother's credit card, which felt really reckless, but I wanted to have it just in case. There was nothing else left. I felt compelled to run to Olivia's room and say goodbye, but I didn't. She would just tell me not to go, and make a commotion.

Pale, thin moonlight streamed through the windows. I stood at the front door and listened to the silence. I could hear the pipes in the walls making noises, but that was all. Then a muffled thump came from my parents' room. My heart jumped into my throat. A confusing mix of emotions flooded me. The rebel in me said I'd better get moving before they found me with my bags over my shoulder, caught in the act. The little girl in me almost wanted to be caught, and then validated with compassion and understanding, but I knew that wasn't going to happen. I walked outside and closed the door silently behind me.

The early morning chill was strong. It was that in-between time when the crickets had quieted down, but the birds and other daytime creatures were still asleep. I breathed in a few last lungfuls of Western Jersey late-summer air, and choked down tears as I turned out of the driveway onto Lomink road. There was always a moment for me between the welling of tears and outright sobs where I either decided not to cry or failed at suppressing them. It always hurt in my throat. My eyes blurred as the road sped by. I passed the spot where I saw a bobcat jump from the top of the bank and run across the road. I'd seen wild turkeys on that road, too. Once, I even thought I saw the ghost of Greta Dorflinger who was allegedly murdered somewhere along the road in the 1800s. Her vaporous silhouette had glowed in my headlights for a moment before she disappeared into the blackness of the night. The road was part of my history. I wasn't leaving forever. I couldn't stop crying, though. Some part of me knew it was because I was never going to be the little girl I'd been for seventeen years. That phase of my life was over.

My mind wandered to Max. He would be surprised to hear that I left. I was going to sock everyone and I loved that. I felt sad for Max, and sad to be leaving him, but we would both recover, and we would have to recover away from each other for a little while. I imagined us together as seniors once I got back. We could patch things up. I planned to write him letters from the road, and hoped his mother wouldn't confiscate them.

When I finally turned my car onto the highway, I could feel the West Coast pulling. Route 80 was like a vein, a pulse drawing me toward the heart of America. I felt free. I turned up the radio and stepped on the gas. I drove across the entire state of Pennsylvania, which was a lot wider than I thought, and finally entered Ohio. I'd been driving for eight or nine hours. "I can make it a few more," I thought, and kept going. My parents would eventually understand. And if they didn't, so be it. I thought maybe I could out-drive the heaviness that I felt bearing down on me, and the strange episodes I'd been suffering from. I was tired of falling down and making a fool of myself. I was starting over. The drive was going to be cleansing.

Olivia would be affected the most; she wasn't ready for me to leave. I loved her, though I never really told her. It wasn't something you said to your little sister. Poor, good Olivia. Maybe someday she would understand me. I knew I'd snapped. Max and my parents were so relieved while I was suffering. It killed something inside of me. My baby died, but I was still alive and I needed sympathy. Even just a sympathy card from Max would have been nice. He was as self-centered as a rock star, but without the ambition or talent. He was just a messed up farm boy trying to be Casanova.

I wanted to drive all the way to Indiana that day. It wasn't even dark out yet. I stopped at a rest area to stretch my legs. There weren't as many trees and the land was flatter and a little dryer. Overall, it was still pretty green, and there were fields of what I thought was wheat, but it might have been something else, soybeans? The rest area was like a mall inside with bright fluorescent lights and sad looking workers in gaudy uniforms. Souvenir shops glared at me like lonely prison cells full of frightening stuffed animals, magnets, and licorice. I went to the bathroom and looked at myself in the full-length mirror. The lights were the kind that made every blemish show up on your face like a purple scar. I was wearing my old Levis. I loved those jeans. The denim was soft and worn down to white threads. My legs were long in proportion to my body, and I suddenly thought that a pair of cowboy boots would look really great on me.

I decided to buy a pair as soon as I found them. I had the money I'd been saving, plus my mother's credit card. Yes, I took it.

I got back in the car and drove until I was delirious and had to stop. I was falling asleep at the wheel. The sun had already set, sinking below the western horizon creating a fierce, blazing sky of clouds. The horizon seemed so much farther away in the middle of the country. I slept lightly and fitfully in my car at a rest area in central Indiana. I could hear cars zooming by on the highway all through the night, and the sun woke me up as soon as it hit the eastern horizon. I started driving early, with no water or breakfast and stopped mid-morning for stale coffee and a blueberry muffin wrapped in plastic. It said, "Homemade" on the wrapper. Somewhere there was a factory full of tired workers who made blueberry muffins in shrink-wrapped plastic for rest areas.

My bones ached from being twisted in a car seat for so many hours. I'd decided to take a more southern route, and I cut down across the center of the country, right through the heart. I crossed the Mississippi in St. Louis and picked up I 70. I couldn't believe how flat it was. Missouri had a strange and fascinating landscape. It wasn't what I expected it to be. On the East coast you picture expansive fields of wheat and corn, but it's really not like that. There are odd land formations that look like they should be called hillocks, buttes, bluffs or mesas. I didn't know what the locals called them. They were smooth and treeless from a distance and had been chiseled by water, which had since dried up. The carved gullies looked like spider veins. I imagined that there was life out there. Probably foxes and weasels and coyotes.

The names of the towns were interesting to say the least. Not all of them, of course, but there were a few that stood out. I wondered if some weary settler landed in this place and was feeling "needful" at the time. Come to think of it, I was feeling rather needful myself. Maybe it was the landscape. By the time I got to

Kansas I felt like I was on another planet. I passed farms with wide-open circular fields. I'd never seen circular fields before and there were bizarre objects in the middle of the flat, dry plains that looked like dinosaurs bobbing their heads down to the grass to eat. I couldn't imagine what they were, so I asked a girl at the rest area in Needful. She told me that they were oil wells. Some were for irrigation, but most were for oil. Something about them really made me feel uncomfortable. They were like evil grasshoppers tapping the blood of the earth.

The sky had been darkening as I'd been driving southwest, and I could see an ominous sky bearing down on me. It was beautiful, actually. I pulled the car over to the side of the road and got out with my camera in hand. To the Northwest was a storm, something like thirty miles away, moving quickly in my direction. The wind was picking up too, and my hair was beginning to swim around my face, whipping across my eyes. I pulled my red flannel shirt from the car and wrapped it around myself. A bolt of lightning touched ground miles to the West. I'd never been able to see a storm from so far away before. I couldn't decide if I wanted to wait for it, or drive. It seemed like maybe it was past the stormy season, but I didn't know.

The air was thick and humid, and had that smell of ozone that comes before a storm. I got back in the car and decided to drive a bit more. I figured if I passed a cheap motel, I'd check in, because my back ached badly and I didn't want to drive in the rain. I had enough money to get a room, so why not? Driving in the rain made me nervous. It was about 4 PM and there was a Super 8 on the outskirts of Hallock, Kansas. What the hell. It was my first time getting a hotel room on my own. I'd only ever shared a room with my parents or Olivia on family vacations. I pulled up and walked inside to ask for the cheapest room they had. It smelled like cigarettes. They had the radio behind the counter tuned to a news station broadcasting information about the storm. It was a violent thunderstorm moving, right toward Hallock.

There was also a tornado warning, which made the hairs on the back of my neck stand up. The key was in my hand. The room was paid for. I wandered out of the mustard colored office full and grabbed my necessities from the car. The storm was getting closer and I could see sheets of rain pelting the earth. I opened my room, put my bag down and then walked back out, past the office and pool to the street where there was a small burger stand called Hallock Cheez'n Fry. I ordered a cheeseburger with everything on it and French-fries. After carrying it back to my room, hot and steaming, wrapped in paper and slapped into a red and white gingham print cardboard boat, I flopped backward onto the bed and melt into the mattress. It felt so good to rest my back flat on the bed like that. I'd never felt anything so good in my life. Then, a clap of thunder rocked the building. I bolted up off the bed and ran to the door.

The rain hadn't quite started yet. The air was thick and green. It smelled like electricity. I pulled a plastic lawn chair in front of my door and sat down to eat and watch the sky. I could hear the hum of air conditioners from nearby rooms and people scrambling to pull things inside before the rain hit. I wanted it to rain. I wanted it to flood. I wanted some kind of cataclysmic thing to happen— something to make my own pain seem small. The air was tense and the clouds were threatening to let go. I could feel the pressure building. I breathed deeply and exhaled and feeling of lightness came over me. I was completely free. How rare those moments were. I hadn't felt this way in a long time and it was a glorious feeling.

I was staring into space toward the swimming pool, letting my eyes relax. I could see the energy. It was shimmering like the heat off a hot blacktop road in August, and as I looked, I realized that all had gone quiet. No birds. I didn't even hear any people. Everything and everyone had retreated. I was alone on the patio facing the pool. Then a bolt of lightning struck the ground somewhere across the street. A clap of thunder roared so close that it shook my eardrums and sent me popping right out of my chair. A car alarm started to go off somewhere nearby.

Huge raindrops were pelting the ground and I moved in under the overhanging roof. The rain was getting heavier and was turning to hail. It was falling in chunks the size of marbles. I loved it, but suddenly it was too cold to be outside. The hail was bouncing up onto my shins from the asphalt and it seemed like all the oxygen had been sucked out of the air. It wasn't that late, but it was eerily dark, so I put on my pajamas and crawled into bed. The cable was on and I flipped through the channels. I paused at the news channel where a frazzled looking woman in a tan trench coat was shouting over the rain. A tornado had touched down near Lonetree and was moving southeast toward Hallock.

"Holy shit." I said out loud to the empty, mauve room. This is how I'm going to die. Not of old age in a rocking chair on my front porch in New Jersey, but alone in a crappy motel in Kansas, in a place I should not be in at all. It was not like TS Eliot said. This was no whimper. I was going out with a bang. Did I want a tornado to rip through the motel, rip through my body sending my limbs flying through the air like tree branches? Would it decapitate me? Maybe it would suck me out of the window and fling me against another building. Would I die instantly? It might be a slow and gruesome death. It shouldn't happen like that, but what if it did? I clenched my hands in a fist near my heart.

"Dear God let the tornado pass over this building, dear God don't let me go like this. I have too many things in my life that I want to do. Dear God, please let the tornado miss the motel."

I sat with my knees curled up against my chest and my eyes shut tight. I felt like running to the people in the room next to me. I wanted some kind of comfort. The wind outside was incredible and I heard the sounds of branches and objects hitting the building. I wanted my journal. I absolutely *had* to write to Max at that moment. If it was the end, I had to write him one last letter. My journal was in my car, so I went to the door, opened it a crack and peeked outside. It looked tolerable — just rainy and windy, even though the clouds looked like ocean waves, bubbling and frothing. My car was only about twenty feet away. I grabbed my keys and hurled myself into the rain.

I was soaked by the time I got there and I could hardly breathe. I opened the door and dug through my bag to find my journal. I felt its hard cover and wire spine and quickly pulled it out. The wind was gaining velocity and I thought it might rip the door right off my car. I had to use every muscle in my body to remain standing. I strained to close the door, and finally looked up. I actually heard the roar before I saw it. The sound of a tornado is something you don't think about. You never think of them having a sound but they do. It sounds more like an angry freight train ripping through the earth than a natural force. And there it was, twisting and charging like a blurry gray snake behind the Motel. It stretched higher than anything I'd ever seen from the angry, green-gray clouds right down to the ground. It was a viscous serpent, spewing debris.

It was moving away from the motel, but as they say on TV, tornados are unpredictable. I didn't know what to do. I didn't see anyone around. There was a siren going off, piercing the thick air. Maybe everyone was already in some kind of underground shelter. I don't know how long I stood there. It felt like I was in a vacuum. Should I get in the car and drive? Run inside and hang onto something? Half way toward my door, I saw Whitefeather standing in my room looking out. My curtains were drawn and he was between the curtains and the window. The curtains were not disturbed. He was following me. Or I was following him.

My heart raced so fast that I could barely breathe. I felt two things simultaneously. One was a bone chilling, nauseating fear. The reality of the moment hit me more clearly than anything ever had before: even more than losing the pregnancy. The other feeling was a sort of other-worldliness that made me feel, strangely enough, like I was in the very best place for me to be. It was like the feeling I had in the car once with Olivia when we were driving and listening to Janis Joplin. Everything was ok.

Whitefeather was still in the window as I approached my door, but was beginning to dissipate as I reached for the door knob. *Don't leave!* I wanted to know what he had to say to me. Then he was gone. Why did he just appear like that? What was he trying to say? I didn't have time to think about it. I was possibly on the edge of death. I remembered hearing something about getting into a solid structure like a bathroom or a door jam. Or was that for an earthquake? No one was coming to my door, knocking to tell me what to do, no one would save me. I just sat on the bed in shock and kept glancing at the window wondering if Whitefeather would reappear.

The TV was still tuned to the news and they were announcing that a tornado had touched ground in Hallock on the outskirts of town. I started my letter.

August 30, 1992

Dear Maxwell,

I'm sorry I left without saying goodbye. I'm in a motel in Hallock, Kansas. There's a tornado outside. I'm putting this letter in my pocket so that if I die, someone will find it and give it to you. I just couldn't stay in Old Mill anymore. It was like the air was suffocating me. I needed some sympathy. Don't you care about me at all? I hope you didn't tell Allyson. It's our secret.

I'm probably a fool for saying this and for still feeling this way, but, I want you to know that I love you. I will never love anyone again like I love you. Especially if I die here in this motel. You were my savior in school, my best friend. You were also my downfall. How can you be all those things at once? There's something between us that transcends this reality. You and I are more than school and church and grades and parents and whatever other shit we have to deal with.

We're like the balance of two polarities. Together I think we are magic. Good and bad magic. We can create each other or destroy each other. I see that now. We have alchemy between us. Do you see it? Am I the only one that sees this? We created a life and also destroyed it. It wasn't all me. You were half of her, and half of why she left me. It wasn't her time. Hopefully this is not my time, but if it is, I love you Maxwell Munroe. You are my first love, and my last. Please don't forget me. I'll be with you until the end of time, I promise.

Love,

Natalie

(PS - Tell my Mom, Dad, and Olivia that I love them.)

I felt like I'd just written the most tragically beautiful love letter in the history of love. I ripped the page out and clasped it against my heart before carefully folding and placing it into breast pocket of my cotton pajamas, still wet from the rain. I felt bad that my family was an afterthought, but I didn't have much to say to them. I thought of calling, but that would just torment them since there was nothing they could do but listen to the howling wind on the other end of the phone. It was dark out and the siren was still going off outside. I turned off the lights and left the TV on, lighting the room with a blue glow until the power went out. Then I laid in darkness. I stayed like that for what seemed like hours, listening to sounds of ripping wood and metal and wind.

12

I awoke suddenly in a dark, silent room. The power was off, but I was alive. I got up and went to the door. The rain was slacking off and the wind had calmed down. It had passed me by; the tornado never hit my building. I was actually slightly disappointed. I didn't want to die, but I wanted some more action. If I had died it would have been a slap in the face to everyone who had pissed me off in the last few months. No such luck. It wasn't my time. Max's letter crinkled in my pocket. Should I send it anyway? I tucked it into my bag.

I was alive, wide-awake and there was no reason to stick around, so I got dressed and checked out. As I left the hotel the absurdity hit me. I'd made all the wrong decisions. I'd unconsciously driven directly into the bulls-eye of a tornado, and instead of driving on, I'd decided to sit still and wait for the thing to hit. Maybe that was my whole problem. Instead of running from trouble, I just went right for it and then waited for it to take me. It was true. I'd done that over and over. I almost felt like I deserved it.

The air smelled of damp earth, wood and gasoline. I threw my journal into the back seat and got in the car. It was early, but there was a buzz in the air. I pulled out of the parking lot and drove slowly down the street toward the highway. To the east I saw a gathering of flashing lights. As I got closer I saw that it was actually a farmhouse that had been completely demolished. In fact, a mile-wide stretch had been wiped out. People were standing outside, some staring, some holding each other and crying. Flashing lights were everywhere and I had to swerve all over the road to miss bits of rubble left behind: a kitchen sink, a motorcycle, what looked like a piano, a small shed, pieces of wood, metal and brick. Others had suffered while I slept. I couldn't quite comprehend it. My suffering was nothing compared to this. I considered stopping to help, but what could I do? I drove past, feeling fortunate and guilty.

As the sun got higher, I could see that the land was getting drier and more barren. To find beauty you had to look closer, get out of the car, and walk through the fields to see wildflowers, gullies carved by streams, cottonwoods clustered around low water. The plains stretched on endlessly as far as I could see. I missed the close eastern forests. I felt like a small freckle on the smooth face of the Midwest. I was headed for Colorado. I wanted to see the Great Sand Dunes National Park. I'd seen an ad for them in some western tour book at the last rest area. I also wanted to see Utah. I thought maybe if they were interesting enough, I wouldn't even go to California. I'd drive to Arches National Park, turn around and head for home. By 6 AM the whole world was a gray-yellow glowing expanse of wheat, soybeans and corn. The oil wells were getting more prevalent. I could see them in my peripheral vision, black creatures bobbing slowly to the ground and back up again. Eventually the sun became a blazing orange fire at the horizon in my rear view mirror.

When I reached Colorado, it was a little anticlimactic. I was expecting the Rockies and there was nothing but vast, dry plains. My Jetta was getting tired. The alignment was off, and she just seemed sluggish. I had to press the gas pedal to the floor to go 65. That was another thing about the West—the speed limit is 75 in many cases. I couldn't believe it. Even after staring at the speed limit sign, it just didn't seem possible.

My hands were curled around the wheel and my feet were stuck in position. My back was stiff, my head ached and my eyes burned, but it was a glorious pain. I felt raw and alive, like layers of my self had been peeled back to reveal an inner core that had been hidden until then. The open spaces were frightening, but I felt like I could finally breathe. I stopped at a gas station in eastern Colorado with a farmer in striped overalls out front working on his truck. His face looked like tanned leather, and while many lines cracked across his face, a smile did not. I was a young, juicy morsel in the midst of a dry desert. He looked up and seemed to take notice of my New Jersey plates, but his eyes didn't linger long. He turned back to the innards of his truck.

The inside of the gas station was equally strange. I'd never seen so much beef jerky in my life. The cashier grinned at me with a sort of "hey you're pretty cute" expression. I glanced away and examined the snack selection. The twang of a country ballad was playing in the background. I picked out a package of mesquite flavored jerky and payed for my gas without saying anything except "thanks." I could feel the cashier's eyes on me as I walked out the door.

Every now and then I passed a herd of black cattle, which I learned were Black Angus. I looked for Buffalo, but never saw any. I guess they didn't roam wild anymore. I was in that half-mesmerized state that happens to you if you drive for hours by yourself lost in your own thoughts. I replayed conversations with Max, Olivia's face when we saw the positive pregnancy test, and when she was shaking me awake in the bathroom. It all felt like stuff that wasn't supposed to happen to me. Maybe it had all happened for a reason. It had jolted me out of mundane life into something much more pungent and authentic. No more sitting at home watching MTV, or eating salad on the porch. I wasn't a victim anymore. I was driving, damn it. I could go anywhere, do anything.

I drove for a while, gazing out the windows, recording the landscape as it passed by, chewing on my beef jerky, which was surprisingly good. It made me feel like either a fierce carnivore, or a rugged cowgirl. I started to covet leather boots. I thought of Serena suddenly and I felt a sting. I didn't tell her what I was doing. She deserved a phone call. I make a mental note to call her when I get to a phone. And then, the Rockies appeared as faint lumps in the distance. Before long, I could see more definition: layer upon layer of high peaks that stretched all along the horizon. I could even see snow on some of them. Toward the north a bank of clouds was hovering close to the mountains like a gray curtain. They were actually sort of purple. That song we all sing about the purple mountains' majesty was right after all. My heart began to race.

I thought about the story of Lewis and Clarke who journeyed on foot through the Great Plains all the way to the Pacific Northwest. I imagined traveling across the continent through areas that were still wild and untouched. No gas stations, strip malls, or highways cutting through the land like lacerations. The thought immediately struck me in the heart like a dagger. This land had been dug up, split, paved, tilled, burned, blasted open with dynamite, washed with torrents of water. The buffalo were gone. Native Americans moved from the lush, fertile places into barren, dry reservations. My eyes welled up with tears. I start to feel guilty for driving my Jetta across the country, guzzling fuel and spewing exhaust for my own selfish need to escape. But what else could I do? I felt like I'd been excavated and blasted open, too.

As I approached them, the Rockies made me pull over to the side of the road and stare with my mouth hanging open. They loomed ahead like giant sleeping gods, like beasts of rock and earth and snow. My mind was blown. I felt like I'd left earth and flown to another planet, only to realize that this was the earth, even more miraculous than I'd ever imagined. All the way to the Front Range I took pictures, stopping every half hour or so. There's something about the gigantic spaces of the west that just cracks your mind wide open. I found myself wondering if the big sky country could actually push you over the edge if you were close to insanity. It seemed that every emotion I felt was magnified by the sky. The tornado had given me some kind of a jolt. I had been spared, even though I stood in the path of it, nearly making contact with it. It was like the tornado said, "No, you keep going, you have more to do." I was completely energized and I had to keep driving.

I left the highway south of Pueblo. I stopped at a McDonald's and sat at a greasy orange table eating a cheeseburger and looking at my map. My plan was to drive to Alamosa to see the great sand dunes and then to head northwest through the mountains to Grand Junction and then on to Utah. I drank a big cup of coffee, preparing myself for the drive. It was still early afternoon and it seems like the tornado had happened days ago, not merely hours. I drove down route 25 to a town called Walsenburg, where I picked up a highway that would take me into the mountains and eventually to the Sand Dunes. My car was starting to work hard to climb up the incline, and around me the earth was growing into larger and larger peaks. I passed through a small town. It was hard to believe that people actually lived in the little mountain towns, but there was even a school and a hospital.

What was it like to grow up there? What kinds of jobs did people have? No thick maples and oaks, no fields of baby white pine and sumac, just wide-open dry grass peppered with scrubby plants. Soon snowcapped peaks came into view. One in particular stood out, luminous and savage, to the North.

13

And then the trajectory of my life was forever altered. I was moving along, awestruck by the landscape, when suddenly there was a pop under my hood and what looked like smoke started pouring out of the front of my car. I couldn't see the road in front of me. I pulled over quickly and sat for a few minutes with the engine running. I knew nothing about cars. The smoke was starting to dissipate, so I made a great decision, as I was so prone to do, and I ignored it. I drove on. After about fifteen minutes the car started lurching and sputtering and the engine stopped. I coasted off to the side of the road and sat there in shock. I could see a town up ahead, but it was pretty far away.

I was on the edge of a high prairie that stretched for miles to the Southwest. To the north were the biggest mountain peaks I'd ever seen. There also wasn't a soul on the road. I got out of my car and lifted the hood, but I really couldn't tell much from what I saw. It was just a swirling mass of black, crusty tubes and shapes to me. I left the hood open and leaned up against my door taking in the view. Soon a wind started to kick up dust and I closed my eyes.

I sat in my car for a long time trying to figure out what to do. Logically I knew; I needed to walk down that road to the town, find a phone, get a tow truck to come get my car and then fix whatever was wrong. But I hadn't planned on staying there overnight. I might even have to stay longer than that. I didn't have money for a car repair. The wide-open area I lad landed in was so foreign, so strange, I was suddenly overwhelmed and started to cry. Everything hit me at once. Who did I think I was? Running away, skipping school, only to end up in such a godforsaken landscape? There was no one around. I missed my parents. My dad would have known exactly what to do; my mother would have kissed my head in her condescending way, but it would have been comforting anyway. I put my head down on the steering wheel and after a few minutes I started to go in and out of sleep. I guess I was more tired than I thought I was.

The sound of a car going by jolted me awake, but it didn't stop. "Bastards" I thought to myself. About twenty minutes later, I heard another car and this time it pulled up and stopped in front of mine. I looked up in time to see a tall man with tan skin and long hair jump out of a yellow truck and walk over to my car. He was wearing faded jeans, tan leather work boots and a graying T-shirt with an eagle on it. His hair must have been down to his waist and it was blowing around his face. I wiped my face, trying to freshen up my tear-streaked cheeks.

He leaned down to my window. I was feeling embarrassingly pathetic and I was also a little frightened by him.

"Hi, you ok? Looks like you got some car trouble." He sounded pretty friendly.

"Yeah, it won't start. It just stopped running and I coasted off the road. Well, actually there was some smoke, and then it stopped."

"Smoke? Well lemme take a look and see if I can tell you anything. Pop the hood for me." He walked around to the front of my car, brushing his hair behind his shoulder. I got out and walked over next to him. As he leaned in, his hair fell over his arms, hiding his face. I still hadn't gotten a good look at him, but his hands were very tan, like he worked outside a lot.

"Well, it looks like you got a busted radiator hose," he said cheerfully as he turned to me, once again brushing his hair away from his face. He looked at me with warm deep eyes and a smile that makes all my problems disappear for a split second. I suddenly wanted to tell him everything. After a few moments of looking at his face I recognized that he was a Native American. He was the first Native American I'd ever met, I was excited and I felt like I wanted to get to know him.

"So, what does that mean, exactly?"

"Well, I think your hose broke and that smoke you saw was really steam. When that happens, you really gotta stop driving, because if you keep going, your engine will seize up."

"Oh."

"Is that what you did? Kept driving?"

"Yeah. I just wanted to get to the Sand Dunes."

He laughed. "Well you'll have plenty of time to see those now. You're gonna need a new engine, most likely."

"How long does that take?"

"It could take two days or two weeks. Maybe longer. I'm not really sure. This is a foreign car, so it can be harder to get parts out here. You're alone?"

"Yeah."

"And you drove here from New Jersey?"

"Yup. I left three days ago."

"Well, I bet the change in altitude is what made that hose pop. You went up to about 10,000 feet over that pass."

"I don't know what to do. I don't have all that much extra money and I don't know where to stay. I don't even know where I am." I was almost in tears again.

"There's a motel in town that's not too bad. You might try that."

"Ok." I paused, not sure if I should ask the question. "Would you be able to give me a ride, maybe? To a pay phone so I can call a tow truck?"

"Sure, no problem."

I sighed with relief. I locked up my car, closed the hood and grabbed my wallet and my backpack. He turned to me once he got to the truck.

"By the way, I'm Christopher."

"I'm Natalie." I shook his hand. He seemed like he was in his early twenties. He was an actual adult, but not that far from me in age. His truck smelled like paint. He backed up and turned around, heading toward the town.

"So what made you drive here from New Jersey? You meeting someone in Colorado?"

"No, I was actually heading for California."

"Oh yeah? What's out there?"

"I don't know. My cousin's there. But I was just driving."

"Running away?"

"I guess, but I wouldn't put it that way."

"I see. Are you in school still?"

"I'm supposed to be a senior this coming year."

"But you decided not to go back?"

"Sort of. I was just gonna drive to California and back again. It's complicated. I have to be back for the beginning of school. My school starts like a week from now."

"Ok, well, if you're stuck here for a while, you can give me a ring if you need anything. I live up on Black Horse Mesa southeast of here." I thanked him. "Okeedoke. I'll stay with you 'til you call the tow truck, and then I'll drive you back to your car."

"Thanks so much. I'll go call."

It was a strange feeling to be helped by this young man when my own family was so cold. I was fortunate in one way, but felt so hurt otherwise. Didn't they care about me? I choked back tears again as I walked into the quick mart and asked the cashier if he knew of any places to call to get the car towed. He pulled out the phone book and looked up the number for Marcus Auto Body and Repair. "Best place in town," he said. I called and they said they would be at the car in about twenty minutes.

Christopher had walked into the market and was standing in the back, watching me. I could feel his eyes on me. I felt lucky that he saw me and stopped. I bought a cherry fruit pie and some Doritos and we headed back out to the truck.

"I'll take you back to the car, and then I'm gonna have to take off. I have to pick up my nephew at the hospital in a little while."

"Oh. Is he okay?"

"Yeah, he's fine. He's just got bad asthma that kicks up when the Chinooks blow. I'm taking care of him while his mom is away."

"Oh. Well thank you for doing all this for me. It's really nice of you."

"No problem." He paused as if to say something else, but didn't. We drove back to my poor little car in silence. He parked behind it and turned off the motor while we waited for the tow truck. "You should be able to walk to the Econo Lodge from Marcus's garage without too much trouble."

"Ok." I looked down at my feet. I was wearing plaid Converse sneakers, which seemed completely out of place. My jeans were dirty and I felt tiny and naive. I looked out the window to the north where a mountain sat, enormous and majestic with snow capping the top.

"That's Tsisnaasjini. Sacred mountain of the east." Christopher said quietly.

"Wow, what a beautiful word. What language is that?" I asked, and turned toward him, shifting in my seat.

"Dine, or Navajo, as most people say. It's my language, though I don't use it much now."

"It's beautiful."

"The Dine believe there are four sacred mountains. The Creator placed the mountains there to represent the four directions."

"Do you believe that?" I asked, because he said it in such a way that he seemed unsure about it.

"I'm not sure what I believe anymore," he said quietly.

"Me neither."

We sat in silence for a little while. I was sitting in a stranger's truck discussing sacred mountains.

"You seem troubled." He turned in his seat to face me. He put his hand on the back of my seat like Max used to do. "What are you running from?"

I took a deep breath and answered him. "I just had to leave. Some stuff happened with my boyfriend, and my family, and I just couldn't stay there anymore."

"Ah, I see. Well, driving can be good for your spirit. Especially if you've got good music. I like to take off and just drive sometimes. Once when I was younger I drove all the way to Mexico when I was upset."

"I've never been to Mexico."

There was another period of silence as we stared out the windows, and then the tow truck arrived in a cloud of dust.

"All right, time to go. Oh, hey, if you're stuck here for a while, call my home number if you need anything at night. During the day I'm at the other number." He handed me a business card.

"Oh wow, thanks. You're really nice. I'm lucky you stopped to help."

"I hope you find what you're looking for," he said as I got out of the truck.

"Bye, thanks again." I closed the door.

I walked over to the tow truck and gave the driver the Ok to load my car onto the truck. As he was backing the truck up to it, and Christopher zoomed away back to town, I looked down at the card in my hand. There was a picture of a white feather in the right hand corner of the card and the writing said,

Christopher Nez
Whitefeather, Inc.
Complete painting and window
detailing for homes in the San Luis
Valley and beyond.

Whitefeather. I stared at the card in disbelief as the wiry and windblown mechanic secured chains to my car. I wanted to catch him and ask him more questions, but he was already gone. I walked to the Econo Lodge like Christopher suggested, checked in and finally called my parents to tell them where I was. I sat with the phone a few inches from my ear while they took turns yelling at me. Finally I found out that Max called, and that when they told him I was gone, he'd gotten frantic. They didn't know anything besides that. I told them approximately where I was (though not precisely), because I was finished with being stoic and secretive. I'd hit a low. I needed my dad. He got on the phone to talk car details with me. In between reprimands, my mother offered to fly out and bring me home. I was really tempted, but I said no. I needed to do this myself. I gave her my phone number at the hotel. Finally I talked to Olivia, and told her about the tornado and the car and Christopher. After I hung up, I thought maybe I'd made a mistake. Maybe I should have let my mom come get me. I spent the rest of the evening watching cable and letting my mind go numb. I was exhausted.

The next day I got breakfast at a diner and sat alone at the counter feeling strange. Completely stuffed with pancakes and bacon, I wandered through town in my old jeans and a white V-neck T-shirt. And then I saw them—black leather cowboy boots in the window of a store called Martin's Leather Emporium. I walked in, spaced out and lethargic from an overdose of sugar and fat and completely in the mood to spend money I didn't have. They had my size and they were fairly comfortable. I stood up and spun around in the mirror. They were $99. There was no question and I wore them out of the store. There wasn't much else to do, so I walked to the garage to check on my car. I asked for Marcus at the front desk and a small, round man with greasy gray hair combed over his bald head sauntered out in a grease covered jumpsuit, wiping his hands with a towel.

"Hi, you Natalie Watson?"

"Yeah."

"Well, your engine took a beating after the radiator hose broke. I'm gonna need to order some parts. I called around, and it's gonna take at least a week, maybe more, because we gotta order the parts from Denver. And I'm kinda short staffed right now. I hope you got friends or something to do here in Alamosa for a coupla weeks."

"Oh. I'll manage. How much will it cost?"

"You're looking at around $800-$900 if not more. I'll try to work out a solid figure for you once we get the parts, because I'm not sure what's gonna need to be done just yet."

I only had $650 left from when I drained my savings account the day before I left. I did take my mother's credit card, but I couldn't afford to stay at this motel for a week or more. I left Marcus the number for the Econo Lodge and walked out. I wouldn't leave my car and fly home, like my mom suggested. It was my car. I was going to have to call my parents again and explain. I was determined to get the car running again, and then drive home. I decided to take a walk and think. I bought a bottle of water and crossed the highway heading in the direction of Mt. Blanca and the Sand Dunes.

It had been half an hour and I'd gotten nowhere. My boots were rubbing my heels raw. I sat down on a rock with a view of the mountain, which was much closer now. I started thinking about Christopher. I contemplated calling him. Maybe he could recommend a place where I could stay for free and maybe work and make a little money. Maybe there was a youth hostel nearby. Interestingly, I didn't have that queasy stomach that I had when Max and I first got together. Instead, I felt a calmness that was new, and somewhere deep inside my mind or heart, whatever you want to call it, I knew I was embarking on something profound, but I didn't know what. I could move on from Max, couldn't I? I could have other boyfriends, other lovers. The thought of Christopher made my heart feel open. I liked it.

I was trying to live in the moment. Still, the regular human games applied, and I couldn't just *call* him, could I? He probably saw me as an immature runaway, but he was the only person I knew there.

I called him at night at his home number taking deep breaths to try and calm down. The phone was ringing… I was ready to hang up, but then I heard the phone pick up.

"Yeah!" a man's voice says on the other end. I felt like I was intruding in his adult world.

"Hi. Is this Christopher?"

"It is."

"This is Natalie, the girl with the dead car."

"Oh." He sounded pleased, but then paused, making me feel uncomfortable. "What can I do for ya?"

"I guess I'm gonna be here for a while, and I can't afford to stay at this motel. I was wondering if you might know if there's a youth hostel here, or anything I can do to stay someplace cheaper. Maybe a place where I can work for room and board or something for a week. I just don't have much more money and the car repair is like $900. Maybe more."

"There isn't a youth hostel that I know of. Hold on a sec." He covered the mouth of the phone. I heard nothing but fuzz at first, but then I was able to make out what he was saying.

Muffled sounds and then "…girl whose car broke down on the road."

A woman's voice replied. "Why's she calling?"

"I gave her a ride to town to call a tow truck. She's staying at the motel but she can't afford it. Needs a cheap place to stay." His voice hushed even more. "She's a runaway. Pretty screwed with that car."

"Will she be ok on her own tonight?"

"Dunno."

"How old is she?"

"Barely eighteen. She wouldn't want to stay here, would she?"

"What's she look like?" asked the woman. "She white?"

"Yeah. From New Jersey. Probably running because she didn't get some fancy stereo for her birthday."

"What nasty bug bit you?"

"I don't know…" he sighed. "She's got honey colored hair with gold streaks. Big green eyes. But she looked at me like I was an alien. I don't know, Tanya."

"Now you're a poet. Ask her to stay here."

"Seriously? She's just a kid."

"Yeah, but so are you. She's still on the phone, Chris."

"Shit."

I heard him fumbling with the phone.

"Still there?"

"Yeah."

"Sorry. I was just um, trying to figure something out. Would you want to stay at my place? I have a pull-out couch. My life's pretty simple. I mean, you won't be in the way." I could hear the woman chuckling in the background. "I mean, only if you're comfortable with it. I'm not a perv or anything." More chuckling. "I also have a tent you can borrow and you can camp out wherever if you're more comfortable with that."

"I don't know. I don't want to be an imposition."

"You wouldn't be, trust me. It would be nice to have a new person around for a little while."

"I guess. I don't know what else to do. But, it's gonna be like two weeks, maybe."

"That's ok. That's nothing in the grand scheme of life. I can pick you up tomorrow morning, if you want."

"That would be good. I'm room 25. I'll just wait for you there."

"Alrighty. See you then."

I hung up the phone and stared at the wall for a moment. My parents were going to kill me. I hoped I wasn't getting myself into more trouble. I had no reason to think he was dangerous, but girls are just raised to be wary of men. I guess I'd learned the hard way that sometimes the men (or boys) closest to you can hurt you even more than strangers.

14

The next morning I took a much needed shower, grabbed a coffee from the diner, packed my bags and checked out. I sat on the bench outside my room and waited. It was so bright outside that the sky was a deep cobalt and the clouds were white as cotton balls. I leaned back and relaxed. Christopher pulled up in his corn yellow Land Cruiser and got out. He was more dressed-up than the day before in a blue button down shirt tucked into jeans. He was quiet as we drove out of town. His hand moved between the steering wheel and the gearshift in a smooth familiar way, like the mechanics were automatic for him. Strange how the body memorizes movements so that the mind can wander, while the body performs any number of activities.

His hands were brown and sinewy, his arms thin yet muscular, and when he turned occasionally to look out the window, or check behind the truck, I could detect a faint spicy citrus smell, like lemon pudding and nutmeg. I figured it was his shampoo or aftershave. It was a pleasant smell and when he turned, he glanced at me with an apprehensive smile. His eyes were almond shaped and brown, his irises were not quite hazel, not a deep brown with hints of a more translucent and silver quality. They sparkled like mica in the moonlight. I watched him, shifting my eyes from his hands to his face and then to the landscape to avoid staring at him too much.

To the east, the land sloped up, speckled with juniper and pine cut occasionally by a dry stream bed, which Christopher called an arroyo. We drove for almost an hour. I felt uneasy leaving the bustling atmosphere of the town. We entered into a wild land unlike anything I'd ever seen before. Christopher turned left onto a dirt road, which stretched straight across a flat plain to the edge of the mesa where the land began to rise upward. There were brightly colored mailboxes, the only colorful objects in a vast expanse of high tan grass. The road was full of holes and ridges where water had rushed down through the red earth. Red dust billowed in our wake.

As we started up the incline, I grabbed onto the door, white knuckled and tense. The road was narrow and the truck was bouncing as if it was ready to pop right over on its side. The truck was pretty bare inside, with just the basic necessities. Christopher had a little leather bundle of something hanging from his rearview mirror, and a box on the floor containing tissues, wintergreen gum, energy bars and a bunch of crumpled receipts. As we flew over a big bump, the glove compartment popped open, jolting me out of my seat. I leaned forward to catch whatever was poised to fall out, but there was nothing to grab. It was all secured by a bungee cord.

"It does that whenever I hit that bump. I got it rigged so it doesn't fall out anymore. Pretty clever, huh?"

"Yeah." I laughed. The truck lurched to the left and then to the right, curving around what I learned are called switchbacks. Christopher said they were cut like that to avoid driving straight up the incline and to control erosion to some extent, though the road was still fairly washed out.

We bounced up over the last incline, and the mesa was revealed, flat and high with occasional houses and trailers. I was experiencing a momentary jolt of panic. What was I doing? Who was this man?

"That's Jim and Tanya's house over there on the left," Christopher said. It was a quaint little A-frame with a green roof. A husky ran out from the house barking at Christopher's truck. Off to the right was Clara Nez's house, Christopher's sister. She had a tan adobe with a small rock and cactus garden out in front. Beyond Christopher's trailer, and out of our sight, lived Maggie Antero, Ben and Mary Altier, Stan Maestas and Charlotte Corn. He pointed out more people's houses. I guess he was telling me this in case I got lost on the mesa or something.

All the houses were somewhat weather-beaten. I guessed that there wasn't much upkeep or gardening to be done at 9,000 feet. My mother would have been offended by the lack of landscaping. While it was mildly disturbing to me to be in a place so unlike anything I'd seen before, there was a certain comfort about the gritty, run-down atmosphere. The road had flattened out and we bumped along for a few more minutes before he turned toward the west onto a narrower road practically hidden between pines. It led right up to a blue trailer. Where the land opened up to the north and west there was a clear view of the mesa and further out, Mt. Blanca and the vast high prairie. Somewhere in the distance were the sand dunes and more mountains.

We hopped out of the truck and I was struck first by how quiet it was. It's amazing how much we adjust to the constant drone of cars, air conditioners, planes overhead, radios, the hum of power lines and generators. All I heard standing outside of Christopher's trailer was the wind.

"Tanya and Jim have my nephew Leo tonight, so you can have a little privacy. They can't watch him all the time, though, so he might be staying here a little bit until his mom gets back."

"Where is she?"

"In rehab. Alcohol."

"Oh."

The door squeaked as he opened it. I hoisted my bags through the door and dropped them on the floor of the small living room that had a sofa pulled out and made up as a bed. The room was decorated with a few subtle and interesting oil paintings, and what I assumed were Navajo pots and some baskets. Christopher walked over to the window in the kitchen and lit an incense cone and placed it in a bowl on the kitchen table. The trailer was really like one long room, except for his bedroom at the far end, and the bathroom, which had doors. Soon the smell of cedar filled the room and I began to relax.

"So, you can sleep there, and I'll just make sure to not disturb you."

"This will be fine. Thank you."

I spent the afternoon writing in my journal and walking around outside Christopher's trailer while he chopped wood. He took a break for lunch and made us peanut butter and grape jelly sandwiches. As we ate, a pang of guilt hit me when I thought about my parents.

"I should probably call my parents."

"Yeah, I thought of that. They must be worried. You can use my phone." He pointed to a small table by the couch. "It's over there."

I called them when he want back outside to finish stacking firewood. My mom answered. I gave her Christopher's number and assured her I would be home for school. It was hard, but I didn't let her talk much. I just told her what I wanted her to know and hung up. It was cold, but I was giving her a dose of her own medicine.

Around four o'clock Christopher asked me if I wanted a beer.

"Sure, I guess so," I replied hesitantly. I wasn't sure he was thinking about my age, and I didn't want to point it out.

I sipped my beer while we sat in plastic chairs watching the sky and a dizzying calm settled in. Christopher was quiet and pensive. In the back of my mind I was aware that school was starting soon and I might not be there to be a part of it. For the first time since my summer-long ordeal, I felt worried about missing school. Matterson was a good place, and I didn't want to be the kind of girl who dropped out.

"I'm taking tomorrow off," Christopher said without any prefacing.

"Oh?"

"Well, I don't want to leave you here alone. I mean, I figure we can go for a hike or something, or I can show you around a bit."

"That's nice of you, thanks."

"No problem. I have a place in mind."

He raised the beer bottle to his lips and watched me. I glanced down at my hands, uncomfortable with his gaze, and he looked away.

"I had a feeling today," he said.

"A feeling?"

"Yeah, when I was getting Leo ready to go out. I stopped to listen to the wind for a minute before we got in the truck, and I just felt something."

"What did you feel?"

"I'm not sure exactly. It's just been an interesting two days, don't you think?"

I laughed nervously. "I kind of wonder what I'm doing."

"Yeah." He turned to look at me again. His eyes had this strange quality to them, as if they were holograms and contained more than one image inside them. They were multifaceted and deeper than normal eyes, like they were made of water.

We heard footsteps in the dry earth and we both careened our necks toward the sound.

"Chris? You there?" a woman's voice was asking.

"Yup!" he said, but it sounded more like "Yeeopp."

A beautiful woman with long black hair appeared from out of the pines. "I just wanted to see how you're doin'. I put Leo down already. He had a day of it with the dog and Jim. He's zonked now."

"Cool, you're the best, Tanya."

"Can I have a beer?"

"Yeah." He got up and stood awkwardly. "Tanya this is Natalie. Natalie, Tanya."

"Hi Natalie." She reached out to shake my hand, and I did the same. Her hands were cold and delicate. She smiled at me with a crooked smile that wrinkled her cheek and made her look shy. She didn't really look like Christopher, but then again, I'd never met anyone who did. He sat down again, stretching out his long legs and leaned back in his chair.

Tanya grabbed a beer from the refrigerator and joined us outside. She looked at Christopher and then looked at me. "You know, I don't think I should stay. Jim's gonna wonder where I got off to."

"You're just taking the beer and running, huh?"

"Well, yeah, in a manner of speaking," she laughed.

"Hold on, I'll walk with you for a minute." Christopher nodded at me, as if I was to understand that he would be right back. He followed Tanya into the pines. I sat there for a few minutes and began to get a little bored. The boredom turned to curiosity as I heard their voices. I got up quietly and tiptoed closer to listen. I could see their blurry shapes through the trees.

"So what're you gonna do if she asks about your parents?" I heard Tanya ask quietly.

"I'll just say they've passed away."

"Just wondering."

"My dad's dead. He must be. We've talked about this before."

"Yeah. Sorry. I was just wondering," she muttered.

"It's not something I discuss with strangers, Tanya. Anyway, she's not going to ask. She won't be here long enough to get into that sort of thing."

"I don't know. I've got a feeling."

"Yeah, I said that today too."

"She's a pretty thing," said Tanya. I felt myself blush.

"Yep, sure is."

"This is gonna drive you nuts."

"Yeah. Well, it's no biggie. Just doing what any nice person would do."

"Of course. You're a nice person, Chris," she said. "Well, you behave yourself, now. Don't be giving that girl too much beer. That's a felony waiting to happen. At least that's what Jim would say."

"Get outta here Tanya. Trying to stir up trouble. She's just a kid."

"Yeah, but so are you."

I heard Christopher's footsteps crunching through the dry dirt and sagebrush, getting louder as he approached the trailer. I raced back to my chair and sat as still as I could with my heart pounding. He sat down next to me.

"Tanya's great. She and Jim are my best friends here, pretty much, besides my friend Jackson. She likes to check up on me."

"She seems nice."

"Yeah, she is."

We sat in silence for a while. I was relaxing slowly, but still feeling edgy, staying at stranger's house—a strange *man*, and just the two of us at that. Eventually the sun set behind the mountains and we both dragged ourselves to bed. I could hear him opening and closing dresser drawers, brushing his teeth, walking around his bedroom with the door closed. They were the sounds of intimacy and the strangeness of it makes me feel like a criminal. Like I was eavesdropping on the minutiae of his life, the things only a wife or family member would know about. I lay awake for hours in the half-light of his small living room with thoughts racing through my mind.

15

We were ten miles back a bumpy four-wheel-drive road. All I'd seen of Colorado was the open prairie and the monstrous mountains bare of anything remotely lush or fertile. I was pleasantly surprised to be in a dense, arid forest full of what Christopher told me were lodgepole and ponderosa pines. The undergrowth was still green with hints of red and yellow as early autumn crept into the edges of the forest. It smelled of pine pitch. We left the truck and hiked back a path that led up a slight incline. I was getting really out of breath, not accustomed to the altitude. The air was so thin, I had to work really hard to get a good, satisfying gulp of air. Fortunately, I'd brought hiking boots with me, and my feet felt good. They were getting dusty as I walked.

Below us a creek stretched out through a canyon. There were strange birds following us along the trail. There seemed to be two particular types: one was black and white, and the other was a dusty light gray. Both were robust, at least the size of a crow. Christopher named the gray one the "camp robber bird" because he said when you camp out, they're the first to arrive pecking for leftovers. I thought the black and white ones were magpies.

We passed through an area that Christopher explained was an avalanche chute. Looking up, the slope of the mountain was steep and rugged, covered with downed trees. Below us it was the same catastrophic scene. He explained that you could determine how long ago the avalanche happened by how decomposed and old the trees were. The one we were looking at had happened fairly recently. In fact, avalanches happened in Colorado all the time throughout the winter. I found the idea terrifying.

"Have you ever seen one?" I asked, not sure if I wanted to hear the answer. An avalanche was as creepy as a tornado to me.

"Well, not a huge slide, but I was caught in a small one once."

"Really?"

"Yeah, me and Jackson like to go backcountry skiing. One time we were skiing down Moonwalker Couloir and I started to feel the snow moving underneath me. It was more than just the regular sliding of my skis. The snow was picking me up and was transporting me down the mountain."

"Were you scared?"

"Yeah, but it stopped quickly, and I knew I was ok. But it is pretty weird to have that happen."

"What's backcountry skiing, exactly?"

"Pretty much just skiing, but not at a resort. You need some extra gear and it's a little harder than regular skiing, because the snow isn't groomed and it's unpredictable."

"I've never been skiing before."

"It's fun. You get a major rush of adrenaline. My favorite part, though, is skiing in deep powder. You can get into a trancelike state where you're actually flowing with the snow, like you're fluid. I think that's probably the closest I've felt to the Creator was when I was skiing deep powder. It's a feeling of oneness with the earth and snow around you." Christopher's eyes were brightening and he was talking with energy and a sense of ownership of his experiences. He also looked younger to me than he had before. Talking about skiing, he was no longer quiet and reserved, but youthful and animated.

"That's cool, I know that feeling, I think. I'd like to learn to ski," I said cautiously.

"Well, if you're here when the snow falls, I'll teach you," he grinned.

Christopher impressed me. I wondered what kind of experience Christopher had with girls. What else could he teach me? I was curious, but in a way I didn't want to know.

We stopped to eat lunch at the base of a snowfield. It blew my mind. In September, still really late summer, there were enormous patches of snow in the mountains just lying there. Some never melted, he said. He ran up to the snowfield and molded a snowball with his hands and tossed it at me, not intending to wallop me, fortunately. I screamed and tried to throw one back. I didn't have a great throwing arm, that was for sure. Christopher told me that he sometimes skied on these snowfields, even in the summer.

The trail at the base of the snow dropped off dramatically into the canyon below and we sat at the edge with our feet dangling in the air. A cold wind was picking up and I began to shiver. There is nothing mellow about the Rocky Mountains. When the wind blows, it blows hard and frigid. Christopher reached his arm behind me and held me close to him, rubbing my arm with his hand. I froze, not sure what to do.

"Thanks," I said awkwardly.

He'd made us peanut butter and jelly sandwiches that we opened and devoured quickly. The breeze was relentless and was blowing my hair around my shoulders and face. Christopher's hair was secured in a ponytail with multiple hair ties spaced about an inch and a half apart all the way down his waist length hair. As a particularly strong gust of wind blew and I grabbed for the plastic bag that once held my sandwich to keep it from floating down into the canyon, I thought I heard my name being called. It was just like that time in the woods behind my house. I looked at Christopher.

"Did you hear that?"

He returned my gaze with wide eyes and a blank stare. "What did you hear?" he asked quietly and closely.

"I heard my name. It wasn't you?"

"No."

"Well, did you hear it?" I asked solidly.

"Yeah, I did," he said with a tone of regret.

"My name?"

"Yeah."

"Well why would *you* hear *my* name? If you heard my name, and I heard my name, then who said it? Someone must have said it."

"I don't know," he muttered. He wasn't giving me what I wanted. I wanted to figure it out, and he was resisting.

"Well, I think it's weird," I said with conviction, hoping he would say more. I was tired of the strange supernatural things that seemed to be following me.

I sat for a while staring out into the canyon. The other side of it was rocky and dusted with scrubby pines. I imagined what it might be like to stretch a bridge across the canyon. It would have to be one of those suspension bridges like in Indiana Jones. I pictured Indiana falling off of it and grabbing it with one muscular arm. And then I heard it again. It was too much. I stood up and looked around me, feeling like I was spinning. Maybe it was a head rush, or a dizzy spell from the altitude, but I could hardly stand up. Christopher saw me swaying like a leaf on the wind, terribly close to the edge of the cliff and quickly caught me in his arms as I lost my balance. He smelled of lemon and spices again, and his arms remained solid, holding me away from the drop below us. I stayed there for a moment, gathering my wits.

"Sorry. Lost my balance there for a second."

"Yeah, I noticed," he laughed, nervously.

I bent down to gather my things and zip up my backpack when I was hit by a wave of nausea. It wasn't normal. I wasn't pregnant anymore. It had to be the altitude. That was all I could figure. I stood up with my hand on my belly, my face in an obvious grimace.

"You ok? Girl, I think you're freaking out," he laughed. I didn't.

"No, I feel really sick all of a sudden."

"Here, have some water." He opened up his water bottle and handed it to me. "Sometimes the altitude can make you nauseous, and water helps. We must be above 11,000 feet and that's pretty high for you, considering…"

I took a big sip and the water in my stomach pushed me over the edge. I ran in the opposite direction of Christopher in time to lose my sandwich over an unfortunate bush with just a hint of autumn red sneaking into its small leaves. Waves of nausea keep coming until my stomach was empty and I was spinning with dizziness. I woke up to Christopher's silvery eyes and cool hands on my face. I was way too susceptible to fainting, I thought as he was singing something in a language I didn't understand.

"Ah, hello. You're back. Can you walk?" he asked when he saw my eyes open.

"Yeah, I think so."

"Well come on then, you need to get out of here. Time to go."

I was still sick, and trying to figure out what the hell was wrong with me. How embarrassing. I was sure Christopher must have thought I was a freak of nature. I was freezing cold and trembling when we got back to the truck. Christopher was acting responsible and mature, but I could tell he was just as unnerved as I was. The drive back was horrendous. He has to stop three times so I could be sick outside the truck. What he didn't tell me is that he heard my name again in that whispering, nowhere voice.

He tucked me into my temporary bed. He put a thermometer in my mouth, and in a few minutes he muttered something about it being 102, and said he wasn't not sure if he should take me to the hospital. He gave me a pill and forced me to take a sip of water. I was starting to see *him*. God, not again! Whitefeather. First I saw eyes, the same silvery eyes as Christopher, and then a face, older and more chiseled than his, but similar in quality. He was dancing in a circle with a headdress of white feathers, cutting the air with an eagle feather. I heard drums in my ears. Maybe it was my blood pulsing in my veins from the fever.

I saw people standing around him and a little boy of about 11. I started shaking violently. Christopher put his hands on me, trying to soothe me. He sang again in soft tones and I heard Tanya's voice as well.

"What do you see, Natalie?" she asked.

"Whitefeather dancing." I said.

"Oh my God," she whispered. "What else, Natalie? Anything else?" She paused. "Chris, she's having some kind of vision. Did she mention this kind of thing happening to her?"

"No, she didn't mention it, Tanya. It's not the kind of thing someone mentions during small talk."

"He's falling," I said, and they hushed.

"Falling?" asked Tanya.

"He's been hit and he's falling. He's bleeding." I heard Christopher sniffling. "Someone killed him." I said.

"Who, Natalie? Who killed him?" Christopher asked with urgency.

16

I must have slept all evening and all night, because I woke to the morning, the empty trailer and a note on the kitchen table.

Natalie,

Had to go to work. There's milk and cereal and orange juice if you feel like eating. Call Tanya if you get sick. Dinner in town tonight if you can eat? My treat.

-Chris

I stood there looking down at the note trying to ground myself, feeling my feet parked solidly on the floor. My heartbeat was regular, my stomach steady and calm. I didn't feel sick at all. I must've had something like food poisoning. What else would make me get spontaneously sick like that? Was it bad peanut butter? But Christopher ate it too. What was wrong with me? My life had become a series of sickness and fainting. I was famished, so I opened the refrigerator and pulled out the milk. He had three boxes of cereal:

Cinnamon Life, Cocoa Puffs and Lucky Charms. The colorful boxes make me chuckle. I choose Life, figuring I'd go with the healthiest option.

I opened the closet near the door. I wasn't really looking for anything, just snooping, I guess. It was a regular closet: a few jackets, a shelf with a flashlight, a pile of magazines, what looked like a bedroll and some boots on the floor. I pulled out a thick red plaid jacket, contemplated it for a moment and put it on. It was chilly inside the trailer. I took my bowl of cereal and walked outside. Clouds were moving swiftly across the sky, sending large shadows across the ground, like transparent beasts sliding slowly through the pines. I took a deep breath and sensed a mixture of pine pitch and wood smoke on the air. The sun warmed me when it peeked through the clouds, but it was a tease, only lingering for a moment. There was an airplane in the sky, groaning out that subtle atmospheric roar that we've all become so accustomed to. It was a comforting sound.

I walked around Christopher's small plot of land. The mesa was high, but flat. The trees were barely trees by my definition. They were somewhere between bush and tree, not growing that much higher than my head. I sensed that something more than just friendly could happen with Christopher and it made me destructively long for Max. Maybe I was afraid of moving on. Could that be? Or did I feel some obligation to him? I don't really know why I longed for him then. Maybe it was more like a habit. Sometimes you know what's best for you, but making the change is the scariest part. It's that time between the decision and the outcome that stings: that in-between time when you've acknowledged the truth, but haven't fully actualized the changes.

I could have called him earlier to see if he was ok, but I didn't. Finally I couldn't resist anymore. I called him collect from Christopher's orange rotary dial phone. I knew his mother Nora might answer, and she did, but miraculously she didn't hang up on me. Instead, she accepted the call and cordially passed the phone on to Max. She must have known something. Maybe they had worked it out.

"How come your mom let you talk to me?" I asked immediately.

"We had a fight and I told her I'm in love with you. She's weird. She'll hit me, but then because she feels guilty, she'll give me whatever I want and she knows I want *you*."

"How long will that last?"

"Who knows? It's been a few days now. So far she's acting like she's ok with it. You need to come home. I can't believe you ran away," he said.

"I just couldn't pretend it was all ok, like everyone wanted me to."

"I get it. I've thought about running away lots of times. Sometimes I think I still might. So, what's it like out there?" he asked.

"It's really amazing. It's like nothing I've ever seen before. The sky is enormous, and the clouds look different. The people are different."

"What are you doing? Are you with your cousin now?"

"No. I'm still in Colorado where my car broke down."

"Oh man, that's pretty nuts."

"I guess. Well, they're ordering an engine from Denver, I think. It'll be done eventually."

"Why don't you just leave the car and come home? I mean, what are you doing out there? School is starting and I miss you."

"I'm not ready yet. I'll come back when I'm ready." I sounded strong in my conviction, even though I was secretly having doubts.

"But you're going to miss the beginning of your senior year."

"I don't really care. Anyway, I'll be back in a week or so. You know, there's more to life than the little cages we box ourselves into. I've realized that. There's a whole world out here so different from our little Jersey hell hole."

"I miss you. I want to see you. Where are you staying, anyway?"

I paused trying to figure out how to explain it to him. "It's weird. This guy who helped me when my car died offered for me to stay at his place until it's fixed."

"You're staying with a guy? Who is he?"

"I told you, the guy who helped me when my car broke down. He's nice and he's harmless if that's what you're worried about."

"That's pretty nuts, Natalie. What's his name?"

"Christopher," I answered. "And there's some weird connection with these visions I've been having. Visions of this guy I call Whitefeather."

"Whitefeather? What are you talking about?"

"Christopher's business is called Whitefeather Incorporated."

"That's a weird name for a business," he said. He was quiet for a moment.

"You ran away from a perfectly good home only to end up shacking up with a man you don't even know? That's insane, Natalie. What will people think? I mean, your mom. Your mom's gonna freak out. What if he hurts you? What do I tell people at school?" he asked, egging me on.

"Tell them I'm taking the fall off to visit my cousin."

"That's it? You think they'll believe that? How about I tell the Headmaster that Natalie Watson is shacking up with some man she doesn't even know!"

"Tell them the truth, then! Tell them what really happened. Tell them everything, Max," I said calmly, even though my heart was racing with adrenaline. "Tell them I'm here because you cheated on me with Allyson Fitzsimons!" Max laughed that nervous breathy laugh I knew so well. He had no reply.

"I want to run away too. We're both part of this. It's not just your drama," he said with calculation in his voice.

"Let's talk about it later. I mean, yes, we have things to work out, but wait till I come home."

"I'm gonna do it. I have a credit card. I love you," he said and then hung up.

Did he just imply that he was coming to Colorado? What was I going to tell Christopher? I was frozen in shock. I didn't want Max there. I liked that this place had no connection to my previous world.

My life had changed dramatically in the last few months. When you get into a regular routine, it clings to you, much like the act of riding a bicycle never leaves your muscles' memory, but if you travel and drag yourself out of that routine, it can be very hard to feel settled again. This feeling of being unsettled is a reminder that you are not your routine. You are not even truly part of what you may call your reality, because your reality can change, and yet, you remain yourself.

I was still Natalie. Natalie of the woods, of Hennessey Creek, of Old Mill, of Matterson. Even if suddenly my entire family and world were obliterated, I'd still be me. Then I was thinking about my mother and how I felt when I was a little girl, when she'd stayed home from work to be with us full time. She made bread then, too, and I remember standing on a rustic wooden stool in the kitchen helping her knead the dough. She often wore her long hair in a bun when I was little and we had matching aprons in a red and yellow floral print.

I knew who I was then. My world was mapped out for me. It stretched from my bed to the kitchen to the woodshed, to the end of the driveway. The players in my life were my cat, my sister and my parents. I remember my dad's beard, his long reddish seventies hair, his office, with its never-ending cycle of pictures cut out from the New Yorker. That world was constant, not static, but comfortable, until Max took that first step into our kitchen. That's when it started to fall apart.

17

Christopher got home when the afternoon sun had escaped behind the horizon in a river of crimson, sending a chill into the dry air. He found me sitting cross legged out near the end of his driveway waiting for him. He stopped his truck and leaned out a little.

"Hey there, Jersey girl. Whatcha up to? You know you can watch TV if you want, or play Leo's Nintendo."

"I know."

"Are you hungry? I feel like getting chili rellenos at La Casa Familia in town. Wanna come?" he proposed through a sparkling grin.

"Ok. That would be good. Can I wear this jacket?"

"Yeah, if you want to. That's my wood chopping jacket. It probably stinks."

"No, it smells good," I replied. It really did. It smelled like pine trees and cinnamon. Christopher's smells were intoxicatingly disconcerting. He smelled like a man. He sat in his truck smiling at me and there was a look in his eyes I hadn't seen before.

"You like how I smell?"

I nodded, feeling myself blush.

"You smell pretty good too," he said with mischievously, "and you look pretty with your hair like that."

I'd pulled my hair back in a messy bun, and touched it lightly, blushing again.

∞

La Casa Familia was a white adobe building with a huge red awning set behind a parking lot full of potholes, pickup trucks and large sedans decked out in rosaries, plastic statues of the Virgin Mary and American flags. I'd never had good Mexican food. I'd been to some restaurants that pretended to be Mexican, but they couldn't compete with this place. The restaurant itself smelled of beer and corn tortillas and the chairs and tables were grimy, but the food was magnificent. I'd never had green chili and I'd never had a chili relleno: a poblano chili stuffed with creamy cheese and smothered with sauce. I inhaled the chips and salsa, which were pungently full of cilantro. Christopher watched me eat, pleasure and satisfaction radiating from his face.

"I knew you'd like it," he bragged. "This is the best Mexican restaurant for 100 miles. I think I need a margarita. You want one?" he asked.

"I'm not 21, remember," I said.

"Shh! Don't announce it! You're so honest. They won't card you here, trust me. Get the Patron Silver, it's the best."

I looked to Christopher for guidance when the waiter asked me if I want it frozen or on the rocks, with salt or without. These are the secrets of adulthood, understanding the minute and seductive qualities of alcoholic delicacies. He suggested on the rocks with salt, so I nodded my head in agreement. I really had no clue. It all sounded fine to me.

"So, why are you here, Natalie? I've been trying to give you space, since I know you're just passing though. It's really none of my business, but I can't help wanting to know," he said.

"Umm…"

"I mean, you're one of the most fascinating people I've met in a long time. I figure you must have a good story to tell. There's got to be a juicy reason why you're not in school for the beginning of your senior year."

"Fascinating? Me? I usually just feel like an idiot." I shrugged.

"An idiot? No way. Maybe too smart for your own good is more like it."

"Thanks, I guess."

"So tell me, what are you running away from?"

My digestion immediately turned acidic, but it didn't last long. I'd started warming to the room, to the paper decorations in bright reds and greens, to Christopher's silvery eyes and his full mouth, which kept turning up at the corners. He seemed to like sitting across the table from me. I was warming to the entire universe, and I thought that at this moment I might do almost anything if he asked me. The words started escaping my mouth, slowly at first, and then faster until my monologue became a steady stream.

I hadn't told my story in its entirety to anyone. It was too new. I didn't have the luxury of retrospect yet. I started out feeling like I didn't deserve to tell it. But Christopher was asking, and his interest was genuine. With every sip of his margarita he moved in closer, seeking more from me. He wanted to know. As I told my story, I began to wonder if it really happened at all. I felt so distanced suddenly, as if I was talking about another girl, some unfortunate thing who was repeatedly victimized. But it was me, it was my story and I had to tell it. That was what I realized as I fingered the little straw in my golden drink with its wide glass. I had to tell it. I'd found someone who wasn't afraid to listen.

"Well I go to a school called Matterson Academy. It's a prep school and I guess what you would call a parochial school. We go to chapel once a week. It's just a sort of non-denominational Christian school. I think it was founded by Lutherans. Everyone there is smart. You have to pass an entrance exam to get in. Anyway, the kids there are all pretty interesting, even though it's got the regular snobs and weirdoes. I'd never really had a boyfriend, but I wanted one really badly. It was something I daydreamed about a lot. I even had an image in my mind of what my true love would look like — tall, thin, dark hair, cool clothes... all the shallow stuff. I had this feeling like he really existed, like he was out there and it was only a matter of time until we met."

Christopher's eyes flickered with understanding and acknowledgement. He knew the feeling.

"And he had to be interesting. That was the other thing. I wasn't interested in the boys who did what they were told to do, who wore their hair in buzz cuts and followed the rules. I wanted someone who was challenging and who understood how I used to feel from the moon and the woods. I liked to feel dangerous, you know? So, when I met Max, I thought he was it. He really met all my criteria. He has this way about him... how can I say it? Like he's only half present. Half of him is someplace else, floating around in the cosmos or inside his mind. It's only recently that I've realized it's not because he's deep and amazing. It's because he's screwed up and doesn't know who he is. That's the conclusion I've come to."

We drained our drinks, and Christopher ordered another round.

"So we started hanging out and I started to feel out of control. My friend Serena was the first person to get me into stuff, but Max was the one who got me messed up. And really, it wasn't pot and alcohol, it was just me. I was searching for something, but I guess I was looking in the wrong places. Max and I have been together for oh, about 7 months now. That's it! I can't believe that's all."

"You're still together?" Christopher asked.

"Well, we never officially broke up."

"I see. Go on."

"Anyway, he's a freaking sex addict. That's the whole problem. I had no idea. But he just started wanting me to do things with him all the time. Sneaking around the school. In the boys' bathroom, in dark classrooms, in the bushes on campus. I thought it was kinda fun, but now I think he's got issues. In June I lost my virginity. We went over to his friend Jeremy's house and put a blanket on the grass behind his house. Max wasn't gentle. Afterwards I decided I wanted to wait before I did it again. Max and I snuck out one night. Oh, that's the other thing, our parents didn't want us to see each other, so we had to sneak around all the time."

"Why's that?" he asked.

"Well, Max's parents are these fundamentalist Christian freaks, and my mom was just being over protective. Anyway, we snuck out this one night. It was a full moon, and it was the kind of night where everything just felt alive. But all Max wanted was to do *it*. I tried talking about stuff with him, stuff I thought he'd find interesting, but he wasn't even listening. I said I didn't want to do it, but he just made me do it anyway."

"What do you mean, he made you do it anyway?" Christopher asked, cautiously.

"I mean, he just did it with me anyway."

"Against your will?"

"Yeah."

"Natalie, that's rape" he whispered, leaning in close to me. I was suddenly on the verge of losing control of myself. Emotion was boiling up from my stomach into my chest like the froth in a tide pool. I gulped it down with my drink.

"Well, I don't really like to call it that," I said, composing myself.

"Shit. That's what it sounds like to me."

"Well, but it can't be. I mean, I know him. He's my boyfriend. Rape is violent and happens to girls in alleys in cities."

"You've got it wrong, Natalie. That's date rape you're describing. Haven't you learned about it in school? In health class? I've known a lot of bastards in my life — men who rape their wives. Just because you know someone doesn't mean they can't rape you."

"Yeah, I know."

"Are you ok? I mean, is that why you ran away?"

"Well, no, there's more. I got pregnant."

"Oh shit."

"It's ok. I got pregnant, because I guess it was just my time of the month or something. Bad timing. We were both really upset, but then I started to kind of like the idea. I decided to keep her."

"Her? You knew it was a girl?"

"Yeah, I guess. I didn't tell my parents or anyone, except Max and my sister. Then I had a miscarriage. I had to go to the hospital and my sister told my parents. It was humiliating. Everyone was just like 'It's for the best.' Max was relieved, because he didn't have to tell his freak parents about it, and my parents were relieved after they stopped being angry, because they didn't have to admit to their church friends that their daughter got knocked up. Everyone was relieved except me. I was just empty, and no one cared about that."

"Oh man, and this all *just* happened to you?"

"Yes, so I decided, well fuck them, you know? I didn't have to stay there and watch them go about their business like nothing happened. It was too painful. And Max, well, I should have told him off long ago, but I never did. I think he was cheating on me too, you know? With other girls at school. I wasn't even enough for him. I don't have any proof, though."

"Yeah, he sounds like a bastard."

"Deep down he's a good person, though."

"I can't believe you can defend even a little part of him."

"I think I understand why he is the way he is. I know it's stupid, but I still love him a little. He just needs help."

"That may be true, but I think that if you really are going to follow through with this running away thing, and make it worth your while, you need to let go of him completely. There's no point in being here if you're still hanging on."

"I'm not really hanging on."

"Yeah you are."

"I guess I can't let go completely. I just don't know how."

"You can. We should talk about this more." He finished the last sip of his margarita and grabbed the bill, which was becoming waterlogged in the condensation dripping off our glasses. I drained the last bit of my Patron Silver and sat back in my chair, taking deep breaths as the waiter cleared the table.

"I want to take you someplace. You feel up to a little ride?"

"Yeah, I feel good, actually. I'm just going to use the ladies room."

"Ok, meet me at the truck."

I stared at myself in the grimy mirror before I went outside. My cheeks were flushed pink and my eyes were heavy, but it gave me a sort of sultry slowness that I liked. I felt different from the tequila than I did from beer. I'd put on a little eyeliner before we left the trailer and I was wearing my black cowboy boots. I ran my fingers through my hair, thinning out the knots and fluffing it around my face. A woman opened the door and squeezed into the stall so I left, snapping myself out of my reverie. Christopher was leaning against the truck. His feet were crossed and his long legs were covered by old, faded jeans. He had his arms folded against his chest and the back of his head resting on the truck. He was looking up at the stars.

I was struck with the oddness of the moment. I was with a man I hardly knew, but was somehow connected to him in a way I'd only begun to understand. He was simultaneously new and intimately familiar. What does it mean when you feel you've known a stranger for lifetimes? It had happened to me twice, first with Max and then Christopher. I couldn't accept it as a result of hormones or a chemical imbalance. It had to mean more. Life could be so empty and seemingly meaningless at times, I had to grasp onto mystery when I could.

He heard my footsteps and raised his head from the truck, smiling silently. He didn't say anything for a long time as we drove north. The moon was full, or close to it. The high prairie was lit from above with a silver white light that was casting long shadows. I could see the hulking shape of Blanca and calculated that we were heading for the sand dunes. We drove for a few miles and parked the car beyond what seemed like a visitors' center.

"Follow me," he said, and gestured for me to scramble up the dunes behind him.

It was hard to walk in the sand, especially uphill, but the height of my boots kept the sand away from my feet. We climbed up a few sandy hills until we were at the top of one of the highest dunes. Behind us were the Crestones, sharp and jagged peaks that looked like fangs in the moonlight.

"Come over here and sit with me," he said, as he settled himself on the sand. "Now lay back and just look up."

The stars are so much clearer to the naked eye out in the vast openness of the west, in places without light pollution. A wind was blowing and clouds were moving quickly across the sky. The moon peeked in and out and cloud shadows were crawling over the dunes.

"It looks like Snowflake Obsidian," I said.

"Like what?"

"Snowflake Obsidian, jet black, but with white flecks. That's what the sky looks like. It's my favorite rock."

"Oh yeah, I've seen that," he replied dreamily. He rolled over onto his side and faced me, leaning his head on his hand, elbow resting on the sand.

"I like to come here at night and think," he said. "When the sky is clear, the stars are like a billion eyes looking down at you. They're our ancestors watching over us, saying hello, we're here for you if you need us. I believe your spirit can fly to the stars. My father did, on his journeys. The stars create a spirit bridge for the souls of people to travel across."

"That's beautiful."

"You're only just beginning your journey, you know. You're so young. Remember that when you look at the stars. You don't need to hang on to anything that isn't good for you."

"True. But do you always follow that advice?" I asked.

"Probably not, but it's good to remember."

We lay on the sand in silence for a while. I was looking up at the sky and could feel Christopher watching me, still propped up on his elbow.

"Do you think about your baby girl?" he asked quietly.

"Yeah, every day."

"She's with you still. I know it."

"I like to think so."

"Souls don't die with the body, Natalie. She is with you. She's one of those stars."

He flopped onto his back again. My hand was resting on the sand when I felt his hand slowly moving over mine. He held my hand like that for a long time. I think he wanted much more of me, but wouldn't allow himself to even consider it. That was fine with me. I couldn't handle anything more, anyway.

What I couldn't stop thinking about was Max and the last thing he said to me. Did he have the guts to buy a plane ticket and run away from his parents? He would be in so much trouble. He wouldn't do it, would he? My body tensed with apprehension. Something told me he just might.

18

On Friday Christopher and I were sitting at his kitchen table eating eggs and cheese on English muffins. He tipped a bottle of Tabasco sauce and let a few drops fall on the corner of his eggs, sandwiched between the muffins, and then took a bite. When he put the bottle down, I grabbed it and copied him. It tasted much more like vinegar than I had anticipated and then my mouth was on fire, but I liked it. I remembered one afternoon at Matterson a guy named Paris Foster and his friends had dared each other to drink Tabasco sauce. Paris had turned bright red. I watched the whole thing from my solitary vantage point. Since then I'd had the urge to try Tabasco, but it wasn't something my parents kept in the house. They liked bland food. This was what I was thinking to myself when Christopher's phone rang.

"I bet it's for me."

"Did you give someone my number?"

"Um, yes," I said slowly, sure that it was Max. He was the only one I gave the number to. I don't really know why I did it. But it should be ok. Christopher wouldn't mind if I got a phone call now and then, right? I was still so young and naive. "It might be Max."

"You gave my number to *him*? Seriously? Damn it, I don't want him calling here."

"I'm sorry. I called him once. Collect. And I just felt like I should give him a way to get in touch with me if he needed to."

Christopher picked up the phone before it clicked over to his answering machine. "Yeah!"

I chewed my English muffin and scrambled eggs, swallowing hard. The toast slid slowly and painfully down my throat in a semi-chewed chunk. I took the phone, which Christopher was handing to me with a scowl on his face.

"Hello?"

"Hey Natalie, it's Max."

"Yeah, I figured."

"I'm at the airport."

"What?"

"The Denver airport."

"Oh my God." I looked at Christopher, hoping he wouldn't be able to read my expression. "Umm..."

"I got a 7 am flight out of Newark."

"But why? We didn't decide that you were going to do that."

"I told you I was coming."

"No you didn't."

"Well, I bought a ticket and here I am."

"That must have been expensive."

"It's no big deal, I put it on my mom's credit card. So, where are you and feather dude living?"

"Damn it Max, what are you trying to do? He's a nice guy. He's my friend."

"Right. Well, I'll believe it when I see it. I don't trust him."

"You're not being fair, Max. Don't be so suspicious."

"Ok Natalie, tell me where you are."

I covered the mouth of the phone. "He's at the airport. In Denver."

"Are you kidding? Did you invite him?"

"No, I didn't. We sort of talked about it, but I didn't tell him he could come."

"Well, he's not welcome in my house. This is your issue, not mine, and I don't want him here."

"I know. I know. I don't know what to do. He's here, and he wants directions."

"Ok, give me the phone," Christopher demanded.

"Hello? This is Christopher." There's a long pause. He paced back and forth in the small kitchen. "I get it. Well, she's here and she's fine and I'm not convinced she needs to see you." Another long pause. "Okay. How about this, we'll meet you in San Luis. Meet at the Star Mart on the main street. It's near the RV place. You can find it. *We'll* be there." He hung up and sat back down at the table.

"It'll take him at least five hours to get here, I'm guessing. The airport is probably 4 hours away and he'll need to find a ride. Are you okay? There isn't much to be done. This puts me in an awkward position," he said, biting his thumb and turning to look out the window.

"It does?"

"Yes, considering what you told me about him, I feel compelled to protect you from him."

"Oh, you don't need to protect me from anything."

"Yeah, that's the other side of it. I don't need to protect you. You can just go with him. Get a room at the Econo Lodge or leave with him. Whatever."

"I guess. But, I don't want to do that."

"You want to stay here?"

I nodded. "I want to get my car and drive back home. I ran away to get away, not to have Max come out here and drag me back."

We finished our breakfast in silence. I didn't like the way he was talking about Max, as if he was an unwelcome stranger, but I had to admit that's what he was. I couldn't blame Christopher. Though it felt like I'd known him for a long time, I hardly knew this man sitting across the table from me. After breakfast I flopped down on the sofa bed, and Christopher got in the shower. It filled the trailer with a thin layer of water vapor and the smell of soap.

He was in his room getting dressed when I did something bold. He opened his bedroom door after getting dressed and I could see him moving around inside. I walked over to the door, my heart racing.

"Can I come in?"

"Um, sure. I'm just trying to chill out a bit. There's nothing that makes me angrier than men disrespecting women. The one person who made my life bearable was my mother, and I believe that about most women. They're the glue that holds us together. I think I'm gonna want to smash his face in."

"Please don't do that. He's just here because he loves me."

"If you say so," he snarled.

I walked in and sat on his bed. He was examining his CD collection. He turned around abruptly, facing me with a look of nervous determination on his face. His eyes were enormous and his hands were hanging loosely at his side.

"Natalie…" He stood there staring at me, biting his lip.

I figured I'd overstepped a boundary. I got up to leave. "I'm sorry, I shouldn't be in here. I think I'm just freaking out." As I moved from his bed to the door with my stocking feet scuffling across the floor, he reached out and grabbed my arm. He was gentle, but firm.

"No, wait."

We both stood there frozen for a moment, trying to read each other's motive. Then he kissed me solidly on the lips. I froze with my eyes wide open, my arms stiff, not knowing if I wanted to melt into it, or pull away. I knew what was going on. Christopher was marking his territory, so to speak. Somehow, without knowing it or intending it, I was in some kind of love triangle. I reached out to him, feeling his shoulders, which were more muscular and larger than Max's, in fact, he was bigger than Max, though not necessarily taller. He was just more filled out. His hands slipped to the small of my back and we moved into a tighter, but hesitant embrace. His hair was wet and was hanging in tendrils around our faces. He tasted like coffee and I was struck with how differently he kissed.

Honestly, I was electrified, but I was also completely terrified, because it meant that my life was becoming even more complicated. I pulled away from him and sat down on the bed.

"Shit, I'm sorry! I shouldn't have done that. I just... I just really wanted to. But you're too young, and it wasn't my place to do that," he said, still standing in the same spot looking bewildered. "Now I've just put more pressure on you."

"It's ok. I think that's why I came in here."

He walked over and sat next to me on the bed. "But you don't need to be confused now, and Colorado isn't your home. We should do ourselves a favor and not even think about what just happened. Neither one of us needs to get attached. I just lost it there for a second. This is hard for me, Natalie. You're just so incredible. I feel like somehow the Creator wanted us to meet, but I don't know why. And now *he's* here. I'm afraid you're going to leave as quickly as you came."

"It's ok, don't worry about it. It was silly for me to come in here, anyway. Let's just not tell Max. I don't know what I want right now, you know?"

"I'm sure it's confusing."

"It is. I'm gonna go get dressed. Maybe I'll take a walk. That might help."

"Ok, I'll leave you alone if you want."

"I don't know what I want!" I said and left the room with loud footsteps.

Christopher slipped outside while I showered and dressed in the bathroom. I could hear the sound of something sharp hitting wood and then the thick thump of something falling on the ground. I pulled the white curtains away from the window to see him fiercely swinging an axe toward a piece of reddish wood positioned on a flat stump. The power with which he flung the axe sent ripples of fear and fascination through me. He could kill Max if he wanted to, I thought to myself. Something about that idea pleased me. "Jeez, Natalie," I muttered to myself and looked away. Max had absolutely no idea what he was getting himself into. Hell, I still hadn't figured out what I was doing.

I primped nervously in front of the mirror as we readied ourselves to go face Max at the Star Mart. I don't know why I was bothering to look good. Christopher insinuated that Max didn't deserve my attention and I knew he was right, but a part of my heart was tugging at me to see him. Another part of me wanted Christopher to take me back to the sand dunes and kiss me again under the huge western sky. I blushed just thinking about it. I'd been gone just less than a week, but New Jersey felt like another world and Max had started to become an abstract idea.

On our way into town the washboard road rattled the truck and made my stomach convulse.

"I don't want to stay in a hotel with him," I blurted out with no prefacing.

"I don't blame you."

"But I can't ask you to let him stay in your house."

"I'd rather not have him sleeping under my roof."

"So I don't know what to do."

"He can sleep outside in my tent."

"Really? Are you sure? God, I can't believe how I'm inconveniencing you, and I don't even know you. You're too nice."

"Not really. I'm guilty of wanting to help a cute girl. Anyway, you're not inconveniencing me. It's not like my life was full of excitement before you showed up."

"Well, you're still too nice."

"I know. It's just the way I am. I believe in treating others how I want to be treated."

"That's a good philosophy. Well, I figure Max will stay the weekend and then leave and then hopefully my car will be ready."

"Ok, well, we'll deal with it, however it works out."

19

Max was already at the Star Mart. His dark brown hair was in a ponytail and he was wearing a new jacket, a navy pea coat type thing, and an eggplant colored shirt. He dressed nicely for obvious reasons, to persuade me. He stood up as the truck rattled into the parking lot. I was leaning on my elbow out the window and I can only imagine what it looked like. Max was standing there like a soldier ready to fight a battle.

"There he is," I said, with apprehensive excitement.

"God, what am I doing?" Christopher moaned, to the truck, the air, or the universe. He wasn't talking to me and I certainly had no answer.

"Thank you," I said and jumped out of the truck.

Max walked dramatically over to me and swept me up into his arms, swinging me around. Then he kissed me. I was facing the parking lot and could see Christopher getting out of the truck. There

I was, kissing Max Munroe outside the Star Mart in Southern Colorado, while the stranger who kissed me earlier watched us from his dusty truck. Who was my heart aching for? It just ached. Christopher's face looked like one of those realistic wax statues that I'd seen in a wax museum in Pennsylvania. His expression was molded into a permanent scowl. We walked over to him.

"Max, this is Christopher. Christopher, this is Max."

Christopher's face remained statuesque, but he did reach out to shake Max's hand. I think it took a lot for Christopher to do that. Neither one of them said a word. Max looked a little bit freaked out. It surprised me, but it made sense. He was totally out of his element, just like I was. I told Max that he could sleep in Christopher's tent and he accepted the offer with a nod, so we all climbed into the front of the truck. I was sitting between them, Christopher smelling like sage and lemons, Max smelling of some expensive cologne.

"So how did you manage to get away from your parents?" I asked, because I couldn't stand not knowing.

"I snuck a call to United Airlines and got a last minute ticket. Kinda expensive. And then at like 3:30 this morning, I got up and crept out of the house. I drove the Jeep and parked it at the airport. That's going to be expensive, too. It's weird to get up in the middle of the night and run away like that."

"Yeah, I know."

"But I figured it all out, no problem. I like airports, actually," he said. Christopher was listening silently from the driver's seat as he maneuvered the truck toward the mesa. "Where the hell are we going? You're really out in the sticks," Max says.

"I don't think they call it that here, Max. I think they call it the backcountry," I said.

"We don't call it either one," muttered Christopher.

Max leaned in close to me and whispered. "You have to get out of here. I can't believe you're staying in a place like this." I turned and scowled at him and he didn't say anything else, though I could feel the tension building.

It was early evening when we got back to the trailer. Christopher allowed Max to go inside to use the bathroom and gave him a bowl of cereal. For all the animosity Christopher seemed to feel for Max, he was being fairly hospitable. I was a little surprised. As Max ate, Christopher was rummaging around in his closet. He pulled out a blue tent and threw it at Max's feet.

"Here ya go. It's easy to put together. Sleep wherever you want, and Natalie, you sleep wherever. Just leave me out of it."

"Oh, I hadn't really thought about it. I…"

"What do you mean? Of course you're sleeping with me," Max said with his mouth full of cereal.

I looked at both of them, turning my head from one to the other, Christopher standing by the closet, Max sitting at the table. "I don't know," I mumbled. I wasn't feeling well. It was all just too much for me.

"Well, let's go outside and talk, ok?" said Max, slurping the last of his cereal milk from the bowl.

Christopher nodded and I followed Max outside. I knew Christopher was going to watch us through the small, dirty window of the living room and frankly, I was glad. I may have claimed to love Max, but I knew that he had the potential to be dangerous, and I sensed conflict building.

"So what is up with you and Feather?"

"His name is Christopher, and nothing, he's just being nice."

"Yeah, I bet."

"Just get over it. I don't know what else to tell you."

"Okay, enough about him. How are you?" Max asked, sweetly.

"I'm fine. But, this whole thing has been pretty crazy. I just wanted to get away, you know? Tell everyone to fuck off. Including you. You never asked me how I was after the miscarriage. You were just relieved."

"No, I knew it was hard for you. But my parents knew something was up and I couldn't call you and I was just, you know, working at the college. I wanted to call you, I swear I did."

"Well, it seemed to me like you were just dumping me or something."

"I would never do that, Natalie, I love you."

"Yeah, okay," I said with sarcasm and stared through the trees to where Mt. Blanca loomed silently. I'd started looking to the mountain whenever I needed to think, or gather strength. Maybe it really was a sacred mountain. The sun was beginning to set and I decided I was thirsty.

"I'm gonna go get a drink. You want something?"

"Yeah, can I come with you?"

"I guess." I walked quietly up to the trailer and opened the screen door, which squeaked. Christopher was sitting on his sofa watching TV. "I need some water. Is that ok?" I asked him hesitantly.

"Yeah, sure. Have whatever you want. I'm having a beer."

"Sounds good to me," said Max.

Christopher flashed me a glance that told me he didn't think Max having a beer was such a good idea and I agreed, but it was too late. Max was popping the top off a can of Coors.

"I guess we'll go back outside," I said to Christopher, once again sharing a lingering glance that communicated much more than we were saying out loud.

The sun was sinking low in the sky and within a few minutes had become obscured by the landscape. The sun always seemed to set earlier in the mountains. Max was putting the tent together in the dissipated radiance from the floodlights outside of the trailer. I could see Christopher's shadow moving across the walls in his bedroom. Max was struggling with the blue nylon and graphite poles that need to be unfolded. He looked like he was doing some strange dance with a flag or a parachute. His skinny body was twitching like a gawky long-legged bird.

"Fuck this thing! Help me put this together, Natalie."

I unclenched my hands, which had grown stiff in the cold night air. With the two of us working on it, the tent lifted off the ground and hovered like a blue blob in the artificial light. Max had crawled inside and was flattening out the bottom, checking for lumps that might hurt our backs once we got horizontal.

"Go ask Feather if he's got any sleeping bags!" he yelled from inside the unpleasantly fragrant shelter.

I was relieved to have a reason to go inside again and see what Christopher's state of mind was. I was uncomfortably aware that I was seriously overstepping my bounds by having Max there and quickly outstaying my welcome, even though Christopher said it wasn't that big of an inconvenience.

He was lying on his bed with a book. He had his eyes closed, actually, and as I crept down the hall, I heard faint music and smelled incense. It reminded me of a kind I used to burn at home. It was Japanese. The book resting on his chest said *The Wisdom of Avalokitesvara the Compassionate Buddha.* He became more of a mystery every day. I leaned into his room.

"Knock" I said quietly. He opened his eyes and folded his arm behind his head. "Hey you. I was just meditating."

"Yeah?"

"I'm trying to practice unconditional compassion."

"Wow, that's cool. I think."

"Yeah, listen to this." He started reading from his book. "The name Avalokitesvara most accurately means 'he who observes the sounds of the world'. Avalokitesvara's great vow is to listen to the supplications, and cries for help from those in the world and to provide them with aid, while postponing his own Buddhahood until he has helped every being on earth to achieve enlightenment."

"Wow. You read that stuff?"

"Yeah, I think Buddhism is great. It really helps me when I feel angry or upset."

"Do you feel mad now?"

"Yeah, I'm working on feeling compassion toward this situation."

"Is that why you let Max stay here?"

"I guess, and I'd rather you be safe. This is better than you and him staying in a hotel room or something, isn't it?"

"Maybe, but you're not my protector."

"No, I'm not. But I guess I feel like I am to some degree. I don't know why. I should just leave you be. In fact, if you want, I'll take you guys back to a hotel. I'm way too involved in this drama already. Shit. Tanya's gonna think I'm nuts. At least she says she's not sick of Leo yet."

"No, I don't want to go to a hotel. This is fine. It's totally weird, but it's fine. Hey, do you have any sleeping bags?"

"Oh shit, yeah. Here, let me get you a Therma-rest and a blanket. I'm sorry, but I don't want him using my down sleeping bag. Take the blankets off the sofa and here, this is warm." He got off the bed and pulled a thick wool blanket out of his closet. It looked a lot like the one we'd used in the pasture.

"I'm here if you need me, ok?" he assured.

"Yeah, I know. Ok, see you later," I replied hesitantly.

Max was snooping around in the bushes, making crunching noises as he stepped on sage and juniper.

"So what is this place?" he asked.

"It's called Black Horse Mesa. Christopher says there are wild horses that still run around out here, but I haven't seen any. There's a mountain over there called Blanca that's a sacred mountain for the

Navajo. It's 14,000 feet high. That's pretty high, Max. This is a cool place."

"I guess, though it sure is big out here. There's too much space. I think I like it better along the Delaware."

"I like that too. But this is cool. It's weird, but I'm having fun."

"So your car will be fixed soon?"

"Yeah, soon. Less than a week is what I'm hoping."

"That's good. So, what's up with you and him?"

"Nothing. Quit asking me that."

"It just seems like something's up. You're all cozy, and that makes no sense to me. You have nothing in common. He's just some blue-collar dude who found you when your car broke down. Why him? I don't get it."

"He's the only person who stopped to help me. Anyway, he's just been nice to me. And we get along well. You're reading too much into it."

"So he's just this saint who does nice things for people? I doubt it. I bet he wants to jump your bones. He's not that much older than us. What is he, twenty-one, twenty-two?"

"I don't know. I haven't asked him. Even if he did want to jump me, I bet he wouldn't. Anyway, took who's talking."

"Whatever. I know how guys' minds work. You'll be fucking in a week. I predict it." Max kicked his foot at the ground sending up dust and rattling the bushes. We were standing in the middle of dwarfed ponderosa pines. Trees grew shorter and wirier on the mesa. They braced themselves against the wind like short, muscular trolls and their branches curl like the gnarled and withered fingers of an old woman. Max grabbed onto a thin branch and broke it off. He raised it to his nose.

"These pines smell good. That's one thing I'll give this place."

"Wait 'til you see it in the morning."

Max moved in close to me and put his arms around my waist. "So how are you, my goddess? Did you miss me?"

"Yeah, I missed you."

"Do you love me?"

"I love you," I said out of obligation. I didn't actually feel it, and that was like a revelation. I realized I was finished with Max. Something had shifted within me.

"I love you too!" he proclaimed and hugged me so hard, he knocked the breath out of my chest. "It's been so long, Natalie!" He leaned down to kiss me, going through his familiar and regular motions of trying to get under my clothes. I let him go to a certain point until I just can't bear it anymore. He'd undone my bra, his hands cold on my skin, and he's gotten my jeans unbuttoned and was using his weight to try and get me to lie down on the ground.

"Max, I don't want to make out."

"Are you kidding? Why not?

"Because it doesn't feel right. This place just isn't… it's not that kind of place. That's all I can say. I feel different now, kind of like being more spiritual or something. More like I just want to talk. Let's walk through the trees and see if we can sense anything. Like spirits or something."

"What's gotten into you? You're getting all new agey on me."

"Yeah, I guess, if you wanna call it that."

"Come into the tent with me."

"I'm not tired."

"Come on!" He grabbed my arm and started pulling me toward the tent.

"Max, stop it. You can't yank on me like that. It scares me."

"I didn't fly out here to be rejected. I love you Natalie. Can't you understand that?"

"I don't know what you think love is, but pushing me around isn't love. It's something else."

"You just aren't listening!" he whispered in a loud hiss.

"Listening to what? I think I want to sleep inside. Let's talk about this in the morning. You're too worked up tonight."

I couldn't give in to Max anymore. Something had happened to me and I just couldn't do it. I slipped away from him, opened the flapping screen and closed the hollow wooden door behind me. I stood behind the closed door and considered locking it. I looked at the deadbolt. I put my hand on the cold metal and turned it. I felt it click into the socket. "I can't. That's too harsh," I said to myself and unlocked it again.

I pulled on my T-shirt and pajama bottoms and crept to the window to spy on Max. The outside light was still on, but he was nowhere in sight. I assumed he settled down and went inside the tent. I flipped the light off and crawled into bed, staring at the ambient, gray light filtering in from outside. A shadow moved in front of one of the windows. I flinched. I was scared, which was absolutely ridiculous. I felt dizzy and my vision was moving between being blurry and unfocused to unwaveringly sharp. My head felt like a bowling ball balancing on top of a thin, wobbly cattail. Christopher was still awake. A warm yellow light escaped from beneath his closed door.

Suddenly the screen door squealed and flopped against the outside of the trailer. I pulled my knees up to my chest. The doorknob turned and Max took a step inside. He was in the shadows, but I could see his dark hair swimming around his face and streaks of what shockingly enough must be tears. The light was glistening and refracting off his cheeks.

"So this is where you and Feather fuck all night, huh? This is the place? Not so great if you ask me!" He kicked a small end table near the door. A clay vase teetered back and forth without falling, making a quiet tick tock, rocking noise. "Is this what you want Natalie? I can't believe you left me for this."

"I didn't leave you. And certainly not for this. Don't be silly."

"Yeah you did. And now what do I do? Huh? Matterson sucks without you. I suck without you. I can't even fucking believe it. You love him?"

"I don't love him Max. You're imagining things!"

He began moving toward the bed where I was folded up, trying to appear as small as possible. I was hoping Christopher would hear him and come out before Max got violent, since that was what he seems to be heading toward. I glanced down the hall and Christopher was there. "Why is he just standing there?" I thought to myself. I could see his face in the pale light, but the face moved as if it was unattached to anything else. The entire head moved, and it moved quickly — too quickly for it to be attached to a body. It wasn't Christopher. It was the apparition again.

"Oh shit." I said out loud, staring at the hallway.

"What are you looking at?"

"It's nothing, just a… maybe a ghost."

"God damn you and your hallucinations!" Max said in a loud voice, too loud for inside the trailer. He walked over to the bed, crawled toward me over the mattress, grabbed me by the waist and started pulling me off the bed.

"Max quit it! I'm staying here. You're embarrassing me."

"No, I think it's the other way around," he yelled back at me. He pulled me off the bed and I fell to the floor with a thud, because I refused to stand up. Christopher's door opened. The hovering face moved with lightning speed across the room, up into my face. I gasped. I was face to face with the transparent head of Whitefeather who had been watching me for several months. He had a fierce look in his eyes and his mouth was curled into a frown. His eyes stared into mine as if to say, "Quit fooling with this crap or I'm really gonna have to get angry." I thought about my uncle Ernie who used to threaten to open up a can of whoop ass. That was what the apparition would say if he could. I was sure of it. I sat there frozen on the floor: furious boyfriend standing above me, hand still gripping my shirt, which was pulled up tightly in my left armpit revealing my bare stomach, and the ghost eyes beaming right into my own. I breathed in and exhaled a long, deep breath, as I gathered my wits and the head disappeared.

Christopher was standing in the doorway of his room, his silhouette backlit by low lights behind him. His hair was down and wild. He moved and the light behind him was obscured.

"What the hell is going on out here?" Christopher demanded.

"Nothing, dude, we were just leaving," was Max's reply.

"Why are you yanking on her shirt like that, and why are you on the floor, Natalie?"

"Forget it. It's none of your business. Come on, Natalie," insisted Max.

"She doesn't look like she wants to go."

"This doesn't concern you. We should leave. Go to a hotel or something. Get up!"

I was still petrified, plopped on the floor with my legs folded underneath me. I could still feel the imprints of Max's hands on my waist, smell the mixture of Polo cologne and sweat.

Why did the ghost appear to me at times when I felt like I was close to losing my mind? It was like the fabric that held reality together got thinner then. Either that or I'd started losing my grip on what was normal and sane and begun treading closer to the unknown territories of my mind. Maybe it was both. I moved to get up, and once I stood, Max pushed me, not terribly hard, but hard enough that I fell back on the bed, bouncing slightly, the air rushing out of my lungs.

"Max, get a grip. This isn't what you think it is," I said when I stopped bouncing.

"Yeah, right. I believe what I see, and I what I see is you siding with him." He pointed to where Christopher was standing in the shadows. "You're the one who doesn't get it. You betrayed me by leaving. You didn't even tell me you were going. We went through so much and you think you can just up and leave like that? It's not fair," he shouted.

"Are you kidding? I don't owe you anything!" I stood up again, stretching as tall as I could. "You hurt me, Max. You can deny it all you want, but you did. And I tried to love you anyway, to forgive you, but then I found out you were hooking up with other girls at school behind my back? Talk about betrayal. Do you know the roller-coaster I've been on this summer? What it's like to get pregnant when you're seventeen? You have no idea. And then to miscarry? Yeah, you were relieved, sure! But you ever think about me? What it felt like to be me? You're the heartless asshole, Max, not me."

And then in what seemed like slow motion, like his hand was moving through water, I saw him raise his arm to hit me. In a moment no longer than the shallow breath I took, he acted out of the only real form of communication he understood. His hand sped up, making contact with my right cheekbone. A dull stinging pain burned into my face. I think I screamed out loud, but I'm not sure. The force of the blow knocked me down, and I lay on the bed, covering my cheek and eye with my hands.

Christopher had been watching quietly, perhaps waiting to see if we'd work it out amicably, but when Max's hand made contact with my face, something snapped. I could feel him bristle without even looking at him. From my pathetic cocoon on the bed, I heard him dart swiftly from the hallway to where Max was staring at his hand in disbelief.

"Don't you fucking EVER hit a woman, you hear me?" shouted Christopher at a decibel my ears could barely tolerate. I hoisted myself up onto one arm. My eye was watering and smarting, but through my clear eye I saw that Christopher had knocked Max down with one swing of his arm. Max rose up from the floor and gave Christopher a forceful push, and Christopher went down too, but only for a moment. Max knocked over the end table by the door, sending the small clay vase smashing to the floor. It was then that Christopher delivered a blow that made me feel sick. Max's lovely freckled nose was bloodied. The sound of it and the thought of what it must feel like nauseated me. Max was lying on the floor and Christopher was standing over him triumphantly.

"That was easy, you little prick. You think you can come into my house and treat this girl like that? You've got a lot to learn about decency and respect. Now get out of my house."

Max dragged himself up off the floor and glanced at me with a look of utter despair on his face.

"Max," I mumbled through tears. "Max, wait…" I reached out to try and grab onto a small piece of him, but he was out the door before I could touch him. The pain I felt turned to relief and then to guilt as I worried about what might happen to him.

20

I couldn't stand the idea of Max running around on the mesa in the black night, with his nose bleeding: his perfectly shaped, pointy and freckled nose. I yelled at Christopher, who had folded onto the floor and was sitting on his legs staring into the gray room. "Damn it! You guys are insane!" I said, needing to find the blame somehow.

"I didn't want to do it," he said.

"Shit! I have to go find him. He needs to take care of his nose." I leapt off the bed and threw on that red and plaid jacket of Christopher's and ran out the door. I was subtly aware of a pain on the right side of my face, but it didn't register in my mind. The night had grown colder and a thin layer of dew was falling, chilling me through my pajama bottoms. My breath came out like puffs of smoke in the cold air and I could see water droplets running down the sides of the tent as I pulled back the fly to look inside. He wasn't there. I looked up and tried to focus on the trees around me for movement, gazing down the dirt road to see if he was there walking.

"Max!" I yelled. "Max, where are you? I'm sorry!" There was no answer, just the rustling of the trees in a wind so subtle I couldn't feel it blowing. "Max? Is that you?" My voice was swallowed up in the velvety paintbrush boughs of the pines and the soft earth. I thought maybe he walked down the road, so I took off running, but quickly slowed to a jog. The long day was catching up with me and my body was tired. I got to the end of Christopher's road, which met another perpendicular dirt road. To the right and left, I could see nothing but reddish dirt snaking into the low, brushy foliage of the mesa. There was a light somewhere through the trees, which I knew was someone else's house, but I couldn't tell how far it was. Maybe that was where he had headed. I turned to the right and started walking, calling out his name periodically.

I stopped near a particularly large ponderosa pine. I reached out to the trunk of the tree and leaned my weight against it. The bark was rough and prickly on my hand and I was out of breath, and slightly dizzy. I thought I saw something move to my right in the shadows of the trees. I flinched. There was nothing in the woods but horses, right? I forced myself to stand there. "Come on, be brave, Natalie," I said out loud to myself. "There's nothing here. Just wild horses." The wind started blowing again, and it almost feel like a response to me, like the mesa itself was breathing a quiet "hello." Or maybe it was something less friendly than a hello. Perhaps it was "be careful" or "go home."

My brain was starting to feel like it was swimming inside my skull — that familiar sensation I seemed to get before a fainting spell. Every time I moved my head I felt waves were lapping inside, making my eyes slosh like marbles in a bowl of water. I took a few deep breaths, trying to clear my head, but it didn't help. I took a step forward, and suddenly the mesa was spinning. While I knew what was happening, there was absolutely nothing I could do. I was fainting again. "I hope this dirt road is soft," I thought as I felt myself going down.

Waking up, I felt silky red earth beneath me. I tried to focus my eyes and saw the universe of stars above me, sparkling. I don't know how long I'd been laying there, but no one had found me. I was already so used to Christopher coming to the rescue, I was actually surprised that I didn't awaken to his gentle songs, or touch. I propped myself up on my elbows. The moon had moved across the sky, so I'd definitely been out for a while. I sat for a few minutes trying to gather my wits. I'd been dreaming about mountain lions. I'd never seen one, but in my dream there were at least three, circling around me.

I stood up and dusted myself off. I shouldn't have even bothered to look, but I decided to scan the scenery in front of me for potential beasts or monsters. I was terrified, though I tried to keep myself under control, because there was nothing I could do. I just had to walk back to Christopher's. I wasn't going to find Max. As I looked around me, I saw something shining on the other side of the road. I concentrated and focused my eyes and as the moon came out from behind wisps of clouds and shone more light on the road, I distinctly saw two yellow eyes staring right at me.

My heart jumped into my throat. I swallowed hard and suddenly I didn't want to move at all. What was it? A wolf? Maybe it was just a dog. I didn't want to turn my back on the eyes, but I really didn't want to remain there having an absurd kind of staring contest. "I shouldn't run," I thought. "If you run, they chase you." I knew this. It was the same with all animals: bears, dogs, mountain lions. I would just back up slowly. I took a few steps backward and the eyes remain fixed. For a moment they disappeared and then reappeared in the same spot. Whatever it was, I thought it had blinked.

I kept walking backward until I could tell that the eyes were standing still. I relaxed just a little. *Okay. It's just watching me. It's not following. I'm going turn around and walk quickly to the trailer.* My heart was pounding as I put one foot in front of the other, slowly and then more quickly until I was running. I couldn't help it. I had to run. As I sped up faster and faster my fear escalated. I was sure it was right behind me. When I got to the trailer I ran inside as fast as I could and slammed the screen door. The outside light was off and I stood there looking out, scanning the woods.

When the moonlight hit just right I could see that the eyes were there in the juniper bush just outside the trailer! The thing followed me home. I never heard a single foot fall or twig crackle under the weight of an animal and at that moment I also realized that I was alone in the trailer. Christopher was gone, probably looking for me. I closed the door, locked it, and flipped on the outside light. I sat on the sofa and began to wait, tapping my foot restlessly on the carpet.

I sat in the shadows for a long time. I was really tired and my face was beginning to throb, but I couldn't allow myself to fall asleep. Max and Christopher were both out on the mesa in the dark with some yellow eyed beast stalking them and it was because of me. The trailer seemed to breathe with the wind. Some invisible draft was fluttering the curtains and the moon was shining through the windows like the milky white soup my mom used to make. She called it vichyssoise. I liked that soup.

The phone rang and snapped me out of my catatonic state. I debated picking it up, but it wasn't my house. But what if it was Christopher? What if it was Max? Who else would call in the middle of the night? It rang once, twice, three times, and just as I finally summoned the energy and gumption to get up and answer it, the answering machine picked up.

"Hey you've reached Christopher. If you have a question about painting or detailing, please use my pager. If not, speak after the beep." There was a pause and then a long tone.

"Chris, you jackass! It's Maggie. What the hell are you doing punching the lights out of a kid in the middle of the night? I've got a kid here who says you broke his nose. What are you up to over there? Jeez Louise. Call me back or get over here and take care of this situation. I gotta get up early tomorrow and so does Lenora."

The phone clicked to dial tone. I stood there staring at the answering machine. Who was Maggie? Max was with someone named Maggie? Lenora? I guess I was relieved. At least he wasn't out in the dark, stumbling around and bleeding, leaving a trail of blood for the yellow-eyed monster to sniff out. I really wanted Christopher to come home. I went into the bathroom and looked at myself in the mirror. A red welt was forming on my cheekbone and the soft, nearly translucent skin under my eye was beginning to turn an ugly reddish purple. I splashed cold water on my face trying to wash it away, but nothing happened. It remained: Maxwell Munroe's cruel signature.

I went back to my bed and curled up, hoping that Christopher would return home soon and find me there, melted into the mattress, needing him. The pillow was soft and as my back relaxed into the mattress, I felt like I'd never be able to get up again, I was so tired. There were still shards of clay scattered on the floor from the poor vase that bit the dust during their fight.

"Dear God, please help me be strong. Please let things work out in the best way possible. Please protect me from the ghost and the yellow-eyed thing," I prayed to myself. I didn't know if anyone was really listening.

∞

We were walking through a flat plain. A warm wind was blowing and lifting a white linen dress off my legs, swimming it around my skin like sheets of lemon meringue. Christopher was up ahead motioning for me to follow him toward the sand dunes. Trying to see the end of the horizon burned my eyes, it was so far away. Christopher moved with agility up and over the dunes. I ran behind him, finding that I had more energy than I ever had before.

I was in bare feet and the sand felt like silk between my toes. I was practically floating over the rises and dips in the dunes. We crossed over the dunes and found ourselves in a valley with a stream mumbling over shiny, round rocks. The trees growing along the stream were tall, drooping cottonwoods and their yellow leaves were falling in the breeze, floating like little golden sailboats on the tide of the wind. Across the stream was a small round building made of red clay. The door was adorned with red columbines and talismans of black cohosh root and tiger's eye. Christopher waded across the stream and I followed him into the building.

The interior was much larger than the outside view should allow and was draped in blood red velvet. The floor was covered with pillows of the same color. To my left was a small altar. It was lit with candles and small pieces of smooth ocean glass. In a clay bowl etched with designs I didn't recognize was a small bundle. I reached out and picked it up, unwrapping it. Inside it was a small baby girl, no larger than an apple or a pear. She opened her eyes and reached out her tiny hand. I held her there for a moment, tears welling up in my eyes.

Christopher was behind me saying, "Put her to sleep now Natalie and come over here with me." I took his hand and he pulled me to the other side of the room as if I was floating. "Look up," he said, and I did. The ceiling of the round building was a planetarium. It looked just like the snowflake obsidian sky when we were laying on the sand dunes together. He pulled me close to him. The room sparkled as if we were inside one of those photos of the Andromeda Galaxy or a supernova. It was a swirl of red and black, with white specs of stars like dust. He stood behind me and wrapped his arms around my waist, resting his face on my shoulder. He began moving, like we were dancing to music coming from across the room, though I didn't hear any. Then his hands moved to my belly. "It's time to create something new," he said softly. He turned me around and began kissing my neck. I reached up and ran my fingers through his hair, returning light kisses on his neck and ears.

Then we were on the pillows and his gentleness turned into urgency, but I wasn't afraid. I felt the same urgency, the tingling on my skin, moistness in my mouth, ready to welcome his lips. He pulled his tunic over his head and let it fall to the ground. My white linen dress had disappeared. His hands traveled over me like warm waves, and I moved against them like the sandy beach welcoming the tide as it moved in. His hands were inside me, around me, under me and as I looked up, the stars in the ceiling were sparkling like mica in moonlight. I knew what he was going to do and I wanted him to do it. For the first time in my life I was open voluntarily, like spring soil opens to seeds.

He entered me like thunder cracking over the wide prairie. He set a rhythm like a storm rolling in from the West beginning with thunder, lightning and eventually rain. Our embrace moved through me like the electricity of lightening penetrating the earth, creating a connection from the heavy clouds to the soil and back up again. We rolled over and under each other, exploring the folds and undulations of our skin until we both needed to rest. He moved away from me and dressed. I pulled on my white linen and rose from the pillows. He motioned for me to leave the room. I entered the building a dry, parched desert ghost and was leaving it a deep pond of fecund water.

When I walked outside, I looked down and see that my stomach has grown full and enormous. I followed Christopher along the stream, watching his feet step carefully around small flowers and moss. He paused and turned to me, placing his hand on my shoulders. "It's time to make something new," he said again.

"Natalie, wake up, come on now," whispered Christopher, who was shaking me awake. "There you are. You were really out like a light. I've been trying to wake you for like ten minutes." He was leaning in close to me, sitting on the bed. He began stroking my hair. "I went out looking for you, but I didn't see you, and then I passed Maggie's house and she saw my truck and came out running, screaming bloody murder at me. Max was at her place. I guess he just walked in the direction of her light. She got his nose to stop bleeding and gave him some kind of herbal tonic with honey or something. I don't know why. Anyway, he was getting drowsy. I guess he's asleep there, I don't know. I don't know if he'll show up here not."

I moaned groggily. "I went looking for him. I stood by a tree. I got dizzy and fainted again. I dreamed about mountain lions. When I woke up there were eyes in the woods watching me. I ran back here, and the eyes followed me the whole way." I turned over in the bed and he laid down next to me, his knees cradled in the backs of mine. He draped his arm over my waist. "And I knew you were out there, too. I was so scared you and Max were gonna be eaten by whatever it was."

"It was just a cat. I saw it, actually."

"A cat?"

"Well, a lion. A mountain lion. It ran in front of my truck. You almost never see them that way. They usually stay in the shadows. They're very stealthy. I think it's a mama cat. She's out hunting tonight."

"And then when I got back here, I fell asleep and I was dreaming. You were in my dream."

"I was? What was I doing?"

"I can't tell you," I said softly, as I drifted back into dreams about mama mountain lions giving birth and nursing tiny baby cats in the thick juniper and sage of the mesa.

Christopher slept the night next to me on the pull-out bed. I don't know if it was because somehow he sensed the dream I had, or if he just felt bad for me. Maybe he wanted to be there if Max returned, ready for more action. We woke up facing each other. I opened my eyes first. The comfort of sleep surrounded me and for a moment it seems perfectly natural to see him next to me. But then the events of the night before hit me and I breathed deeply trying to comprehend it. He was awake too, and he stared at me for a moment and then a look of pity glanced across his eyes. He reached out and lightly touched my face and said something in a different language. I imagined that it meant "poor thing," but I didn't know.

Neither one of us spoke. He just got up and walked into the kitchen, poured a glass of water and then got in the shower. He emerged a few minutes later and we traded places. I rubbed the fog off of the mirror. My eye looked hideous. I was having trouble acknowledging that Max did it to me, that he could have done something so blatantly abusive. Christopher was pouring cereal into a bowl and brewing coffee.

"He might come back over here, you know," he said.

"Yeah, I know. I'm worried about him. I mean, you really punched him hard."

"I think he deserved it."

"I guess he did. But still, I feel bad about it."

"Yeah, I do too. It's certainly not something I do every day."

"Can we go over to Maggie's house?"

"Naw, I don't want to go over there."

"Why not? Max is still there, I'm sure of it. In fact, you don't need to come with me. I'll go myself. It's my thing, not yours, anyway."

"She lives on the other side of the mesa near the lake."

"There's a lake?"

"Hell yeah, that's where the expensive real estate is. That's where Jim's always trying to sell."

"Is it close enough to walk to?"

"Oh sure, but you don't have to. I'll take you."

"You will?"

"Yeah, I mean, if you really want to. It's just that Maggie … Well, Maggie used to be married to a friend of mine. An ex-friend. Now she's with Lenora."

"Oh." I was trying to figure out what he meant.

"Daryl hit her. It's kind of ironic that Max ended up at her place."

21

Maggie's house was a step up from Christopher's trailer. It looked like one of those homes that arrived on the back of a truck, already built. Her house was pale yellow with a gray, cement foundation revealed in its bleak glory. It needed some shrubbery, or something. She had a rainbow windsock hanging from the small roof over her front door. Christopher rang her doorbell, bracing himself for something. I didn't know what. A young woman with spiky blonde hair opened the door.

"Hey, come on in. The kid isn't here," she said with a sneer. She turned around as we followed her into the house. "You must be the infamous Natalie. I'm Maggie, and this is Lenora." She pointed to another young woman who was sitting at the kitchen table reading a magazine. She had a similar haircut, but her hair was brown, and she looked a little older than Maggie, in her 30's.

"Where's Max?" I asked, trying to hide the nervous urgency in my voice.

"Lord knows I don't give a shit," said Maggie defiantly.

"What's up? What happened? I thought I was the bad guy, at least that's what it seemed like last night," said Christopher.

"That little turd has a lot of nerve. Lenora and I stayed up for hours with him, putting ice on his face. She'd changed into her pajamas and was standing there and he turned to me first and said something suggestive about her." She tried to mimic Max's voice by talking in a deep voice that reminded me of a feminine Barry White. "I think he was kidding, given the state of his face and all, but honest to god, what was he thinking?"

"He didn't do that for real, did he?" I asked, hoping it isn't true.

"He sure as hell did," offered Lenora from the table.

"And it looks like somebody swung a good one at you, girl," said Maggie, inspecting my face and giving Christopher an inquisitive look. "I've got some good stuff to put on it. Come with me." She grabbed my hand and pulled me upstairs. I followed her into a room that would have been a bedroom, except it had been converted into what looks like a studio/meditation room of some sort. The other room down the hall looked like a master bedroom.

"Does Lenora live here too?" I asked.

"Yep, she does."

"So, you both sleep in there?" I asked as I looked toward the bedroom.

"Yeah, we sleep together, hon. Ok, come here," she whispered. She pulled a glass jar from the shelf above us and scooped up some yellowish paste, getting ready to smear it on my face.

"Wait, what is that?" I asked.

"Oh, no need to be afraid. It's a homemade ointment. It's a base of beeswax and olive oil with herbal extracts. The combination of stuff is good to bring down swelling and heal. I make salves and magical ointments."

"Wow, I never met anybody who made magical ointments."

"Yeah, it's fun. I just dabble in it, really. Christopher's sister taught me a few things about Native stuff, but I'm more into Wicca."

"Christopher's sister does stuff with herbs?"

"Yep. Hasn't he told you anything about his family?"

"No."

"He's silly. Always the quiet, sullen one. Never talking about his father or his inheritance."

"Inheritance?"

"His calling. Some folks believe that if you are meant to be a medicine man or woman, a shaman, you are called to be one."

"How are you called?"

She smeared the ointment on my face. "Well, it can be a lot of different things, but I think in Christopher's case it was getting sick and fainting."

"Really?"

"Yeah, I think some people go sort of mad when they get the calling. Others get really sick, or have an encounter with an animal. Chris went through a bunch of fainting spells and some mysterious sicknesses a few years back. They say if you ignore it, the spirits will keep calling you, though I don't think he's been sick lately. And you know, not many people get the calling and now when they do, they usually ignore it. At least that's what his sister Clara tells me. I remember, when he'd just graduated from high school, like three years ago, he'd moved to the mesa to be near Clara and he fainted in the middle of the road up there near Nelson's arroyo. Don Saulter found him when he was driving his Jeep up to check on something at Nelson's old house. He was just lying there, out like a light. Lucky someone didn't come by and run him over."

"Oh man. The road is a bad place to faint," I said.

"Yeah, I'd imagine so," she replied. "So, is Max your boyfriend?"

"Sort of. Not anymore," I answered. The ointment was cooling my throbbing face.

"Did he do this to you?" she asked, hesitantly touching my cheek.

"Yeah. That's when Christopher punched him."

"Shit, I wish I hadn't laid into Chris like I did. I just didn't know the whole story. He used to hang out with these guys from town, you know. One of them was my ex-husband Daryl. They were a bunch of woman hating assholes. Into some bad stuff, too. Chris doesn't hang out with them anymore, by the way. Shit, Chris even got arrested once for holding stolen property at his house. He just said he'd keep it for this guy, and whaddya know, he gets arrested. I think he's got a record now, felony theft by receipt or something."

"Yikes. That sounds bad."

"Yeah, it sounds bad, but it's nothing. We've all got at least one dirty little secret up our sleeve."

"How did you learn to make these ointments?"

"I got a job working in the herb shop in San Luis after high school. Now I manage it. It's pretty cool. You know the San Luis Valley is the UFO sighting capital of the whole country? There are more sightings here than anywhere else. Cow mutilations, too. This is one weird place. I love it. I moved here from Taos with Daryl, but he used to get drunk and hit me like Max hit you and now he's gone off to someplace, Lord knows I don't care where. Now it's just me and Lenora. We're like two peas in a pod. She's the best thing that's ever happened to me."

I couldn't stop thinking about the "inheritance" Maggie had mentioned. Christopher used to get sick and faint, too. Why didn't he say anything about that when it happened to me? He must have recognized what was going on. I had to talk to him about it.

Maggie led me back downstairs.

"Where do you think Max went?" I asked as she walked with us to the front door.

"Well, my guess is he walked back out to the main road and probably hitched a ride or something. He said he was leaving, so maybe he figured out a way to get back to the airport."

"I noticed that his bag was gone from the tent," I said. I wasn't sure how I feel about him leaving like that. I was partly relieved, but the whole thing made me sad.

"Well, let's hope he just got a ride back to Denver," said Christopher.

"Ok guys, I'll see you later," said Maggie, urging us out the door and smiling at me with eyes that seem to know things. We hopped back in the truck.

"I need to go into town to drop off some tools for my friend Jackson. Do you mind coming along? It'll only be like 20 minutes," asked Christopher.

"That's fine," I replied.

I liked the idea of getting off the mesa. Maybe we would pass Max on the road. But, Christopher took a different route. Instead of driving west, like he normally did, he drove north. We picked our way down the mesa, avoiding large gullies in the road, and eventually found ourselves in a quaint area of town full of Spanish looking buildings. Most of them were white with delicate, ornate decorations along the roofs. The streets were narrow and he turned between a church, "Our Lady of the Springs" and a deli. He pulled onto a dusty dirt road that led to a small house that was painted a light turquoise. No one was home. He stopped the truck with a sputter of the engine and got out to unload some stuff from the back. I sat and waited. The little house had lace curtains and I tried to look through the window, but all I could see was the reflection of the bright sunlight and Christopher moving behind me. I wanted to ask Christopher about the fainting, but I was waiting for the right moment.

He leapt back in the car smelling slightly of the dampness of sweat.

"Okay. All set. You want lunch?"

"Sure, that sounds good."

He drove back to Our Lady of the Springs, turned right and parked in front of a small diner that boasted green chili and burritos for $2.50. I decided to treat Christopher for lunch. It was the least I could do. We walked in and sat down, opening the greasy plastic menus. The waitress fills our water glasses and then walked away.

"Christopher, I need to talk to you about something."

"Okay."

"Maggie said something about an inheritance. Your calling. What did she mean?"

"I don't talk about that."

"Well, when I was back in Jersey I started fainting. It started around the same time I got pregnant, so I thought it was just from that. But it didn't stop. I mean, you saw me faint when we went on that hike. And it's not just fainting. I see things. I've been seeing this man with white feathers. I saw a bear once too. And I hear my name being called. It's the kind of thing where I could just say it's my imagination, but it's happened enough that I can't ignore it. I mean, I fainted in the middle of the road last night. Maggie said you fainted in the middle of the road once." I bored holes into him with my eyes, waiting for his response. He scratched his chin and stared at me.

"Yeah."

"So what do you think?"

He sighed deeply. "What's happening to you used to happen to me, but I ignored it. I didn't want to face what it meant."

"What did it mean?"

"That I was to follow my father's path. He was a medicine man, you know," he looked directly at me and his silvery eyes were pained, but imploring. "Do you know what a medicine man is?"

"Yeah, I do."

"My dad used to tell us about our ancestors. He would sing to us. Sometimes he'd stay up all night singing until the moon moved across the sky. He'd heal people, too. He knew the right prayers to say for a sick person. He told me a little about these things. But then he left us."

"He left you?"

"Yes, one day he never came back."

"Do you know what happened?"

"I don't. I think he must have passed away, but I didn't think that for a long time. For the longest time I thought he just left us. Maybe he didn't love us, or maybe he wasn't such a great man after all, you know? Why would I want to inherit something if all it did was make him leave? What kind of a man is that?"

"I see a man who looks like you, but older and with white feathers."

"I know."

He stared at me with that look again. It was as if he wanted me to put what I saw in his eyes into words. He crumpled a napkin with his hands, twisting it and then unrolling it.

"Christopher, am I seeing your father?"

"I think you might be."

"But why? Why would I see him in New Jersey before I even met you?" I asked.

"I can't explain it," he shrugged.

"Don't you want to know?"

"Yeah, I guess I do. I don't know what to think."

"Well, I think he's trying to tell me something. He talked to me once. He said he wanted me to do something for him."

"He talked to you?"

"Yeah. He's been trying to get my attention." I twisted my napkin between my fingers.

"Do you think it's his ghost?"

"I'm not sure. He seems more like just a spirit than a ghost, but I don't really know how to differentiate. It's not like I see this stuff all the time."

"Clara told me that when you are meant to be a medicine man or a healer, that sometimes you'll get sick or have something happen to you that basically jolts you out of your normal reality. It's like the spirits are trying to get your attention."

"So that happened to you and you ignored it and now it's happening to me? And somehow I was supposed to meet you?"

"It looks that way."

"Wow. So what do we do now?"

"Maybe this is it. Maybe we were just supposed to meet each other," he said with a slight smile.

"Maybe."

The waitress was waiting to take our order, but we were leaning in, concentrating intently on each other. There was a tension building. I watched his eyes and his mouth, wanting to get closer, maybe even kiss him. But what was I thinking? I sat back in my chair, grateful that the waitress was there.

"What can I git ya?" she said. We both ordered burritos.

We relaxed a bit now that the intensity of our conversation had died down. It was September and the aspens had begun to turn yellow. I could see one out the window of the diner.

"There's a place I want to take you tonight," said Christopher. Something about the way he said it sent shivers through me.

"Okay."

"You up for a hike to some hot springs?"

"Yes, definitely."

22

Something had changed between Christopher and me. I guess I shouldn't have been surprised. I'm sure if anyone had been watching us, they would have seen it coming. To be fair, even though it seemed much longer, I'd only known him for two weeks and I suppose it was partly the natural progression of getting to know someone. Max felt like a distant memory now, even though he had just been there. I think the awful scene in the trailer completed something for me, because I didn't feel that longing for him that I felt before he arrived. Now my attention was on Christopher and what this strange turn of events meant. There was no doubt we were supposed to meet each other. There was some force at work in our lives. I felt like I'd received permission from the universe to be with him.

I could tell that something was changing in him too. At first he was hesitant to touch me, and even that time he kissed me, he was awkward and cautious. Now he was laughing with me more, horsing around, putting his hands on my shoulders, looking at me with openness rather than caution. At first he was sullen, maybe even depressed. Now he was smiling and there was a light skip to his walk. I thought I knew what it was. I thought we might be falling in love. But, I only let myself think that once, for real. I pushed it aside, because it was impossible, and way too fast. My car would be fixed and I had to go back to school. I still didn't know how old he was. All I knew was that he was over twenty-one and that scared me just a little bit.

After lunch, we drove back to the trailer and I called the garage. A part was backordered so it was going to be another day or two before they would be finished. I was beginning to think they were a bunch of idiots at Marcus Auto Body and Repair. The truth was that I was starting to hope that the repairs took a long and indefinite amount of time to complete. Once my car was done, I would have no excuse to stay with Christopher. My eye was clearing up quickly after Maggie applied her ointment and now it was just a pinkish purple, instead of an angry red. I felt good.

That night Christopher took me to the hot springs outside of town. He turned onto a road that twisted up into the enormous and looming mountains. It was pitch black outside the car.

"What makes them hot?" I asked, staring out the window at the dark nothingness.

"I think it's from magma at the center of the earth."

"Really?"

"Yeah, it heats up steam or water that travels up through cracks in the earth."

"Wow. That seems so primal. Creepy." What if hot lava started erupting out of the spring and cooked us to a crisp? I shifted my feet and clenched my towel a little tighter. I could tell that there was a steep cliff outside my window, but I couldn't see how far down it went. I feel like I was about to take a step toward something I could never turn back from, like I was going to jump off the edge of the road into the canyon below. If I pursued a relationship with Christopher, what did that mean for my future? I was about to complicate the heck out of my life, but if I did it joyfully, that seemed to make it alright. I guess that's what matters most, right? Maybe the whole, weird ordeal had simply been about meeting Christopher. Maybe he was my true love.

We turned onto a dirt road that was made of the same red earth as the roads on the mesa. It seemed to go on forever, charging through mesmerizingly repetitive dwarfed trees and bushes until we found a small area for parking cars. We each had a towel with us, the clothes on our backs and that was all. Christopher insisted that it was best to go naked into a hot spring and that it would be pitch black so I didn't need to be bashful. He said he wouldn't see a thing, wouldn't do a thing. I trusted him, and it wasn't my first time skinny dipping.

We were in the middle of the woods and on either side of us the mountains sloped upwards. It was almost like a canyon, but Christopher said it wasn't. It was more of a valley. We followed a path along a stream for a short distance.

"Here we are," said Christopher in a hushed voice. I could see steam rising off of invisible pools.

"It's so quiet here," I whispered.

"Yeah, isn't it great? Not so many people know about these springs. There's another spring where the tourists go." I could tell he was starting to undress in the dark as he was talking. The moon was out, but it wasn't full and it was still low in the sky. All I could see was his telltale shape moving quickly because the air was a little bit cold. "Go ahead and just do what I do," he said. I could see him moving toward the pool, testing it with his foot and then stepping in. He disappeared quickly and all I could see was the faint hint of his head hovering above the water. "Come on, it feels great!"

"Okay, but don't look." I took off my shoes and socks and sat them on a rock. I carefully removed my jeans, then my T-shirt, and rolled them up in a ball and placed them on top of my shoes. My underwear was all that separated me from the cold mountain air. What the hell. I took them off too, and tucked them into my jeans. Naked and embarrassingly pale, I stepped from rock to rock, trying to avoid the mud. I couldn't tell where the bottom of the pool was and Christopher reached out his hand to help me steady myself. I took his hand and eased myself into the water. It was hot, though not as hot as a Jacuzzi. The water was fantastically soft against my skin and I could feel myself relaxing immediately. I let out a big sigh.

"Yeah, isn't it nice? I like to lay back and just watch the stars," said Christopher.

I had a hard time getting over the fact that we were naked in a pool of water in the middle of the woods, completely alone. If Max knew what I was doing he would totally lose it. Thinking about him made my stomach uneasy. Poor broken-nosed Max. I'm sure his parents were unbelievably furious when he returned home, but I was done worrying about Max.

Christopher seemed very comfortable being naked and was letting himself float a little, lolling about in the water. He was acting fairly uninterested in me, which I knew was his way of being decent and honorable. I appreciated it, but it wasn't what I wanted at that moment.

"Christopher, how old are you?"

"I just turned twenty-two."

"Really?"

"Yeah, why?"

"I thought you were like twenty-five."

"Yeah? Why's that?"

"Because you have a business and a house."

"Naaw, my sister owns the trailer. And the business, well me and Jackson kind of started it together. We figured, we had some skills, we might as well make money doing them, you know? It just happened. I didn't go to college, so I've been out of school now a few years. I needed to do something and there isn't that much around here to do."

"Yeah, that makes sense."

"And you're seventeen?"

"Yeah. Eighteen in December. So we're five years apart. Is that a lot?"

"Not really."

"I guess not."

"No, not in the grand scheme of things. It's not much at all. Why are you asking?"

"No reason."

He stretched his long legs across the width of the pool and he could almost touch the rocks next to me with his toes. I reached out and tickled his foot. I felt like being daring. He laughed, but didn't take his foot away. I moved my hand over his foot again, applying a little pressure as if I was going to give him a foot massage. He still didn't move, but he became more still, sensing that I had an agenda.

I moved my hands up his legs a little and let myself float over in front of him, moving slowly in the water like a cat stalking its prey. Moving my hands further up his legs, I could tell that he wanted me, but he was silent and afraid of what I was doing.

He mumbled quietly, "Are you sure you…" I cut him off mid-sentence.

"Yes."

"But I think you…" I silenced him by kissing him on the mouth. We'd been burning for this moment for days. He starting to kiss me with urgency. I don't know why I was being so bold, but I knew what I wanted and I wasn't being taken advantage of. I was directing the pace and the progression of events. His hands were becoming less timid, moving over my skin underwater. He kissed me like he was dying of thirst and my lips were cold spring water. We were wrapped around each other, slipping on the slimy rocks and the muddy bottom of the pool. We laughed. This was how it needed to be. I felt like my spirit was lighter, unburdened.

"Look at that tree," he said, breaking the momentum and pointing toward a cottonwood that had become more visible as the nearly full moon rose higher in the sky. "Doesn't it look almost like it's moving?" he said quietly.

I turned to look in the direction he was pointing and immediately saw the blurry figure of a man hovering in the tree. The stars were out beyond the tree and I focused my eyes there before looking directly at the tree again, hoping that what I just saw was gone. It wasn't. I saw arms moving as if the figure was swimming.

"Oh god, not again. Not now," I said.

"What?"

"I'm seeing him again."

"You are? Now?"

"Don't you see anything in that tree?" I asked, hoping he saw it too.

"I thought I did, but now I don't."

"It's like he's floating in water. He's moving his arms like he's swimming."

His feathers were rippling in an unseen breeze and he was mouthing words that I couldn't hear. His hair was long and black, and swirled around him like long tendrils of underwater hair.

"What do you want?" I shouted out loud toward the tree.

"Do something for me," the apparition said.

"Do you hear anything?" Christopher asked.

"Yes, he says he wants me to do something for him."

"Take my son and go to Milk Creek, look below where the rock runs yellow and find me there."

"Where is that? I don't know what that is," I said.

"Where what is?" asked Christopher.

"Find Milk Creek, where it runs below Gunbarrell Pass. Find me there," said the apparition.

"Milk Creek?" I repeated.

"Milk Creek?" asked Christopher.

Christopher's father was giving me instructions! I felt the need to write them down, but I had no paper, no pen. Then he was changing. His eyes were turning utterly black, the whites blending into the dark sky behind him and I thought I saw blood dripping down the side of his face from the top of his head. He was beginning to shrivel, so that the outlines of his skull were becoming more and more visible. I felt like my own body was shriveling along with his. I screamed and backed up toward the rock wall of the pool.

"What is it? What's happening?" asked Christopher.

"He's changing. It's like he's shriveling up. He's dying!" I shouted, pointing at the tree. "He said he's your father. He's gone now," I said matter-of-factly. And he was. He had disappeared into the black sky and it was just the tree again with wiry, gray branches. "What's wrong with me?" I asked, through tears, which I couldn't control. "Why does this keep happening? I don't want to see him. I don't ask for it."

"I don't know."

"I'm sorry."

"Why are you sorry?"

"Because I ruined the moment."

"Don't worry about it. There will be other moments," he said and pulled me close to him. "What did he say?"

"He said to go to Gunbarrell Pass, find Milk Creek and look for yellow rock."

"I think that's in New Mexico."

"Really? You've heard of it? It's a real place?"

"Yeah, it is. That's crazy."

"I think we should go there," I said.

"I'm afraid of what we'll find."

"Yeah, but I'm afraid that if we don't, this freaky stuff is going to keep happening to me."

We floated in silence for a long time watching the stars. At one point we heard coyotes calling somewhere to the north. They didn't sound like domestic dogs, exactly, nor did they sound like wolves. They almost sounded like they were laughing, but it sounded slightly sinister to me. The moon was close to full. How many full moons ago had I gotten pregnant? It felt like a thousand. In truth, it had only been four.

Sometimes the universe seems more open and I almost get a feeling or recollection of what it must be like to be a soul unattached to a body. When I think about it I get a sensation of being in a borderless, airy place, where communications with other spirits happen in vibrational frequencies, rather than words and movement across great distances is immediate. I wonder if we can go there in our sleep. I think I went there when I was with Max in the pasture and in the birches when I got pregnant. In fact, maybe I went there whenever I was scared. Maybe that was why I saw Whitefeather at those times. It was when I was freaked out and left my body just a little — just enough that I entered into whatever space he occupied.

Maybe that was where Christopher's father was. He's in that place of spirits. He was just a whisper, a faint breath of air in a calm room, or a flickering shadow.

23

Christopher and his friend Jackson Pacheco walked ahead of me through the forest at the bottom of Gunbarrell Pass. The closer we got to the spot, the more nervous I became. Gunbarrell Pass was on the border of New Mexico and we were hiking in part of the northernmost forest of the state. A pass is always the high point of a mountain road, where the weather is generally colder and fiercer than at lower elevations. Gunbarrell Pass wasn't bad in September, but Jackson told me a story about a harrowing excursion over Monarch Pass on the way from Crested Butte to Denver the previous winter. He said that many of the roads don't even have guardrails and you can literally just slide right off the mountain if you're unfortunate enough. I longed for the rolling hills of New Jersey. Ice is a problem back east, but at least there aren't white-knuckle passes to roll off of. Wasn't it Jack Kerouac who said you can't fall off a mountain? I think he may have been wrong. Just talk to someone from Colorado.

Jackson was Mexican American and about the same age as Christopher. He had a fondness for light beer apparently and had a case of it in the back of the truck, for celebration perhaps? It seems a little morbid to me. His hair was lighter than Christopher's, though still a dark brown. He was wearing overalls with a narrow navy blue and white striped pattern. They look like train engineer overalls.

Since we didn't know how far we would have to hike, we were equipped with all the basic camping necessities. My pack was the lightest, though I still felt like I was carrying an extra 100 pounds. I'm sure it was only about 20.

A dry creek stretched through the canyon. Christopher said we were near the Rio Grande, though I couldn't imagine it. The Rio Grande sounded like a huge river and the dried up creek I was looking at seemed like a pathetic tributary. "Actually, at certain times of the year, the Rio Grande is dried up completely," said Christopher. As we hiked further into the canyon, the walls grew higher and looming shapes of rocks at the rim looked like faces watching us. It was so quiet. It was even quieter than the mesa, if that was possible. We hiked for hours with no results. The rock never changed and we never saw anything that remotely resembled Milk Creek. Christopher didn't actually find Milk Creek on the map, but he figured that it had to be in the area, simply because it was the only place below Gunbarrell Pass with the possibility of running water.

I was in over my head a little bit. The thought of Matterson and our immaculate, preppy campus seemed distant from the quest I was embarking on. We stopped at a wide part of the canyon where the water had started to run more steadily. It was deep enough to wade in up to our ankles. "It's getting late," said Christopher. "I think it might be best if we camp here and start out early tomorrow morning. I have a feeling we're in the right place." He dropped his backpack with a thump and began rifling through it, pulling out his blue tent. Jackson did the same and soon there were two dome tents: one blue and one yellow, neatly positioned on the flat, sandy area near the creek. Christopher and I were going to share the blue tent. Jackson got out a small stove, which he said was fueled with white gas. I had no idea what that was. He started boiling water and adding some dehydrated stuff that was theoretically going to turn into beef stew. We filled our small camp plates with food and sat in a circle to eat.

Night fell quickly and it was getting cold. Just as Jackson cracked open a beer, which was one of six that he'd lugged with him on his back, Christopher started talking.

"So, I've been thinking a lot about my dad and when he disappeared," he offered cautiously. "We lived on the res then, and he had a lot of people he worked with. He'd work on healing illnesses, prescribing herbs or chants to help people. Then he started helping out this guy who was trying to heal his cancer. My dad started visiting him. It was one time when he went out to meet this guy that he never came home again."

"I blocked all this out of my mind for a long time. I guess I just decided that he'd deserted us for a woman. My dad wasn't a saint or anything. He had his weaknesses, but he was a good man. I was really angry at him for leaving us. I was 12, I mean, you know what it's like to lose your dad at 12? It's like losing a part of yourself. I didn't know how to become a man. I was really angry. I even ran away for a little while. Clara just started drinking with her high school friends. My brother Sam was the only one who managed to act like nothing happened."

"Do you remember his name?" I asked.

"Who?"

"The man with cancer."

"Oh, yeah, it was this guy named Larry Begay. Right after my dad disappeared we went to his place in town and asked him about it. He didn't know anything. He said my dad visited him as usual and then left in the evening to go home."

"So you don't think Larry had anything to do with it?" I asked.

"I don't think so. We just figured my dad left us. We didn't want to think about the other possibility."

Christopher was staring up at the stars. Jackson and I had instinctively grown quiet out of respect. The canyon had become a dark corridor with a lighter, indigo blue sky stretching like a speckled carpet above our heads. Coyotes were beginning their mournful howl and I shivered. No one would ever believe this story at Matterson.

It was the middle of the night and my dreams were wild enough to wake the dead. I think maybe the dead *were* awake. At least one dead man.

I was sitting at a bar with a drink in my hand. It was the color of Scotch. I was wearing an evening gown covered in red sequins. Like a shiny red fish, I slithered off the bar stool and walked toward the back of the room. I looked down at my fingers and noticed that my fingernails were like cat claws. I began to slink like a mountain lion, silently padding over the concrete floor. There was a room in the back full of casino games — tables with people playing cards, slot machines and colorful gadgets. There was odd music playing that reminded me of the strangely unnerving jingle that emanated from ice cream trucks in the summer. I crept around the tables, half fish woman in sequins, half cat.

Through many more identical rooms, I crept, and finally found a solid green door that I pushed open slightly. It led outside. Beyond the casino door was a dusty road lined with a few plastic garbage cans and a dumpster. I slithered over the dry earth and began to journey down the road. I passed a few storefronts and a peeling, wooden bench. I sensed movement ahead of me. My cat claws picked up the pace and I was flying over the road, red sequins glittering in the moonlight. I turned down an alley and saw a man pushing a young woman up against the brick wall of a building. The man's blonde hair was short and he was wearing faded jeans and a red T-shirt. Her long black hair was in a messy ponytail. It looked like maybe he had been pulling her hair. Her dress was yellow with small red flowers and her feet were bare. I saw a sandal near my feet and instinctively looked for the other one. I saw it further down the alley.

He gave her a push and she turned her head. I could see her face — tear filled eyes and a small red mouth, half open in a silent cry. Her hands were against the bricks. A silver bracelet with a large turquoise stone shone against her brown skin. He reached for his belt buckle. He lifted her skirt. I felt nausea wash over me. I couldn't watch. He was going to rape her. I knew it. My bones were on fire with rage. I flew at him, tried to pull him off of her, but I could do nothing. It was like I wasn't there. I was just watching it as if it was a movie. Suddenly there was another man in the alley. He walked past me. It was Christopher's father, Whitefeather.

"Hey!" shouted Whitefeather. The man turned in shock and stared at him.

"Get the fuck out of here!"

"Let her go," said Whitefeather.

"This ain't your business," said the man.

Whitefeather walked faster. He dropped his bag and ran toward the man, who took his hands from the girl. Whitefeather flew at him and knocked him down. The girl looked toward me, almost as if she knew I was there. Our eyes met for a fleeting moment and then she was off, running down the alley with her black ponytail flying behind her.

Whitefeather and the blonde man were scuffling on the ground. At first Whitefeather was winning, but then the man pinned him. He reached toward a garbage can and grabbed something in the shadows. I couldn't see what it was. He hit Whitefeather with it. "Stop it!" I screamed. He was hitting him over and over again. I hear the sound of metal hitting bone and I cringed in the shadows, retching, because I could smell the familiar metallic pungency of blood. While the man was bludgeoning Whitefeather, I noticed that a wallet was laying open on the ground. I walked over to it. Bending down, I could see a photo ID inside. The name of the man who murdered Whitefeather was Leonard Norwood. I looked up at him in time to see that the thing in his hand was a tire iron and Whitefeather wasn't moving anymore. With what sounded almost like a growl, Leonard stopped bludgeoning Whitefeather and looked at me. He grabbed Whitefeather by the collar and held him up in the air so that I could see his lifeless face. His skull was crushed and caving in on one side. "Is this what you want? You want to be next?" He shouted at me. I screamed.

I screamed so loudly that I woke myself, Christopher and Jackson out of a sound sleep. I was shaking. My pajamas were soaked with sweat.

"What? What is it?" he asked, with slurred speech.

"It was just a dream. I just had the weirdest, goriest dream."

"What was it about?" Christopher asked.

Jackson was kneeling at the entrance of the tent. "You ok?" he asked.

"Yeah, it was just a bad dream, go on back to sleep," answered Christopher. We heard Jackson shuffle back to his tent and the familiar high-pitched zip of his tent flap.

"So what was it about," he asked again.

"Oh, I don't know if I should tell you."

"Well, you have to tell me now that you said *that*. You like to keep me in suspense with these dreams of yours."

"It was about your dad. I think I might know how the murder happened. And I might know the murderer's name."

"From your dream?"

"Yeah, if you trust my intuition. I don't know."

"Girl, if I trust anyone's intuition, I trust yours."

"Ok, well I was in this bar/casino type place and I walked through it and ended up in an alley. I saw this blonde guy pushing a girl up against the wall. He was going to rape her. I could tell. I wanted to do something, but I couldn't. Then your dad walked up to the guy and told him to stop. The guy turned on him and started hitting him with a tire iron. The girl ran away, but your dad was just lying there on the ground in the alley. The man just kept hitting and hitting and there was blood on the ground and then he started talking to me, asking if I wanted to be next, and your dad's head was all smooshed." My voice was shaking.

"A tire iron?" he asked, his voice cracking with emotion.

"Yes."

"What was the man's name?" he asked hesitantly, wiping his tears from his eyes.

"Leonard Norwood. I saw his wallet laying on the ground, so I looked at it."

"You are amazing."

"I don't know if it's all true. I mean, it was just a dream."

"Makes me wonder what other stuff you could find out if you tried. You should try to have a premonition about the winning lottery numbers for next week." He was trying to be light hearted, but I could hear the sadness in his voice. He lay back down in his sleeping bag and I thought maybe I heard him crying. I rolled closer to him and wrapped my arms around him while sobs shook his body until he fell asleep. I lay awake for a long time thinking about the dream and what it meant for me to have these visions. With knowledge comes responsibility, I decided, as I listened to the sounds of the early morning.

The morning was cold and damp with small droplets of water running down the nylon faces of our tents like silverfish. When we emerged, achy from sleeping on the warty face of the earth, Jackson was already squatting in front of the camp stove. His belly rolled out over the waistband of his cargo pants and created a soft round bulge under his red fleece jacket. Jackson was fiddling with the small gas tank, no bigger than a water bottle, trying to get the flame to burn correctly to boil water for instant oatmeal and coffee. The sun didn't reach into the canyon as early as it did on the high plains, so we were in cool shade for a long time. The camp robber birds had found us and were hopping around with their necks bobbing, maintaining a safe distance from us, but watching feverishly for a dropped morsel of food. The sound of the creek comforted me. Christopher and I stretched, our muscles slowly moving out of the stiff, cold dormancy of the night, and we walked over to the stove. The three of us sat around it hoping for the sun and eating our oatmeal.

By the time the sun cracked over the rocky edge of the canyon and sending shadows darting across the water, we were on our feet and moving again. We had hiked for two hours when Jackson pointed out that the water was cloudy. It looked like somebody's dirty dishwater or skim milk. My pulse sped up. As we hiked on, the water became even more obviously clouded with some opaque, white substance. The canyon widened out a little and we noticed that to the North the rock wall was slightly yellowed. In fact, just up the slope was an entrance to an old mine. Christopher recognized it first. There was a small hole in the rock and what looked like runoff coming out of the opening. The entire north side of the canyon was peppered with old mines and their yellow tailings.

"This is the spot. It has to be," Christopher announced. "These old mines sometimes pollute creeks and rivers with stuff that changes the color of the water. That's why this water is cloudy. I don't know what it could be, but that's it. I camped once down in the San Juans at a place where the stream was literally rust colored from iron in the water. Whatever you do, don't drink it," he said.

"So, whaddya think? It's a big area to dig up, Chris," said Jackson.

"Yeah, but we might not have to dig it all up. First, let's all separate and look for any sign of a grave or anything unusual," said Christopher.

It was still very early in the day, about 9 AM. We dropped our packs and scattered, combing the creek bed and canyon walls, which sloped upward at an angle that allowed us to walk up to the mines. We were slipping and sliding on the loose silt. The ground near the creek was overgrown with short, scrubby brush, which made anything on the ground difficult to discern. Even if there were a grave, it would be completely covered with bushes. We searched for about 45 minutes until we all flopped down on the ground near our packs.

"I just don't see anything," said Christopher.

"Neither do I," I replied.

"But you know, why would we? We're talking about a criminal here, who wanted to hide a crime. He wouldn't mark it with a stone or something like 'here lies the man I murdered.' You know? It's going to be hidden," said Jackson.

"He *did* say to dig right?" Christopher asked me.

"Yes."

"Could it be in the water?" asked Jackson. We all get up and looked at the creek. It's too filmy to see the bottom.

"It's a good possibility," said Christopher. "The water would hide any tampering, though I can't imagine digging a hole in a creek, I mean, it would just keep filling up with water, and it would also more quickly dislodge bones, you know?"

"Unless the body was all bundled up and weighed down like a rock. Then it might not go anywhere," said Jackson. "Or, what if he buried him when the creek was dry?"

"Now there's an idea," said Christopher.

"When I saw him in the tree by the hot springs, he was swimming. I thought it looked like he was swimming in the air, but maybe it meant that he was actually in the water," I said.

"But why would someone choose this spot?" Christopher pondered out loud. "It's a long haul in here and back out again. It doesn't make sense. I mean, I guess it does in one way. It's not a place many people would pass by. I want to walk a little further up the canyon and see what's up there. Why don't you guys stay here? Have a snack or something," he said.

He took off without his pack, just a water bottle and a red bandanna to put over his head. His legs were so long that in a few strides he was out of sight. The way his body moved makes me shiver.

"You want some apple cornbread? My mom's specialty. I got some wrapped up nice and fresh in my pack," asked Jackson.

"No, that's ok. Thanks, though," I replied, staring at the water. I got up and walked over to the edge of the creek, took off my hiking boots and socks and rolled up my pants.

"You gonna walk in there? I'd be careful if I was you. Can't see the bottom," Jackson warned.

"I know, I just think maybe this is a good place to look. I mean, it sort of makes sense."

I tested the water with my toes. It was ice cold. I put one foot in and then the other. It wasn't terribly rocky; the bottom was soft and mucky. My feet sank a few inches into the sand. It made me feel a little queasy, but I took a few more steps. As I adjusted to the temperature and texture of the creek bottom, I walked around more, testing the feeling of the sand with my feet. The canyon wall on the opposite side of the creek was virtually vertical, which was why we ignored it. There was also no beach: the wall jutted right up out of the water. I walked upstream in the direction Christopher went and stopped abruptly, my breath quickly leaving my lungs in a burst of adrenaline. There was a vein of golden colored rock running through the vertical wall.

"Jackson! Come over here!" I shouted downstream.

He came running. "What? Did you find something?"

"Yes, look at this. He said to go to where the rock runs yellow. This makes more sense than the old mines," I said.

"You think we should dig in the water?"

"Maybe. Look at that boulder right there. Maybe we should look underneath it. That would be a good way to make sure nothing floated to the surface. Put a big rock over it," I said. A big black, shiny rock was sticking up out of the water like the hump of a hippopotamus. It was so big and looked so natural there that I hadn't thought about it before.

We both stood there staring at the rock with apprehension. The stream of milky water was rushing around my knees and I had to constantly try and regain my balance. Jackson remained on the edge of the water, chewing on his apple cornbread, not wanting to take the plunge and get wet.

"I don't know. That's a big rock," he said.

"Yeah, I think we'll need all three of us," I replied.

"And, why do we need to dig him up anyway? Don't we already pretty much know what happened, more or less?" he asked. "Chris is doing ok. No need to dig up old baggage. No pun intended," he chuckled.

"Well, I think we need to do this. *I* need to do this so he stops bugging me," I said.

"Oh yeah, right. I forgot," he said with a hint of sarcasm.

We were both startled by the scuffling of Christopher's feet in the brush. He was running back toward us. The first thing I saw was his red bandanna stretched tightly over his head and then his thin legs in faded jeans stepping high over the weeds. He was out of breath.

"There's a road right up there! This isn't as remote as I thought. It's a county road," he wheezed. "I bet the dude just drove his car up to the edge of the canyon and then hiked in. There's even a trace of an old mining road that comes down in here. This used to be traveled by miners pretty heavily, I bet."

"Christopher, look at this," I said. "See that yellow streak in the wall? He said to go to Milk Creek, under where the rock runs yellow. This has to be it. And look, there's this big rock here. I'll bet you a hundred bucks he's under this rock."

Jackson removed his overalls, threw them in a heap beside the creek and revealed bright red boxers underneath. He said he didn't want to get his pants wet. Christopher plunged in without even rolling his jeans up. The three of us pushed against the rock, which didn't want to budge and our hands slipped across its slick surface.

"We're gonna have to go from underneath," Christopher said hesitantly.

We all bent down and try to get our hands under the rock. Keeping my clothes dry at this point was futile, because in order to get my hands under the rock, my face was nearly underwater. The rock did have a bottom. We were all able to get our hands underneath it. Christopher leapt out of the water to get his shovel, which he then wedged under the rock as we tried to move it with our weight and strength. It shifted little by little as we fought against its girth and the pressing of the water. Together we got it to begin rolling ever so slightly down stream. The current was helping us. It left its resting place with a strong suction of mud and sand and revealed its underbelly, which was slimed with muck and minute water creatures.

"Okay..." said Christopher with fearful anticipation. We all stared down at the water, terrified of what we might find.

"What should we do?" he asked.

"I'm afraid to put my hands in there," I answered.

"Me, too. You should dig in with the shovel," said Jackson.

Christopher looked at us with utter bewilderment on his face. It was one of the few times that I could see how young he was. His solemn, quiet exterior generally lent him a mature demeanor, but running through the canyon had flushed his cheeks and standing there with such wide eyes, he looked like a boy about ready to discover that his father had left for good.

"I'm scared," he said quietly.

We both just looked back at him, mirroring his fear. I nodded silently as if to say, "do it" and he understood. It's hard to put it into words, but at that moment it was almost like I understand why everything had happened. The entirety of those six months seemed to make perfect sense, though I really don't know how to explain why I felt this way.

I was dizzy and my equilibrium was off. I braced myself in the current as Christopher dug the shovel in for the first time. He pulled up a large glob of mud. He moved toward the shore and dropped it there. He did this repeatedly until there was a large pile of muck on the ground and the water had become tan instead of filmy white.

"You want me to dig, man?" offered Jackson.

"No, I want to do this," he replied. "But it just seems like endless mud. I mean, what else would it be anyway?"

"Dig a little deeper maybe," I said.

Christopher pulled out a few more globs of mud and then struck something. The color drained from his face. He looked at me for some kind of reassurance, his silvery eyes pleading with me. I didn't know what to say. I just stared back.

"I think I'm gonna be sick," he said.

"Why? What is it," I asked.

"Nothing. I just feel something down here, and I don't know if I want it to be him, or if I don't. I sort of don't want it to be. I mean it's sick. It's just sick! This whole thing is fucked!"

Jackson chimed in with support. "It is sick, man, but you gotta do it. We're here now, and if it's him, you need to know. You'll hate yourself later if you don't go through with it. I know you."

"Right," Christopher replied, gathering some nerve.

He plunged the shovel back into the water more deeply this time, pushing it underneath something and then lifting up. It gave him some resistance and he was working hard.

"Ok, I've got it," he said.

He put his hand in the water to feel it, I guess, or steady it on the shovel and looked up at us with his worst expression yet.

"What is it, Chris," said Jackson.

"It feels like a plastic bag," he replied. "But I don't know. Clear out of the way, I'm gonna walk it over to the ground."

I felt sick. When I was a little kid, my cousin Leanne and I used to make up murder mysteries. One of our neighbors had an old antique cast iron stove discarded in the woods behind his house, along with a lot of other strange and random refuse. For some reason we decided that he'd murdered someone and put them inside that stove. We made up stories about it, crept around it at night and enjoyed scaring ourselves. I never thought I'd be involved with a real murder in my lifetime and I definitely never thought I would be the one to solve the mystery. I never expected to see the remains of a dead man, and I really didn't want to.

Christopher put a large plastic sack on the bank of the creek. It was covered with muck and slime from the creek bed. What relieved me slightly was that it wasn't the shape of a human body. It was a rounded bag, about the size of a 14 gallon garbage bag. A human man couldn't fit inside a bag like that.

Christopher cleared some of the slime off the bag with the shovel and stared at it for a painfully long time.

"Ok, I'm gonna do it," said Jackson.

Jackson knelt down and took hold of the bag and ripped. The first rip didn't reveal much, just more layers of black plastic. He walked over to his overalls and pulled a Swiss Army knife out of the pocket. He sliced through the bag from one side to the other, like he was performing surgery on the abdomen of a large bellied person with a scalpel. What he revealed both set my mind at rest and horrified me more than anything I've ever seen.

It was full of bones. Human bones. But they weren't just loosely gathered in there. They were organized. Jackson pried it open a little further and all three of us stared speechless. Christopher hurried away from us and retched. Jackson lifted a flap of the plastic and moved a few small white shards, which looked like finger bones, and a bundle of long, thin femurs or something and revealed the skull. The bone underneath the crud from the creek was white and smooth, except for the side and back of the skull, which was shattered and caving in. The strangest thing was that as we looked more closely, it was becoming apparent that the arms and legs had been fastened together as if they were removed and then secured together with tape, which was now gaping without flesh around it to keep it adhered tightly.

The murderer had cut him up and then taped his arms and legs, hands and feet together. Thigh-bones were joined together with old, decaying tape, as were the calf bones, upper arm bones and hands. The pelvic bone was on its own, as was the rib cage. The end of the spine where the neck would have been showed signs of cutting or sawing. Jackson was spreading the bones out, examining them when Christopher returned, his eyes bloodshot and his face stained with the salt of tears.

"It's him," he said with conviction.

"Of course it is," replied Jackson.

"That sick fuck!" shouted Christopher to no one in particular.

I was surprised that there was no smell of rot. There was just the smell of a damp fecundity, the watery fishiness that accompanied any creek containing living, organic matter. And where did all his flesh go? The only thing that was left was a knotted mass of black hair near the skull.

"What do we do now?" I asked.

"We have to take him back with us," said Christopher.

"That's going to be messy," said Jackson.

"We'll bundle these garbage bags around the bones and then I'm going to put it into my nylon stuff sack for my sleeping bag. I have to honor my father. I've waited ten years to find him." We both looked at Christopher and I rubbed his arm. "Plus, if we leave it like this, and Leonard what's-his-name comes up here for any reason he's gonna know someone's found him out unless we do our best to cover this all up."

"Who cares if he knows?" asked Jackson.

"I don't want him to know, because then he might run, and I want to find him and surprise the shit out of him," said Christopher.

Christopher started shoveling the mud back into the creek and we all got in and rolled the rock back to its original location. The wet muddy spot on the bank would dry quickly in the high desert. Still, it did look like someone had messed around in the creek. We could only hope that Leonard didn't pay regular visits to the site.

We hiked together back the way we had come. Christopher carried the bag of bones inside his stuff sack at a distance from his body the whole time. His arms must have gotten tired, but he didn't complain.

24

I should have felt a sense of closure and relief, but I didn't. We arrived back at the trailer drained and filthy. We left the bag of bones a few yards from the house in a cluster of pines. After long showers, Christopher announced that he was going to make flatbread. Balancing the phone between his ear and shoulder while clanking in the kitchen, he called his sister Clara and his brother Samuel to tell them the news. The atmosphere was somber, but there was a lightness in Christopher along with sadness. I left him alone to talk to his siblings and walked outside to a high area of the mesa, about a thousand feet from the trailer, and sat down. I could see Blanca and the wide prairie to the west.

I had just helped a man solve the mystery of his father's disappearance. It was the strangest feeling. My heart leapt with pride and pleasure at my intuitive abilities. What did it mean for my life? Would I continue to have visions and be drawn to unknown places? Was this mystery the reason all the strange and awful things happened to me this summer?

My eyes burned when I closed them. My muscles felt like they wanted to melt right into the ground. My head ached a little and there was a slight buzzing in my ears. Through the noise I heard a tiny voice. I didn't pay attention at first, but it wouldn't stop. It was almost like the incessant buzzing of a bumblebee, but it was sweeter than that. "It's not over yet," I thought it said. What? "It's not over yet. Go home." Was it my inner voice? My conscience? Of course I would go home. "Your journey isn't finished. Find Max. Find the river. Listen. You are not alone. I never left you. There are things to tell you." I opened my eyes and shook my head, hoping that the weirdness was from my delirium and my aching body.

I stood up, stretched and looked back at the trailer. The sun was getting low in the sky and Christopher's lights were beginning to glow. He was stringing blue Christmas lights along the roof. I could see his lithe body moving up and down a ladder. Why was I still hearing voices? I thought that would be over. I shoved my hands in my pockets. *Go home, find Max, find the river.* Why? *I never left you.* Who never left me? Could it be? Could it be the one person who *did* leave me? The one I wanted to stay the most? My baby? I breathed in lungfuls of the thin mesa air and was overcome by a feeling that something was wrong. I felt like it was Max, but I didn't know for sure. I needed to go home. It was time. Something wasn't finished yet.

I could see Christopher moving around in his woodpile. My heart ached for him. I still didn't really know him that well, but I wanted to. Knowing that I might never see him again stung, but there wasn't much I could do. He was walking toward me now, stepping over small bushes and sagebrush. He had a candle in his hands.

"I thought you might like some light," he said when he was within earshot. "Clara and Sam are gonna come visit. They want to see the bones. I'm gonna bury him here on the Mesa." I smiled at him, trying to hide what I was feeling.

"You're going to leave, aren't you," he said regretfully.

"Yes. I mean, I need to wait for my car to be done, but as soon as it is, I have to. I can probably still finish this year and graduate when I'm supposed to. If I leave now."

"I know. And you should. The garage called, actually. While we were gone. It's finished."

My heart sank inside my chest. "It is?"

"Yeah, I just listened to the answering machine a little while ago."

"Well, then I guess that's it. Great timing."

"Yeah. Looks like it's time for you to move on."

"But I don't want to leave."

"I know. And I feel like my life is just starting now. Finally. There's so much more I want to show you."

He leaned down to kiss me and I rose up on my tiptoes to meet him. He covered my face with kisses, running his fingers through my hair, pulling me firmly to him with his hand at the small of my back. I leaned back into his hand, completely surrendering.

"Maybe I'll drive up to your prep school in my rusty truck and propose marriage," he said when we paused for breath.

"Everyone would be shocked, that's for sure," I replied. "I think you should do it."

"Maybe I will. When do you turn 18?" he chuckled and turns to lead me back to the trailer.

"December 17th. I'll watch for you from Willard Hall. You can steal me away in my school uniform."

"Oh, don't even tell me you wear uniforms."

"Yup. Well, sometimes. For special occasions."

"Ok, well then, I think I should arrive on a horse, don't you?"

"That's perfect."

∞

It was morning and it was chilly and overcast — an unusual day for Colorado. I'd learned that even at eight in the morning the Colorado skies usually gleamed bluer than pictures of the Caribbean Sea in travel brochures. It actually felt like snow. "First snow's gonna fall within a few days, I bet," Christopher said thoughtfully as we pulled up to Marcus Auto Body. I was trying to soak up every detail of the area that I possibly could. The only place I didn't want to visit again was the Sand Dunes. That memory was complete and I didn't want to alter it.

Next to Marcus Auto Body was a square building painted the color of dull lima beans. On the building's side-wall, which was a flat expanse devoid of windows, were two enormous letters painted white. It said RV. Behind the building it looked like all the Winnebagos and Starcrafts in the United States had been let out to pasture. An old woman on the roof, wearing a bright robin egg blue raincoat and sweeping with a broom. Her hair floated off of her head like a purpley-gray puff of smoke.

"Look at her up there!" I said with amazement to Christopher, who was gloomily pulling into the garage's parking lot.

"That's old Mrs. Carter," he said. "She always does that before it snows — sweeps the pollen and twigs and leaves off her roof. Says the roof will rot with that stuff on there if the snow traps it in. She's a little weird. At least the roof is flat. She won't fall off."

I went inside and paid Marcus for his work, splitting it between my mother's credit card and my cash. After I paid, I threw my stuff in the back of my car and walked over to Christopher, who was leaning up against his truck. His yellow truck was speckled with red dust, as were our feet. He had his head back against the truck like he did that night when we went to the Sand Dunes. I felt my throat tighten into that aching lump that always precedes tears, but I swallowed it down. I was strong. He was strong too, though I knew how he was feeling. He moved away from the truck and embraced me. He pressed my face to his chest and the scent of nutmeg and lemon overwhelmed me.

"You know I was falling in love with you, right?" he said in my ear.

"I know."

"I'll see you again," he said, looking me in the eyes. He lifted my head and kissed me sweetly on the mouth. "Now get going. Don't be late for school."

25

My well-oiled machined purred like a cat, quieter and smoother than it ever had before as it crept up the mountain's gradual incline, past where my radiator hose burst nearly three weeks before. This time there was no strange and ominous steam, just the rumble of my wheels over gray pavement. Blanca was visible in my mirror and the mountains to the South stretched on toward New Mexico, a seemingly endless ripple of undulating earth and stone. There was a dusting of snow on their peaks and they were luminous in the low morning light. The sun was glinting off microscopic water crystals miles from where I was. "I'm coming home." I said out loud. "I'm coming home everyone."

I hadn't called my parents again. They had no idea what I was doing. I liked it that way. They would be beyond angry, but I didn't care. It was a miraculous change. *I don't care. I exist to live and experience. I can handle pain. I've faced pain and conquered it and I am still alive. But I've had enough and it's time for joy.* My heart leapt as I charged over the highway and turned up the radio. The only station I could find was playing Blondie: *Call Me.* I started to sing at the top of my lungs, feeling for Christopher's business card in the breast pocket of my shirt. My voice cracked and fogged up the windows, but I kept singing. I felt wonderful and freer than I ever had before.

Kansas was a tan, flat pancake of prairie hardly worth mentioning, except that with the sight of the barren and flat plains, the desperate cottonwoods and chiseled stream beds, I recalled the fierce memory of the tornado. I remembered seeing Whitefeather in the window of my room. For a moment I thought I might miss seeing him. I breathed in a great sigh of thanks to whatever power allowed me to live through that tornado and kept driving.

When I got tired, I pulled over and slept in my car. I ate .99-cent burgers at rest areas and fueled myself with coffee and water. While I slept, I had vivid dreams about fat bellied truckers in stained white T-shirts stopping to talk to me, asking if I'm ok, and inviting me into the backs of their trucks. They spit tobacco. I tossed and turned in the backseat of my car. I had one dream in particular that I couldn't ignore. It was the sweet bumblebee buzzing voice again. She told me cryptic things and hovered in front of me in a cloud of shimmering air. I couldn't see her face. "It's time to create something new," she said. "Gather the bones and bury them in the birches. Sing over them, watch what grows. It's time to sing over the bones."

When I reached Ohio, green was beginning to creep back into the landscape. The rolling hills weren't the tan color of deerskin, but green like astro-turf. I felt myself relax. The leaves were a tapestry of green, orange, yellow and maple syrup brown as I passed into western Pennsylvania. Once I reached the eastern edge of the state I was in ecstasy in the soft light of dusk.

It was night when I turned onto Lomink Road. I stopped the car at a wide spot along the shoulder of the road and stepped out. My body was a creaky, achy, rusted thing in need of stretching. I raised my arms into the air in a luxurious stretch and yawned. The smell hit me like a deep and rich inhalation of a peppery drug. I'd temporarily forgotten the smell of fallen leaves. And this wasn't the peak of autumn by any means. The peak wouldn't be for another few weeks. I still had time. I stood there for a long time breathing in the smell of the woods. *My* woods. Then I thought about Max and his broken nose, and a subtle fear started creeping up my spine into my belly.

He was the only one who even half-way understood what I'd gone through. The only one besides Christopher. At the moment, Max was my only friend and my biggest enemy. At the same time I realized that I smelled like Christopher. The smell of his laundry detergent and soap was still on me, as was the subtle scent of his trailer — lemon and pine, aged firewood and beer. I forced myself to get back in the car. Two more miles and I would be home.

Anxiety was beginning to win out over my excitement. I was going to be in trouble. I also had to catch up on almost a month of school. It wasn't going to be easy to justify why I'd been gone, and why I hadn't been in contact with them. I knew my dad could pull some strings with the Headmaster of Matterson, but that wasn't all I was going to face. The kids at school would wonder where I'd been. They would ask questions, make up rumors about abortions, felonies and my crazy parents. I figured there was an element of truth to almost any rumor they could dream up. I couldn't decide if my parents were going to make a big scene or be subtle about it. They could go either way. My mother was usually cold and passive aggressive in her silence. She might just give me a hug and a dirty look and shoo me upstairs to my room to get cleaned up, leaving a lingering sting of guilt in my stomach. She might cry and tell me how hard it was to have me gone. There wasn't much in her manner that didn't inspire guilt. My father would be silent and voice his feelings to her later in the privacy of their room and I would hear about it second-hand after it had stewed and festered in my mother's mind and become something much larger than was when it started.

Olivia was the one I wanted to see. I'd realized over the time I'd been gone just how important she was to me. I thought about her strawberry blonde hair and her green eyes. She was shorter and smaller than me, but there was no guarantee that was a permanent quality. She was also smarter in some ways and for once I was ok with that, because I'd found something within myself that was unique, that she could never come close to. I liked that. Somehow it made the thought of connecting with her more possible. I was over comparing myself to her. It just wasn't necessary anymore. At least that's how I felt driving my car swiftly down Lomink Road, hugging the curves as if I was in a red Ferrari.

The road opened up into a clearing at the Lacey family farm. Out of the corner of my eye I could see the dark nothingness of the field and then luminous, hulking shapes. I tensed up in the contoured seat of my Jetta, startled and on edge. At a second glance, I realized they were horses, their fat bellies glowing in the subtle moonlight. I wanted to pull the car over and run out there with them, leap on their backs and ride, but I kept driving. I remembered the day I saw wild turkeys half walk, half fly across the road, their wings barely lifting their fat breasted bodies off the ground. They were dark gray with skinny, floppy heads. My dad saw an owl fly across this road once and my mom in a moment of forgetfulness had lost her favorite pair of shoes there. She'd put them on top of the car as she was loading it up and forgotten them there. If someone had been behind us on the road that day they would have seen brown leather sandals flying through the air like strange featherless birds. She combed that road for days afterwards. She found *one*.

I laughed to myself as *Ramble On*, by Led Zeppelin followed Steppenwolf's *Magic Carpet Ride* on the classic rock station. It seemed appropriate. I was rambling on, though I couldn't decide if I was leaving or returning. The driveway hadn't changed. I don't know why I expected it to. Three weeks wasn't that much time. The only thing that had changed was that I could smell autumn through my open window and see fallen leaves on the gray-blue gravel. The lights in the house were on, sending a warm yellow light into the yard and the field beyond. I could see the shape of my mother's head in the kitchen window. I knew by the way she was pacing and moving that she was talking to someone on the phone. It was probably Nancy Rettzinger, the Assistant Pastor's wife. They spent long hours on the phone talking about things that would put me to sleep.

As I got closer to the house I saw Ladybug's quiet gray shape sitting on the front steps. I felt tears welling up in my eyes at the sight of her pointy little ears, her head and dainty feet. She was waiting for me like she knew I was coming. I stopped the car and leapt out, bounding quietly over the gravel to the steps. I scooped her up in my arms and started to dance. We spun around, waltzing like two reunited lovers. She gazed at me with yellow-green eyes, drooling as cats do when they are in joyful ecstasy. I stroked her little silky head and closed my eyes, listening to the sounds of the autumn woods. The katydids and cicadas were nearly silent, replaced by subtle crackles and crunches of dry leaves.

She strained to get down and I let her drop to her feet. I looked up at my window. The lights were off, but the curtains were open. Something was keeping me from going to the door. The Jetta was finally relaxing, settling into the driveway like a horse let out to pasture. I could hear the fan running under the hood. There was no more putting it off. I walked up to the porch, through the screen door, across the aging oak floor to the blue door. I had the urge to knock, but that would be too strange. I grabbed the knob, which was cold in the night air, and turned it, listening to the satisfying click as the latch released. I pushed it open and the smell of my house hit me. You don't think about your house having a smell. It was a pungent mixture of spices from my mom's cabinets, old wood and wool. There was also the slight odor of paint, or maybe nail polish and other more human smells, which were unidentifiable.

As I opened the door I heard my dad's laugh. Music was wafting down the stairs and I knew where my mother was. She was the one I feared the most.

"Hon, did you make your sandwich for tomorrow or should I do it?" she yelled from the kitchen. I jumped out of my skin.

"It's in the fridge. Just come sit down and relax," replied my dad.

Her footsteps began to patter across the terracotta tiles toward the door where I was standing. I waited, not breathing. She crossed from tile to wood, the tone of her steps changing from padding to creaking. That's when her eyes meet mine. I'd startled her, standing there like a ghost in the unlit foyer. I didn't smile, just stared, trying to read her expression. Her face was blank for a moment before it softened into relief.

"Natalie!" she said quietly, not loud enough for my father to hear. "Oh honey, you're home," she cried, and ran to me, hugging me to her soft chest. She was in her robe — a pink and white striped terry cloth atrocity. She smelled of Emeraude. She put her hands on my cheeks. "Why didn't you call us? We've been worried."

"I just wanted to drive. I wanted to surprise you."

"Well, you did! Come on, see your father."

She led me into the living room. He was in position on the sofa, flat on his back with his neck propped up on a pillow staring at the TV with the newspaper resting on his chest. He turned his head when he saw us, his chin wrinkling at his neck and his graying strawberry blonde hair pushing up against the pillow so that when he sat up, it lifted off his head in a puff.

"Natty! You decided to come home!" he said, jumping off the sofa. They both embraced me with heartfelt hugs before they dug in.

There was always an electrified pause before my mom scolded me. I knew what was coming.

"What were you thinking? Your father was beside himself, you know. All sorts of things can happen to a girl like you on the road."

"Things can happen to a girl anywhere," I mumbled to myself.

"What was that? Don't mumble, Natalie. Say something for yourself." My mother was sitting on the edge of the pale blue, corduroy easy chair, too tense and full of the need to reprimand to relax into its cushions. "Did you realize the kind of danger you were in? Where did you sleep? How did you pay for a month at a motel? Do you have any idea how worried we were?"

"Yeah."

The TV was still on and the weatherman's voice was competing with ours. He was talking about a cold front moving in from the Great Lakes and something about 5th graders measuring rainfall. My dad picked up the remote and turned it down. My mom stood up and walked over to me.

"I'm sorry to come on so strong. It's just that we were really really worried. I'm so glad you're home." She hugged me again. "I still don't understand why you didn't call us."

"Where were you for three weeks?" my dad asked.

"I was staying with a friend."

"A friend? What kind of friend? How could you have a friend there?" he asked with suspicion.

My mom was still hugging me, pressing my face into her shoulder. I pulled away from her to look at my dad.

"It was a nice person who helped me when my car broke down."

"A person? Does this person have a name?" he asked.

"Christopher."

"You stayed with a man?" remarked my mom, horrified, stepping backward and almost falling over a stool. She lifted her hand to her chest as if to halt a heart attack, her voice wavering.

"He was really nice to me."

"Yeah, I bet he was. I don't even want to imagine why," moaned Dad.

"That's got to be the most foolish thing I've ever heard, Natalie. I can't believe after all the hard work we've put into raising you to be a responsible young woman, you pull this kind of stunt. First you get pregnant, god knows how or where, and then you run off to live with some *man* in Colorado. What on earth has gotten into you?"

"I finally feel like myself. Just as I was driving here, I realized that I finally feel like myself," I said.

"You feel like yourself? What does that mean?" sobbed my mother.

"See? You don't understand! You have no idea what it's like to be me! Believe it or not, I've turned out better than lots of other kids." They were both silent. "Pastor Steuben has no answers for me. Just telling me to make peace with the Lord, to repent. Well, repenting didn't keep me from getting raped by Max, didn't keep me from getting pregnant or miscarrying. All the criticism, the Holy

Communion, they didn't make me a better person. They made me want to escape, so I did."

My parents were staring at me open mouthed.

"Raped?" said my mother with skepticism in her voice. "Natalie, he was your boyfriend."

"That doesn't mean anything," I said. It was pointless to try and explain.

"Matterson and Church are good influences, Natalie. We chose the best places for you to spend your time. It's the choices *you* made that created this. Carey Marshall, for example. Look at the way she's chosen to live her life!"

"I don't care about Carey Marshall! She's not me! She's nothing like me!" Carey has to be one of the blandest, dishwater-dull girls I'd ever encountered. She'd given a sermon once at our Church, her pasty moon face beaming from the pulpit like white mushrooms on an overcast day. I heard she'd gotten into an all-women's school in the South. I bet they still wore white gloves there.

"I know she's nothing like you. It's just an example. You have many choices to make in your life and we want you to make the right ones," said my mom.

"I think the *right* decision is a matter of opinion. Don't you even want to know what I experienced in Colorado?"

"You can tell us about it later. Right now I need to go to sleep. Believe it or not, I've lost quite a bit of sleep with you being gone," said my mom. "Your dad will arrange something with school tomorrow and we'll put this behind us. We'll get you back there by Monday. And you're going to church with us this Sunday. It'll be good for you," said my mother matter-of-factly.

As I sat there on the edge of the ottoman and watched their faces wrinkle and pucker with agitation, I knew I *did* have choices, like she said, but they were different choices than my mother or father could ever imagine. I could choose to get up and walk right back out the door. I could get back in my car and drive to Serena's house. I could tell them how out of touch they were with reality. Or I could go upstairs and see Olivia. I actually wanted to leave again at that moment. I also felt the pull to fall softly into bed and curl up with Ladybug and my stuffed animals, to laugh with Olivia, to tell her about Christopher.

"I'm sorry, but I'm tired. I just drove for 15 hours. You can continue criticizing me tomorrow, but right now I need to rest. It's nice to see you, too," I said snidely, leaving the room and heading for the bathroom.

"We're just trying to help you, hon," my mother yelled through the bathroom door.

I didn't answer her.

"Well, we'll see you tomorrow. Sleep well," she said.

I stared at myself in the mirror for a few moments. I'd gotten a lot of sun in Colorado. My face was tan and my honey-colored hair had white-blonde streaks. I liked how I looked. I opened the door expecting to find an empty hallway. Instead, my mother, who had led me to believe she was going to bed, was lurking in the shadows of the hall.

"Natalie," she said.

I jumped. "What? Mom, you scared me."

"I don't feel finished. I want to talk to you about this Christopher. Were you intimate with this man?"

"No, Mom. It doesn't matter anyway."

"Yes it does matter, Natalie. Having sex is no small matter. Do you know all the awful things there are out there? Sexual diseases. I was just reading an article about cervical cancer. It says that women with multiple sexual partners are more likely to have it."

"Are you trying to scare me?"

"No, I'm just trying to tell you that you need to get this sex drive of yours under control."

"What are you talking about? My sex drive is normal! I'm seventeen!" I was shouting.

"Hush, you'll wake your sister," she whispered. "Natalie, you knew what you were doing, sneaking around with Max. What did you expect to happen? Sex doesn't happen in church, or sitting on the bus, or at restaurants."

"That is NOT true! I can't believe you! Why won't you listen to me, mom?"

"I think you're just a little lost, that's all. We can guide you through this. You're not alone."

She was so much like my grandmother—her mother. Strict and reserved and cold most of the time. Occasionally some warmth would come out, but mostly the way she loved me was through criticism and control. I was determined not to be like her. I was going to embrace life and allow people to be themselves. I was going to start with allowing myself to be free.

"Well, I feel alone! Tell Olivia I love her," I said angrily, and suddenly I was walking out the door again.

26

I was back outside in the cool night air, right back where I started. I wanted to go inside, to sink into my bed with my cat and to hear Olivia's innocent voice asking me to tell her all about it. I'd snapped again, though, and I wouldn't give my mother the satisfaction of me going back in there.

I walked past my car toward the lower woods between our house and Lomink Road. I didn't want to get back in the car. I paced back and forth until I turned toward the house and saw my mother in the kitchen window watching me. She thought I asked for it. She was so sure she was right. She was so hung up on sex that she didn't want to hear about Christopher and wouldn't believe me if I told her he was a kind and gentle person. I knew she didn't actually expect me to take off again. She thought I would blow off steam and go back inside. So, I decided to surprise her. I walked right over to my car, opened the door, pulled my car keys out of my pocket, turned on the ignition and tore out of there leaving a cloud of gray dust.

I planned to stop again, but I thought my parents might follow me so I kept going. I unconsciously turned right. Right was the way back to the highway, and toward Max's house. Left was the way to Serena's house. I kept driving, past the entrance to the highway, north toward the road that twisted along the Delaware. Leaves were dancing like butterflies in my headlights. I opened the window and breathed in the river air. I slammed my brakes when a deer darted across the road, but besides that, I drove on, mindlessly. I drove until I found myself turning onto Max's driveway. I parked my car and walked up to the front door. His house was neatly manicured with a brass door knocker on the wide, dark wooden door. Nora opened it as I was raising my hand to knock.

"Is Max here?"

"No, he went out. Can I tell him you stopped by?" she asked sweetly.

"Do you know where he went?"

"We're not sure."

I'd never actually met this woman face to face before. I'd seen her pick Max up at school and I'd talked to her on the phone, but we had never been formally introduced. Did she know who I was?

"Can you tell him Natalie stopped by? Do you know when he'll be back?"

"Natalie. Oh. Well, I didn't expect to meet you like this. Isn't it late for a visit?"

"Yeah. I'm sorry. I just got back from... a trip."

"We heard all about that trip."

"I bet."

"Max just had a bit of a fuss. We argued and he left. He likes to take off and not tell us where he's going. We were thinking about going out and searching, but he's probably over at the Miller's."

"What did you argue about?"

"You."

"Oh. I'm sorry. Is he ok?"

"Probably not. Why don't you just go on home? He's off doing what he needs to do. He's just blowing off steam." From inside the house, I heard his dad shout toward the door.

"He's not just blowing off steam, Nora. You heard what he said."

"Shut up Kenneth! He was just being dramatic." Heavy footsteps pattered down the hall toward the door, and his dad peered out at me. His face echoed Max's angular chin and nose.

"Natalie, you might find Max at Ackerman's Falls. He's threatened before to go there and jump," said his dad.

"Jump? He'll die!"

"Yes."

"And you're just sitting here doing nothing?"

"He's not going to jump!" Nora said, rolling her eyes.

"We don't think he will, but I don't know," said his dad.

"Well, if he does, then it's God's will. That boy's got the devil in him."

"Ackerman's Falls? Is that along the river?" I asked, disgusted with Max's parents.

"Yes, just about a quarter mile up from Storm's Ferry," Max's dad said.

"Ok, I'm going," I replied and turned on my heels.

I knew where Storm's Ferry was. We went hiking there once. If Max's parents didn't give a shit about him, someone had to, right? I'd never be able to forgive myself if I went home and he actually jumped. I got back on the river road and drove north. I passed the sign for Storm's Ferry, one of those state park signs in brown with tan lettering.

I was hoping Ackerman's Falls had the same kind of sign. It did. I pulled into the parking lot. It was just a gravel circle, no lights, no picnic tables, nothing except Max's Jeep.   I didn't have a flashlight. I walked toward the woods and could vaguely see a dark corridor that opened up in the trees — a trail. The night's damp air was creeping around my face, chilling my fingers,

What is it about some people that makes us run back to them again and again even when they treat us like we're worthless? If I found Max, would he hit me, or garble and try to kiss me? I felt like scaring my parents, telling them I was going to jump, but maybe they would ignore me like Max's parents.

And then I remembered the words I heard in my head on the mesa. Go home. Find Max. Find the River. *Oh my God, that's what I'm doing.* Movement ahead of me jolted me out of my thoughts. I tried to focus my eyes, but could only see dark lumps, which I imagined were rocks. I walked forward slowly as if stalking prey.

"Who's there?" shouted a voice that I immediately recognized as Max. I felt stunned, mute. I walked a little closer.

"Who the fuck is that?" he said with fear in his voice.

"It's me."

"Who?"

"Me," I said again and walked more quickly so that I was further out into the clearing. Max turned on an industrial sized flashlight and shone it right in my face. It hurt my eyes. I squinted and he turned it off.

"Holy shit. What the fuck are you doing here?" His voice wavered with shock and a nervous laugh.

"I just got home. I went to your house. Your dad said to look for you here."

"You just never stop, do you?"

"Stop what? I wanted to see you. They said you were suicidal."

"Suicidal? I'm just going to put an end to a wretched and meaningless life, that's all."

"Don't be so dramatic, Max."

"This isn't a drama. I thought you were never coming back."

"Is that why you're here?"

"I wanted to go back to Colorado, to apologize. I was going to make it right, but my parents wouldn't buy me a ticket."

"Is that what you fought about?"

"Well, that, and a million other things. My grades, sex, girls, church, you name it."

"That's typical stuff, Max."

"Yeah, well I'm sick of it." He moved away from me in the dark. I could hear his footsteps receding into the distance. "Come over here and look down," he said through the chasm of night air.

"What is it?"

"It's a cliff. It's beautiful."

Something in his voice scared me. He sounds disembodied.

"Max, you're making me nervous."

"My mom says the devil is inside me. She says he's got his claws dug in. What does that mean? Well, how did he get there, huh? That's what I asked her. How did he get there, Mom? She says because I'm weak. I say it's because she let him in. She's like the devil herself. I told her that. I called her the devil. Then she hit me. That's the devil if you ask me. Not sex. Sex isn't a result of the devil. It's a result of us being animals. I can't help it if there's a Neanderthal in me. It's just a need, like needing to eat. You know what I mean? That's not evil!"

"Yeah, you're right," I said quietly.

"You think?"

"Yeah, I think you're right. Mostly."

"Fuckin' A."

I walked over to him, close enough to see his face. I could see his eyes glistening in the moonlight.

"See this?" he asked. "I'm bleeding. She made me bleed. My mother." I could see a dark stain moving from his ear, down the side of his neck. "Jeremy says pain is an illusion. He says we're just trapped in our bodies momentarily for this life on earth. Like eventually, we'll all just go poof! Evaporate into spirit and rise out of our bodies. He says it's a blessing to be able to be alive. He told me this last night. He said it's a shame to end your life early when there's so much more to be experienced. He says it's weak to check out early. What do you think?"

"I think he's probably right."

"Yeah, well I think it's a shame to stay here if your life sucks, that's what I think. I don't care if it's weak, I can't take it anymore. Do you like your life, Natalie?"

"My life's ok."

"Then why are you here? Why aren't you home with mommy and daddy and your sister if you just got home?"

"I left again."

"Your life's that great, huh? See, you and me, we're the same. We're like two sides of the same coin: key and keyhole, brother and sister."

"I don't know," I hesitated.

"Can't you see it? We're in a twisted karmic drama together. That's what Jeremy says. I see it. I never meant to hurt you. I had to show you."

"What?"

"That you were mine. That we were meant to be together. I knew it as soon as I met you. We've known each other before, like in a past life or something," he said under his breath.

"You think? You believe in that stuff?"

"Jeremy's been teaching me. He has all these books." He moved closer to the edge of the cliff.

"Max let's walk back to my car. We can talk more there."

"See? See how beautiful it is? Can't you just see yourself flying? I want to learn to fly, don't you?"

"No."

"I think when you die it gets easier. I think it's like suddenly gravity doesn't matter anymore and you just rise up like a helium balloon. I just want to rise up into the sky."

I thought about wanting to climb up a rope into the sky and escape.

"Look down, Natalie. Look at the water." He was leaning over the edge. I walked closer to him and held onto his arm. He was wearing the sheepskin coat I used to love so much. I ran my hand over the leather, feeling its supple texture, searching for his body underneath. Every now and then I could see the faint ripple of the water moving. I tried to see how far down it was. It could have been 20 feet or 100. It was too dark to tell.

"It's beautiful Max. Let's go back to the car now. I'm cold."

"Let me kiss you." He leaned down and wrapped his arms around my waist, pressing his lips to mine. I pulled away. "Max, let's go now."

"Just a little longer," he said hastily. He tried to kiss me again, his energy becoming more fierce and urgent. "I love you Natalie. I need you. I don't ever want to be apart from you. We both need this," he breathed into my ear.

"Need what?"

"This." He leaned down and kissed me and then with trembling, but solid muscles he ran toward the edge of the cliff, pulling me with him.

As soon as his body left solid ground, his hand slipped from me and we separated. I grasped for the cliff, scrambling up away from the open air, my feet slipping on wet rock, my fingernails digging into thin soil, ripping out tiny plants. When I finally felt my feet steady on the cliff, I looked down.

For a second I could see his tan shape disappearing below me into the darkness. *Oh my God, Max. What do I do?* I had to find a way down. I looked up at the sky for a moment and saw Orion's Belt again, guiding me away from the cliff. The Milky Way was a river of light. Was his life going to end in the river, under water, just like Whitefeather's?

I started running along the cliff, looking for a way down. I ran until I found a rough path that twisted steeply to the water. I stumbled down loose gravel and rock. Bushes snagged my legs. How was I going to get him out of there? I was getting whipped in the face by pine branches. Falling over rocks, I tumbled onto the flat beach of the Delaware. The beach narrowed so much that I had to get my feet wet in the river.

I found him lying on his back in shallow water with his arm twisted unnaturally underneath him. He didn't respond when I grabbed his wrist to check for a pulse. Max was alive! Looking up, I still couldn't tell how far he fell, but I was guessing it was 15 feet. I sat down on a wet rock and took a few breaths, trying to calm down.

"I'm going to get help." I said to him, though he had no response.

It had been easier going down that it was going up. I slipped and nearly fell over and over again. My knees were covered with mud. By the time I got to the top I was a bedraggled mess. I jumped into my car and tore down the road. I drove to the closest house and called 911.

There was nothing else for me to do but to go home. My body was beyond weary. I felt like I could just nod off while I was driving. It wasn't the homecoming I was expecting, though truth-be-told I hadn't known what to expect anyway. I parked my car outside my dark house, walked carefully up the steps and closed the door silently behind me. My mother was sitting in the dark living room. Her pale night gown glowed slightly in the dim moonlight through the window.

"Natalie…"

"Mom, don't. I'm fine. I'm going to shower and go to sleep."

"But, where were you?"

"There was something I had to do."

She was quiet for a moment. To my great relief I realized she sensed that it was best to just let me go upstairs. I stood there in the dark for a few uncomfortable moments before she said, "Go to sleep, Natty. We'll talk in the morning." She sighed a deep, sad sigh.

After a glorious, hot shower I fell instantly asleep.

∞

I was hovering in the sky looking down at the river valley. I could see Max lying there unconscious. Thin clouds were sliding past me like vapor as I started to move west through the sky, faster and faster. Soon I found myself perched on a telephone wire. Below me I saw a town. On the edge of the town were some trailers in various pastel shades, some ranch style houses and a few small sheds. I noticed two shapes darting quickly between the buildings. I strained to see more and was suddenly on the ground behind them. It was Christopher and a man who I knew must be his brother Samuel. They both had black knit hats pulled down over their faces and their hair braided tightly down their backs. Christopher, the smaller of the two, was wearing an army green jacket. Samuel's large shoulders were wrapped in a plaid wool shirt.

They were acting like panthers stalking prey, sneaking silently over the red earth. Christopher stopped and leaned against a small shed and I could see that the sinews and veins in his hand were tense as he clenched his fingers. I could even hear him breathing. He was nervous. Samuel was calm.

"This is number 105. It should be up there a little way," said Christopher. They started walking again. The moon was a thin sliver, which provided almost no light in the desert. The village looked as if a jar of ink had been spilled over it. Samuel reached into the waistband of his pants and adjusted a gun. I shivered. They started walking again across the open desert toward a cluster of small buildings. As they got closer, they passed charred and rusted metal barrels, plastic flower pots, a Big Wheel, a wiffle ball bat, clothes lines and car parts. I followed, a silent creature moving unseen and unheard behind them.

Samuel and Christopher were twitching with anticipation and probably fear. I was scared too. Scared of what they were going to do. I was the reason this was happening. Another crime was going to be committed and it was because I told Christopher about Leonard Norwood. Did I do the right thing? Maybe I should have kept it to myself. It was too late now. I started to float ahead of them as they walked, as if I knew where they were going. This was a dream after all. I stopped in front of a small square bungalow with dirty windows. There were yellow curtains in the windows. One window was taped with duct tape. I decided to go inside. Christopher and Samuel hadn't arrived yet, but I knew this was their destination. There was a red Harley parked outside next to a tricycle. Could a child possibly live there? Was Leonard a dad? I flew past the Harley and through the dirty window like a ghost.

The house had three rooms: a living room/kitchen/laundry room, a master bedroom and a smaller bedroom. No one was home. The bedroom was a mess with clothes flung in all directions, cheap furniture and a waterbed with a regular mattress in its frame. The walls were mostly bare, but the few decorations I could see were a mixture of sports posters and thrift store art.

I heard the front door open as I moved into the next room. I caught a glimpse of a He-Man bedspread and a wrestling poster on the wall before I was drawn back into the living room. Leonard was walking through the door. He threw a bag down on the olive green corduroy sofa and went over to the refrigerator, which was also a sick shade of green. He cracked open a can of beer. It made that familiar cold crack and fizz sound that was so enticing. I felt thirsty. Leonard chuckled at something with a deep, gravely laugh. He looked older now than he did in my previous dream. His face was chiseled with lines that reminded me of the gullies carved into the road on Black Horse Mesa. I suspected that in Leonard's case it was from years of pain instead of erosion. He reached into his breast pocket and pulled out a pack of cigarettes and lit one, inhaling deeply and exhaling a sigh that sounded like relief.

I noticed him start to relax and as he was heading for the sofa to sit down, the front door crashed open. It was Christopher and Samuel. After a moment of shock, Leonard shouted, "Who the fuck are you? Get out!" Samuel had his gun out and aimed it at Leonard.

"Shut up and put your hands on your head," ordered Samuel.

"No, I don't think so, punk. There ain't nothing here you'd want."

"Are you Leonard Norwood?" asked Samuel. Christopher was silent, watching, fighting the urge to kill.

"Yeah, so?"

Christopher lunged at Leonard, knocking the burning cigarette from his hand. I watched it fall to the floor and roll under the base of the sofa. Christopher swung the first punch, but Leonard was not weak or afraid. He responded with a fist square in Christopher's jaw. I wanted to run to Christopher, soothe his injured face. They were scuffling on the floor when Christopher, gaining the upper hand, pulled a switchblade out of his pocket. I heard the blade release from its sheath with a quiet, metallic ching. He held the knife to Leonard's throat.

"You killed my father. Don't you remember? Was he nothing to you?"

"I don't know what you're talking about," said Leonard.

"I think you do. I think you know exactly who I'm talking about." He pressed the knife to Leonard's neck, breaking the skin. Leonard flinched and a thin line of blood started to run down his neck.

"I was in Vietnam. I killed lots of men," he said with subtle desperation rattling in his voice.

"I'm not talking about a war. I'm talking about our father." Leonard didn't reply.

"Stand up," ordered Samuel. Leonard got up when Christopher nodded his head, the knife still pressed to his throat.

"Twelve years ago you tried to rape a girl in an alley. Our father tried to stop you and you killed him."

"How the fuck do you know about that?" asked Leonard.

"It's doesn't matter how we know. We found him. Don't bother denying it. We know the whole story," said Christopher.

"But how could you? I never told nobody."

"What matters is that we know," said Samuel.

"You don't know nothing," mumbled Leonard.

"Oh yeah? I know that I lost a father. I hated my father for leaving us when I should have been hating you!" yelled Christopher. In a fit in adrenaline, he began knocking things off the counters: an old ceramic lamp, an ashtray, a vase.

Christopher pulled a roll of tape out of his jacket and ordered Leonard to turn around. He bound his wrists tightly. Samuel slapped him across his face with the gun and Leonard slumped, blood beginning to swell on his cheek, which had split open.

"It was so long ago. So long... I never thought..."

"Yeah, well maybe you should have thought!" yelled Samuel, whose rage was building. He pushed Leonard who fell to his knees. I cringed at the sound of metal-toed work boots hitting flesh and bone. Christopher was kicking him and Leonard curled up in a ball of pain. I watched from the corner of the room and between me, the brothers and Leonard, I noticed a thin ribbon of smoke rising up from the sofa where the cigarette fell. "Hey!" I yelled. "Watch out!" but of course they didn't hear me. As they continued to kick and pummel him, the smoke began to gather into a thicker trail, until small flames erupted around the skirt of the sofa.

At the same time, the front door squeaked open. A woman and a little boy walked in. The woman screamed.

"Daddy?" whimpered the boy who tried to run to Leonard. The woman caught him and held him back. Christopher and Samuel stood up straight, stunned. The sofa's synthetic cushions exploded into flames.

"Fuck, man..." said Samuel under his breath. Christopher didn't say anything. The woman ran out the door with the boy.

Christopher and Samuel instinctively started dragging Leonard outside. I followed and watched as they stood proudly over the battered body of the man who moaned quietly while smoke rose out of the small house.

I woke to pale strands of sunlight stretching across my bed as I tried to bring my consciousness back to where I was. I'd been dreaming, but it was a dream so real that I knew it had really happened. A lump formed in my throat as tears threatened. Christopher and his brother had attacked Leonard, but they didn't kill him. Maybe they never planned to. Maybe they spared him, because he was a father. After all, they knew what it was like to lose a father. I knew they wouldn't do that to another boy. Still, they had disrupted a family and harmed a man who thought he was free. He deserved it, I guess, but I lay there in bed, sniffling and thinking about whether or not revenge was necessary. Maybe living with his own conscience would have been enough punishment for Leonard.

I was proud of Christopher, though. It was a gruesome dream, but I knew he had found closure and that ultimately he was a good man, the kind of man who would spare the life of his father's murderer to protect an innocent child.

I thought of Max, and I was suddenly overcome with sadness. I knew he wasn't dead. He had to go on living. That was the most pathetic suicide he could have dreamed up. A moment later reality hit me like a thud in my chest. I had to return to school. And, while the anxiety twisted in my gut I also felt something new rising within me.

I got up, slipped on some clean clothes from my dresser, pulled on my flip flops and walked outside into the chilly morning air. My cat was thrilled that I was home and she followed me as I crunched through the late summer woods. I found my spot in the birches and sat down. I breathed in the wonderful smell of home and did something I'd never done before. I closed my eyes and deliberately reached out mentally to see if anyone was there to answer. "Whitefeather, are you there?" It took a moment of concentration, emptying my mind of any stray thoughts before I heard a voice.

"Yes."

I took a deep breath and smiled to myself. I knew he would answer. "Are you free now?" I asked with my eyes still closed.

"Yes, thank you. You broke the chains that bound me. I am home."

I smiled again. No one would ever believe me if I tried to explain this mystical adventure. They especially wouldn't believe that I could communicate with a dead man. Regardless, I felt a great sense of peace flowing through me, knowing I accomplished something so profound and significant. I stretched my arms and legs and got ready to stand up. My stomach was growling for food. I was startled as Whitefeather's words rang in my mind again.

"Remember your light. It will always be with you. Your inner knowing is strong and true. Never doubt yourself. Return to school, Natalie, but know that Christopher is waiting for you."

Christopher was waiting for me? I wasn't expecting that. I hadn't really considered a future with Christopher. He was too far away, and part of a different life. How could our worlds ever blend together? Would he move here? Could I move out west for good?

Those were the thoughts that occupied my mind as I spent the next few days getting ready to return to Matterson Academy, ready to see my friends and classmates again, ready to tackle all that my senior year entailed.

27

Summer 1993

Seeing the wide open, tan fields of Colorado again was such a relief. It was like breathing in the sweetest, clearest breath of fresh air. Headed south on Highway 25, my father was nervous, gripping the steering wheel, ordering my mother to check the map every few minutes. Olivia was silent next to me with headphones in her ears. I smiled to myself, reveling in the brilliance of my plans. With the help of Ms. Gagliardi I was able to find a good college that happened to be conveniently located; Adams State was as close to Christopher as I could get. My goal was to major in Anthropology with a minor in Women's Studies.

"How can a person drive out here and stay awake? It all looks the same!" complained my mother.

"I think it's beautiful," I said in defense.

GATHER THE BONES * 274

"Good thing, since you're the one who's going to live here," she said with a touch of regret.

My mother had tried hard over the last ten months. I gave her credit for that. She had so much resistance at first, but as I talked to her and explained my experiences to her she began to soften. She began to believe me. Ironically, it helped that Olivia began dating a guy named Andrew from our high school. She fell madly in love and became even more obsessed than I had been with Max (at least I like to think so). I was eternally grateful to her for taking some of my parents' attention away from me. In fact, as I glanced over at her in the car, she was scrawling a note to him, completely oblivious to the amazing landscape around us.

Returning to school in late September was simultaneously strange and uncomfortably normal. All the mundane activities of the school year resumed almost as if they'd never ended. I received back-breaking piles of books, impossible amounts of homework and a generous amount of teacher-instilled anxiety. There was one major difference about me, though. I had an unwavering confidence that everything was going to be okay. I'd faced my demons and lived through it. In fact, I'd faced *other* people's demons and conquered them! I also turned 18. I was officially an "adult". And I couldn't help hearing Whitefeather's words reverberating in my mind. Christopher was waiting for me. Not long after I had that cosmic communication with Whitefeather, I wrote Christopher a letter telling him what happened to Max and mentioned Whitefeather's message. Christopher wrote back quickly and our relationship blossomed through the mail. It was so romantic. It was intoxicating reading Christopher's words and feeling his love from afar.

We had been in the car for a few hours already and as I stretched to relieve my aching muscles, my ring flashed in the sun light. I extended my arm and admired it for a moment. Olivia saw me do it and rolled her eyes. I stuck my tongue out at her. The symbol of our love was that ring. Feathers carved into sterling silver wrapped around my finger, holding a large, bluish opal that reflected the light. I felt like it held some mysterious magic. I twisted the ring lovingly on my finger.

It had arrived in the mail the day before my high school graduation along with a proposal. It wasn't a marriage proposal, though it almost felt like that. Christopher asked me to wear it as a promise that we would see each other again. A little corny, maybe, but it was like the universe had started a wind blowing at my back, pushing me forward. I floated through my graduation, the happiest girl in the world.

At graduation, we all stood awkwardly in our white dresses and suits outside on the lawn, smiling for photographs after the ceremony. My smile was completely genuine, unlike quite a few other people, especially Max. He had returned to school after some time in what he referred to as "therapy." He made one attempt to get back together with me in November. It was a memory I'd never forget, sitting on the sun on a crisp day, not too far from Thanksgiving. I told him I was done with our twisted relationship. He acted hurt, but not long after that he began dating Allyson Fitzimmons. I wasn't even jealous. I'd seen it coming. They broke up right before graduation though, and Max looked sullen and dejected in most of the graduation pictures.

∞

We headed southwest. At my parents' request I had arranged for them to meet Christopher, presumably so that they could give him their stamp of approval. I figured I would humor them. I called him from our hotel in Denver and we made plans to meet in Crestone outside the diner where I'd bought myself many coffees, not quite a year ago. In a way it felt like another lifetime. I'd become a different person. How quickly a person can change.

My stomach was all tied up in knots as we got closer to the San Luis Valley. We were in the mountains and their hugeness was still a shock. As we approached Crestone and I saw the familiar mountains that Christopher told me so much about, I swooned from anticipation. I hadn't actually fainted since we solved Whitefeather's mystery. I wondered if returning to Colorado might make it happen again, but I felt solid.

We parked the car a short way from the diner. I was wearing a long skirt with a rust and gold sunflower print and a black tank top. I felt the weight of the ring on my finger and it eased my nervousness slightly. Then I saw his yellow truck parked a short distance away on the opposite side of the road.

"There's his truck!" I said with excitement, pointing at it.

"Well, let's go see him then," said Olivia. She smiled at me and hooked her arm in mine, guiding me down the sidewalk. As we walked, she tipped her head slightly and rested it on my shoulder, just for a second. She was only a little bit shorter than me. I think her gesture meant that she believed in me, maybe that she would miss me. I feel myself get choked up with emotion, but I swallowed it down.

Then I saw him. He was sitting at a table outside a café a block away from the diner. His hair was pulled back in a braid and he was wearing a black T-shirt with a silver medallion around his neck, glinting in the sun. I stared for a moment, smiling, and then he turned and saw me. In an instant he was up and running and before I could say a word I was in his arms and he was lifting me off the ground in a huge, trembling hug. He put me down and held me there for a moment, a little longer than my parents would probably have liked. Then he pulled away and just looked at me, smiling with his beautiful eyes.

"So, this is your family," he said, knowing he needed to do the right thing and shake hands with my parents. "I'm Christopher Nez."

My dad reaches out and shakes his hand. "Mr. and Mrs. Watson. Nice to meet you."

Christopher nodded his head in such a way that said, *I respect you, sir.* I could tell my dad appreciated it. "Would you like something to eat?" he asked politely.

"Yes, let's go get something to drink at least," said my mother nervously. "We need to stay hydrated to avoid altitude sickness." Olivia looked at me and we both tried not to laugh. Our mother was always looking for things to be nervous about. Lucky for her I presented her with many opportunities.

We joined Christopher at his table outside the cafe and ordered our food. I was still on edge, wondering if my dad was going to give Christopher the third degree. Sure enough, he wasted no time. "So, Christopher, what is it that you do for a living? Natalie said construction?"

"Yes, I've been working for myself, doing painting and carpentry, but I recently began studying passive solar technology. I think it's going to be really important someday in the future. And I can make a good living building passive solar homes."

My dad raised his eyebrows, but Christopher had snagged his interest. "When will you be done studying this?"

"It doesn't take too long. A series of classes over the summer. I'm aiming for certification as soon as I can. I want you to know, sir, that I plan to support Natalie however I can." They were the words my dad wanted to hear.

"I'm glad to hear that," said my dad in his most fatherly tone."
Olivia and I both exchanged glances.

My family checked into a bed and breakfast in the middle of
town. My parents were out of their element, but I could tell that they
were also enjoying themselves. My dad had a lightness to his walk
that I didn't always see and my mother was smiling more than I
expected. Christopher even managed to charm them a bit during our
meal, making my mother laugh and blush a few times and impressing
my dad even further with his knowledge of solar power. While my
parents checked into our rooms I stood outside with Christopher.

The bed and breakfast was like nothing we would ever see back
east. Wind chimes and prayer flags flutter in the breeze.
Southwestern style architecture paired with multitudes of potted
plants add to the feel of it. It had a spacious front porch with brightly
colored wooden chairs, and Christopher sat down.

"The ring looks good on you," he said. "I knew it would." He
took my hand, touching the silver feathers, squeezing my hand with
just the slightest pressure. "I knew you would come back to me."

I nodded my head and smiled at him. My smile was sincere,
though I couldn't say I always knew I'd be back. I had so much to
figure out. It was the message from Whitefeather that gave me some
hope of seeing Christopher again. I found myself wondering if I still
had the gift or if it was gone, along with Whitefeather.

"What's on your mind?" he asked.

"I'm just remembering those visions I had when I was here.
Wondering if that will ever happen again, or if it's all over."

"I don't think it will happen like that again. The visions were so
intense because you weren't paying attention and needed to wake up
to your gifts. You can choose to use them now when you want to. It

will be different. There are a lot of people in this area who can help you." I nodded in agreement and took a deep breath, smelling the fresh air; it had a slight hint of sage. "Actually, I have a surprise for you. Do you think your parents would mind if I took you for a little drive while they settle in?"

I ran upstairs to our rooms and asked for permission to leave with Christopher. It seemed silly to ask, but I knew it made my parents feel good to give their approval. They agreed and asked that I be back in time for dinner. They'd found a restaurant boasting an award-winning chicken with green chili sauce.

Once I fastened the seatbelt in Christopher's truck, and felt the air rushing past us as we accelerated, I realized I was holding tension in my body. I took a deep breath and exhaled, relaxing into the old truck. I closed my eyes for a moment. It was hard to describe the sense of relief that I felt, but it was combined with something else. Maybe just the slightest twinge of fear, and also an overwhelming sense of potential.

Christopher turned onto the road that led to Black Horse Mesa, but instead of heading straight to his trailer he turned left and headed northwest. The tan, dirt road was narrow with thick junipers and pinion pines on both sides. He stopped the truck in the road and turned to smile at me. "We walk from here," he said with a twinkle in his eye.

We walked, kicking up reddish dust as our feet crunched down the road. The aroma of the pines smelled like heaven to me. I remembered that strange night when Max was there, lost for a while in the darkness. Remembered my dream of the mountain lions circling me. I loved the wildness of the place. After a few minutes more a clearing came into view. I could see a large shape through the trees.

"What's over there?" I asked, squinting.

"Something I've been working on. Come see."

He took my hand and we began walking again. He picked up the pace a little bit and I could tell he was nervous. We reached the end of the road and at first I was confused. It was a house with a beautiful wrap-around porch. It looked very new.

"Who lives there?" I asked.

"You do. We do. That is, if you like it."

I stared at the house in disbelief for a moment and then my eyes focused on the mountains in the distance. "The view! Christopher, it's amazing. How did you..."

"I bought the land from old Jim Sanders who owns a lot of this mesa. He doesn't ask much for it, just has certain requests about how it's used." Christopher was nervous, I could tell. "Come on, take a look inside. It's not totally finished, but you'll get the idea. I thought you might want to pick out the paint."

The porch and siding were made of cedar and smelled wonderful. The inside was empty, but the rooms had high ceilings and bright southwestern light was pouring in. The hardwood floors were a warm caramel color. I walked through each room, smiling to myself. It was all too wonderful.

He led me upstairs. "There are four rooms up here. You can have your own, plus a study. Look, I'm not going to rush you just because we live together. Then there's this room." He walked into a room at the back of the house. It was a sunroom with an incredible view of the mountains. He already had some plants on a table in the sun. There was a stereo in the corner and he turned it on. It was jazz, and it complimented the peaceful feeling in the house perfectly.

"What do you think?"

"I think it's amazing."

"Do you? Is it okay?" He searched my eyes. "It's not that long of a commute to the college."

"It's perfect," I said softly, and I kissed him.

He wrapped an arm around my waist, grabbed my hand and twirled me in a circle, dancing slowly to the music. I felt a bright swelling of happiness building in my belly as he spun me around and I laughed out loud. *This is what joy feels like.* Christopher stopped spinning me for a moment as the music slowed down. We turned and looked at the mountains again. I could see for miles and miles.

"Welcome home, Natalie," he said with a smile.

Also by Andrea Kresge

What would you do if you suddenly had the ability to manipulate energy with your hands and move things with your mind? Stella Westfall is still grieving her mother's death when a latent magical ability is sparked in her after a motorcycle accident. With her new ability comes an invitation to join a group of witches. They are a quirky assortment of country people, including unnervingly handsome, but narcissistic Charles, and earthy, grounded Derek. She finds herself in a love triangle, but that's not the real challenge. She navigates the magical underground of witches and shapeshifters and ultimately uncovers something terrifyingly sinister. Will she also find out the truth about her mother's untimely demise?

A Note from Andrea Kresge

Thank you so much for reading my book! If you enjoyed it, please consider leaving a review with your favorite retailer. I love to hear from readers, so please visit my website where you can contact me, sign up for my newsletter, be notified of new releases and read my blog. You can also find me on social networking.

http://www.andreakresge.com

www.ingramcontent.com/pod-product-compliance
Lightning Source LLC
Chambersburg PA
CBHW030034180626
46810CB00001B/372